HOW DO YOU EXTORT SIX HUNDRED THOUSAND DOLLARS FROM A DYING MAN?

Someone had done just that to Dr. Fortner Geis. And although the trail was nineteen months cold when Travis McGee arrived in Chicago, certain apparently unrelated events began to form an unpleasant pattern.

- A jovial, singing fellow had kidnapped the doctor's grandson and, evidently losing his nerve, had let him go unharmed in a downtown park.
- His wife's Mercedes had been wired with one of those silly torpedo things they sell to practical jokers.
- His nurse's cat had been skewered by a prowler and left to die on the kitchen floor.

To McGee these were symbols of violence. Demonstrations. As if someone had said, "Kindly note, Dr. Geis, that I could have strangled the kid instead of turning him loose. I could have wired the little Mercedes so it would have blown Glory Geis into small pieces. I could have skewered the nurse instead of the cat.

"So let us start negotiations, Doctor, sir, and maybe you can give me six hundred thousand arguments why I should not improve upon my tricks."

That was how it was done. Now McGee had to find out who, for Travis had a sick, uneasy feeling that the twisted intelligence behind the crime would not be satisfied with money alone. McGee knew he was right when he looked into the single, staring yellow eye of the mutilated corpse in the deserted Illinois farmhouse.

Fawcett Gold Medal Books
in The Travis McGee Series
by John D. MacDonald:

THE DEEP BLUE GOODBYE   13604-3 $1.50

NIGHTMARE IN PINK   14097-0 $1.75

A PURPLE PLACE FOR DYING   13879-8 $1.50

THE QUICK RED FOX   14098-9 $1.75

A DEADLY SHADE OF GOLD   13815-1 $1.75

BRIGHT ORANGE FOR
  THE SHROUD   14100-4 $1.75

DARKER THAN AMBER   13563-2 $1.50

ONE FEARFUL YELLOW EYE   14146-2 $1.95

PALE GRAY FOR GUILT   14148-6 $1.95

THE GIRL IN THE
  PLAIN BROWN WRAPPER   13768-6 $1.75

DRESS HER IN INDIGO   13732-5 $1.75

THE LONG LAVENDER LOOK   13834-8 $1.95

A TAN AND SANDY SILENCE   13635-3 $1.75

THE SCARLET RUSE   13952-2 $1.95

THE TURQUOISE LAMENT   13806-2 $1.75

THE DREADFUL LEMON SKY   14148-9 $1.95

ONE
FEARFUL
YELLOW EYE

JOHN D. MACDONALD

FAWCETT GOLD MEDAL • NEW YORK

ONE FEARFUL YELLOW EYE

Published by Fawcett Gold Medal Books,
a unit of CBS Publications,
the Consumer Publishing Division of CBS Inc.

A shorter version of this book has appeared in
Cosmopolitan Magazine.

ISBN: 0-449-14146-2

Printed in the United States of America

30   29   28   27   26   25   24   23

ONE
FEARFUL
YELLOW EYE

one

Around and around we went, like circling through wads of lint in a dirty pocket. We'd been in that high blue up yonder where it was a bright cold clear December afternoon, and then we had to go down into that guck, as it was the intention of the airline and the airplane driver to put the 727 down at O'Hare.

Passengers reached up and put their lights on. The sky had lumps and holes in it. It becomes tight-sphincter time in the sky when they don't insert the ship into the pattern and get it down, but go around again. Stewardesses walk tippy-dainty, their color not good in the inside lights, their smiles sutured so firmly in place it pulls their pretty faces more distinctly against the skull-shape of pretty bones. Even with the buffeting, there is an impression of silence inside the aircraft at such times. People stare outward, but they are looking inward, tasting of themselves and thinking of promises and defeats. The busy air is full of premonitions, and one thinks with a certain comfort of old Satchel's plug in favor of air travel: "They may kill you, but they ain't likely to hurt you."

It is when you say, "What am *I* doing here?"

I was here because of the way Glory Doyle's voice had sounded across the long miles from a Chicago December down to a balmy morning aboard *The Busted Flush* at Slip F-18, Bahia Mar, Lauderdale.

"Oh Trav," she said, a wan voice, deadened and miserable, "I guess there's only one word. I guess the word is help. It's a lousy leverage, huh?"

"But I'd use it on you if I had to, Lady Gloria."

"You'll come up here? You really will?"

It was a valid assumption she was a few thousand feet below me, below layers of snow flurries and pockets of sleet. And then we dipped a sickening wing, leaving my stomach back up there at ten o'clock high, stood precariously still on big flaps, then steadied down into the runway lights streaming by, bumped and squeaked, brake-blasted, and everybody began smiling at everybody for no special reason, and began gathering gear, as the hope-you-enjoyed-your-flight-aboard-the speech came on, articulated by one of our stewardesses over a PA system which seemed to be constructed of an empty tomato can and a piece of waxed string. The speaker systems, and the interior beanwagon plastic decor seem planned to give the air passenger the minimal confidence in the unseen parts of the mechanism. As if the brass did not expect the fad to last.

The sludge upstairs was rain by the time it settled onto Chicago. When I was ten feet into the scurrying cross-traffic of the terminal building, amid fluorescence and PA instructions, Glory Doyle—correction—Glory Doyle Geis, or alternately Mrs. Doctor Fortner Geis, or acceptably, widow of Dr. Fortner Geis, came flying at me, to hug and hiccup and make glad sounds, lift a mouth up as high as she could get it, which is perhaps a little over five feet off the ground when she is in four-inch heels.

It had been four years for us. She was thinner than she should have been. Deep vertical creases between black brows, lines bracketing the mouth, smile lines deep at the corners of the eyes. But even so, looking younger than the thirty-four I knew she had to be. After the kiss, I held her off a half-step, hands on her shoulders, to look at her. She tilted her head, made an upside-down smile, and her brown eyes filled quickly with tears.

"McGee, McGee, McGee," she said. "God, it's so *good*!"

Hers is a moppet face, mostly eyes and a mouth made for laughing, helter-skelter crop of black hair, tidy little figure, and remorseless energies.

She looked at her watch. "Let's talk over a drink before we have to plunge into the damned traffic." She guided us into a three-deep bar, and moved around to the far side, around a corner, and while I was putting our order in, she managed to ease onto the last stool as it became vacant, hitched it close to the wall to give me a leaning space, my back to the neighboring stool.

"Your luggage?" she asked.

"Just what I carried off. Just this."

"Always simplify. Peel it all down. One of the rules of McGeeism." I could see what four years of marriage to Geis had done for her. She had far more assurance. She wore a dark green knit suit under a tweedy rain cape, and a frivolous little Sherlock Holmes hat that went with the cape. The diamonds in the wedding ring winked in the backbar glow as she lifted the Irish and soda to touch the rim of my gin over ice, and said, "To crime, Travis dear."

"And little women."

She drank and smiled and said, "But you had eyes for all the great huge broads, sweetie. What was that funny name everybody called that dancer? The one named Mc-Call?"

"Chookie. She married one Arthur Wilkinson, who builds spec houses and makes her very happy indeed."

"And Meyer?"

"Sends his love. He's as hairy and bemused as ever."

"And the Alabama Tiger?"

"The party still rolls on, never really quits."

"It's a lot cozier aboard the *Flush,* Trav. Golly, I miss that whole bit, you know? If Fort hadn't come along just when he did, I could have turned into a beach girl forever, and ended up as one of those nutty old biddies who go pouncing around after seashells. It was just right, you know. My whole damned life fell all to bits and pieces, and you helped me put the pieces back together, and then I had to have somebody who needed me instead of the other way around, and Fort came by. But . . . it was too short. Four years. Not enough, Trav. Very good years, but not enough by half."

"I would have come up, but I was over in the Islands, and when I got back your letter was two weeks old at least."

"He was buried on October tenth. My God, a beautiful day, Trav. One of the greatest you could ever see. A real sparkler. We knew. Right from the first night I dated him, he leveled with me. I went into it knowing. But you kid yourself . . . when you're that happy." She lifted her shoulders slowly, let them fall, then grinned at me and said, "You are certainly a pretty spectacular sight, man, around this pasty old town. I never saw you out of context before. You're a little startling. I was aware of people looking at you, saying with that size and that much tan, he's a TV actor hooked on sun lamps, or from an NFL team in Texas or California, or some kind of rich millionaire playboy up from Acapulco, or you have this big schooner, see, and you go all over the Pacific. Hell with them. Let them wonder. Now let's go home."

The rain had stopped but it seemed darker. The highways were wet. She had a very deft little hunk of vehicle, a Mercedes 230 SL, in semi-iridescent green-bronze, automatic shift. I am no sports-car buff. But I enjoy any piece of equipment made to highest standards for performance, without that kind of adornment Meyer calls Detroit Baroque. She said, "I better drive it because I'm used to the special ways they try to kill you here, and the places where you've got to start cutting out of the flow or get carried along to God knows where."

"Fine little item."

"Fort's final birthday present, last May. It's a dear thing. If I do anything that bothers you, McGee, just close your eyes."

Glory and the car were beautifully matched. They were both small, whippy, and well-made, and seemed to understand each other. There was that good feel of road-hunger, of the car that wants to reach and gobble more than you let it. We sped north on the Tri-State, and she had that special sense of rhythm of the expert. It is a matter of having the kind of eye which sees everything happening ahead, linked to a computer which estimates what the varying rates of speed will do to the changing pattern by the time you get there. The expert never gives you any feeling of tension or strain in heavy traffic, nor startles other drivers. It is a floating, drifting feeling, where by the use of the smallest increments and reductions in pedal pressure, and by the most gradual possible changes in direction, the car fits into gaps, flows through them, slides into the lane which will move most swiftly. She sat as tall as she could, chin high, hands at ten after ten, and made no attempt at chatter until the stampede had thinned.

"We jump off this thing at Rockland Road," she said, "and take a mess of shortcuts you couldn't possibly find again, and end up at Lake Pointe, with the terminal E, twenty-five bitch miles from O'Hare, where awaits a shaggy house, shaggy beach, shaggy drink in front of one of the better fireplaces in the Western world."

"Will I be staying near there?"

"In there, stupid. Not in the fireplace. There's a ton of room, and help to run it. And a lot of talking to talk, dear Travis."

On some of the curves of her shortcuts she showed off a little, but not enough to break the rear end loose. She knew the route through the curves and laid the little car on the rails through each one, steady as statues.

She laughed, and it was a fond laugh. "That man of mine. That Fort. Do you know what came with this thing? Lessons from a great old character named Kip Cooper who raced everything on wheels on every course there is. When old Kip finally approved, then and only then was this my car. Have you still got that absolutely ridiculous and marvelous old Rolls-Royce pickup truck?"

"Please, you are speaking of Miss Agnes. Yes, but lately I'm feeling wistful about her. She's becoming obsolete. You have to be up to speed when you bust out into the turnpike traffic, or you're a menace, and the old lady just hasn't got enough sprint. She accelerates like the average cruise ship. I'm going to have to save her for back roads, lazy days, picnic times."

We slowed and went between fat stone columns. Private. Slow. Lake Pointe. Residents and guests only. In the gray light through the branches of the bare black trees I saw fragments of houses, a wall, a dormer, a roof angle. When the leaves were out it would be impossible to see them from the smooth curves of wide private asphalt road.

Glory drove to the far end of the area, by a sign that said Dead End, and into a driveway. She parked by garages. The house faced the dunes and the lake. It was a long house, of gray stone, pale blue board and batten, dark blue tile roof. We went in through a side door into a foyer, and a big broad smiling woman in an apron came to meet us.

"Anna, this is my old friend Mr. Travis McGee. Anna Ottlo."

"I am please to meet," Anna said, bobbing her head.

"Trav, you're in the east wing. Anna will show you the way. This is going to be just the two of us, informal. I'm going to change to a corduroy jump suit, if that clues you."

"Miss Glory, the Mr. Andrus was phoning again. Best thing, I told him, you phone him in the morning, yes?"

"Perfect, Anna. Thanks."

I started to contest Anna to see who would carry my flight bag, but she looked so distressed I had to let her have it. I was put in a fine room, more apartment than room. There was a hidden unit of stove, sink, and refrigerator for breakfast. She showed me the button that rolled the panel back to expose the built-in television set. She showed me where the light switches were, and where I could find more clean towels.

After she left me, I unpacked, changed from the suit to the pair of slacks and gray flannel shirt I had stuffed into the bag as an afterthought. An ancient and treasured shirt, that good Limey wool that turns softer as it grows older. French doors opened onto a planked deck facing the expanse of dunes and wind-twisted dwarfed trees between the house and the lake shore. The temperature was dropping, the wind increasing out of the north, and in the last grayness of the day I saw a full line of red in the west, like distant cities burning. The cloud cover was breaking up and I saw the first star. Wish I may, wish I might . . . I found myself wishing that Glory Doyle Geis would find some good and rewarding thing to do with her life from now on in, find someone who would sense how much she had to give, and how badly she needed someone to need her—as Fort Geis had.

The wind began to search out my tropic bone marrow, and I could smell a sourness in the wind. I remembered that it blew across a dying lake. For a hundred years the cities had dumped their wastes and corruptions and acids into it, and now suddenly everyone was aghast that it should have the impertinence to start dying like Lake Erie. The ecology was broken, the renewing forces at last overwhelmed. Now the politicians were making the brave sounds the worried people wanted to hear.

Now they were taking half-measures. Scientists said that only with total effort might the process be slowed, halted, reversed. But total effort, of course, would raise havoc with the supposedly God-given right of the thousand lakeshore corporations to keep costs down by running their poisons into the lake. Total effort would boost the tax structure to pay for effective sewage disposal systems.

So in the night wind, the lake stank, and I went back in out of the wind, and thought of the endless garbage barges that are trundled out of Miami into the blue bright Atlantic. People had thought the lake would last forever. When the sea begins to stink, man better have some fresh green planets to colonize, because this one is going to be used up.

I found my way to the big living room. High beamed ceiling. Low fat lamps with opaque shades. Off-white walls, with good strong paintings. Islands of furniture, demarked by bright rugs, and between those areas, a floor of pale planking in random width, polished to semi-gloss. Slate fireplace big enough for an ox roast, with a broad hearth raised two feet above the floor level. Bookshelves on either side of the fireplace, and, built into the shelves on the right, a high-fidelity installation, doors open, reels turning on the tape deck, making a sound of indolent piano in the room, at a volume just high enough to be audible over the crackle of logs and the wind sound around the corners of the house.

Glory sat on a crimson cushion on a corner of the hearth away from the direct heat of the fire. She wore a pale blue wide-wale corduroy jump suit, silvery where the nap caught the light.

She sat huddled, drink in her hand, looking into the flames. I stood and looked at her for a few moments. By some trickery of firelight, I could see how she would look when she became very old. She would become one of those simian little old ladies, wrinkles leathery against the round bones, eyes bright with anthropoid shrewdness.

So I put a heel down on the polished wood as I approached, and she snapped her head around, her brooding look gone in an instant. She motioned toward a chair which had been pulled close. "Did I say it was a great fireplace, McGee?"

"It's a great room."

The drink tray was on a low table between my chair and where she sat. Into a heavy half-sphere of Swedish glass she dropped three ice cubes, then with a knowing, mocking look showed me the label on the bottle of gin before pouring it over the cubes.

"Good memory," I said.

"What do you mean? For heaven's sake, remember how we had to practically go on an expedition from that crazy cottage on Sanibel so the lord and master could restock the Plymouth gin supply? I remember that day so well. When we got back, finally, you walked me so far along that beach that before we got back I wanted to sit down in the sand and cry. I've never been so pooped in my life. I thought you were being cruel and heartless. It wasn't until later I realized it was one of your ways of putting the jumbled jangled lady back together. And then I wondered why you bothered. I certainly wasn't much good to you or anybody until later."

"I used to wonder too."

Four and a half years ago I had gone dawn-walking and found Glory Doyle sleeping on the public beach. She was twenty-nine. She was broke, loaded with flu virus, hysterical, suicidal, and mean as a snake. I packed her back to the *Flush* like a broken bird. As she was mending, reluctantly, I pried the story out of her, bit by bit. She had no intention of telling anyone her troubles. She had no people. At twenty-two she had married a man named Karl Doyle. He was a chemist doing industrial research for a firm in Buffalo. He was handsome, amiable, competent, and an emotional cripple. He was not capable of love because of his deep feeling of insecurity. The more she gave, the more he demanded. His jealousy of her was like a terrible disease. They had a daughter, and he resented the child deeply because it took some of her attention from him. After their son was born, he became worse. As he became ever more violent and unpredictable, she begged him to get professional help. She fought to make the marriage work, and she was a fighter, warm, understanding, gutsy. One night after he beat the little girl for a minor infraction of his ever more stringent rules, she took the kids to the home of her best friend and stayed there with them. When he called she said that when he started going to a psychiatrist, she would come back to him. One Saturday morning when it was her turn to do the marketing, she came back to the house to find that her husband had broken in, had killed the friend, both children, and himself. She could not remember very much about the next few weeks, but finally, after everything was settled, all she had was the car, her clothes, and a few hundred dollars. She headed south. Somewhere in the Carolinas the car got low on oil and the motor burned out. She sold it for junk and continued by bus. She had planned to get a job in Florida. But when she got to Lauderdale and rented a cheap motel room a few blocks from the beach a strange lassitude came over her, the end product of her conviction of guilt. She slept twenty hours a day. The money slowly dwindled away. She began to hear voices, and she knew that when she went out people nudged each other and pointed at her and told each other of the terrible thing she had caused. She was warned about the rent until one day she came back and found a new lock on her room, found that they were holding her possessions. She was feverish and dizzy. I found her on the beach the following dawn. She had fallen asleep while awaiting the necessary energy to walk into the sea and swim out as far as she could.

Somehow you can tell the real crazies from the broken birds. This one was pure bird. She'd had just a little more than she could handle. She had to have somebody to hang onto, somebody who could make her see that her disaster was as much her fault as is that cyclone or flood or fire which takes all but one of a family. Her nerves were shredded, digestion shot, disposition vile. She was without hope or purpose, and she had gone a dangerous distance along the path toward despising herself. But in the end it was her sense of humor which saved her. There was a compulsive clown carefully hidden away, who had almost forgotten tricks and jokes and absurdities. When I got her weary enough and healthy enough, the clown part began to make tentative appearances, and the good mending started. After it had turned into a physical affair between us, another danger arose. She began to become too emotionally dependent on me. She was a very affectionate woman, needing and giving the casual touches and pats which to her were as necessary a part of communication as words. I felt too fatuously delighted with myself for bringing her back into reality to let her slip into another kind of fantasy. So, after helping her get a job as a dining-room hostess in a Fort Lauderdale hotel on the beach, I firmly, gently, carefully disentangled myself.

It was through her job she met Dr. Fortner Geis. He was staying alone at the hotel.

A log shifted in the fire. She sighed audibly. The music

ended and she went over and punched the button to reverse it, so that it would play the other half of the tape.

"I loved this house," she said.

I looked at a large painting on the opposite wall, the colors vividly alive, the composition very strong. A small gallery spot shone on it. I got up and went halfway to it, and then made out the artist's signature and went back to the chair.

"An incredible old man," I said.

"Fort and I picked that out in New York three years ago. It had just come into the gallery. Fort met Hans Hoffman once, years ago. He told me that Hoffman had such an almost childlike quality of enthusiasm, that youthfulness that comes from being eternally inquisitive. I told Fort he had exactly the same thing. He looked so startled I had to laugh at him. Golly, I'm going to miss that painting."

"Do you have to sell it?"

"In November, two weeks after Fort died, a very polite and considerate man showed up with a perfectly legitimate bill of sale for that Hoffman. He's a Chicago collector, and he paid Fort seven thousand five for it. He said that he had added it to his fine arts rider on his insurance policy, and he insisted on leaving it here until I decide what I'm going to do. It wasn't a shock, Trav. Not by then. By then I knew I couldn't consider anything mine. Not even the house."

"I don't understand."

She took my empty glass and said, "The lady yelled help. Remember?"

two

I knew she must have planned how she would tell me, but when she started, I could see that it seemed wrong to her.

She stopped and hopped up and began pacing around.

At last she stopped in front of me and said, "Okay. Look at it this way. Look at me and Fort from the outside, the way his son and daughter saw us. Their mother, Glenna, died eighteen years ago, when Roger was eleven and Heidi was seven. So they were the privileged children of Dr. Fortner Geis. Money *and* prestige. Money in the family from their mother's side, plus what Fort added to it by becoming a great neurosurgeon—and the prestige of being the children of a man who'd made himself an international reputation. Fort told me he'd made a lot of mistakes in his life, but the worst one of all was the one he made five years ago, after the diagnosis was absolutely certain, after the prognosis was definite, deciding to tell Roger and Heidi that he probably had not more than three more years left. Damn it, Trav, he wasn't looking for sympathy or being dramatic. He was a doctor. He knew a fact pertinent to their lives. So he told them. He'd always worked too long and too hard for the relationship with his kids to be terribly close. They set up a death watch, practically. They started dropping in on him, full of brave and noble cheer. And it started depressing him to the point where finally he had to get away by himself. He canceled out everything for a month and came down to Fort Lauderdale and didn't let anybody know where they could find him. He told me he had some adjusting to do. He said he had been too busy to think about dying. And if a man was going to die, he should have some time for contemplation, so he wouldn't die without coming to any decision about what it had all meant. He wanted to walk on the beach, look at the birds, read something other than medical journals. And he started coming into the dining room at odd times for coffee when I could sit with him and we could talk. Dammit, Trav, I had *no* idea he was important. I knew he was a doctor. I knew he was a widower. He said he was taking his first vacation in twenty-five years. There was that wonderful . . . simplicity about him."

"I know," I said. "That long nobbly face and the spaniel eyes and the slow grin."

"Loneliness," she said. "Both of us. We never talked trivia. We started talking from the heart right off. He'd loved Glenna deeply. He still missed her. And when we finally had a date, he told me what was wrong with him, and how long he probably could keep operating, and how soon he would die. We'd each taken our lumps. I told him . . . what had nearly sunk me without a trace. He was fifty, Travis. I was twenty-nine. Something in us responded to each other. He said it was because we knew what some things cost, and why other things were worthless, and too many people never found out. Then he asked me to marry him, and he said that if I felt squeamish about his being sick, I'd better not, because he desired me, and that was the kind of marriage he wanted with me, along with being friends and in love. He said he would have two years anyway before there was any outward sign or feeling, and it would get bad, but not too bad, when the medication stopped working. So I thought it over for two days, and knew I wanted him, and proved there was no squeamishness, and married him with the idea we'd be going back to some sort of old frame house with a downstairs office and waiting room in front, and some old dragon of a nurse. We had three and a half good years, Travis. We laughed a lot. I tell you, we laughed a hell of a lot. The pain started last April, but it didn't get as bad as he thought it was going to. And in September, he just started . . . dwindling away. Very quietly."

She sat down again. "Anyway, he was like a kid when he brought me back here to Chicago. I'd been too dumb to know who he was. He had this house designed and built for us, and sold the one in town. He cut his work back to just the experimental part. He didn't do any routine operations. It gave us more time. But you can guess what his friends and his kids thought. They made him so mad. They looked at me as if I was some kind of a bug. They acted as if marriage was some act of senility or something. I was the smart little operator, a waitress type, who nailed the poor guy when he was depressed about knowing he wasn't going to get anywhere near three score and ten. And the inference was that I probably liked it better that way. Roger was the worst. He's twenty-nine. He's a market analyst. He's a self-satisfied fink. He had the gall—and the stupidity—to go to Fort and suggest that inasmuch as I'd married him so late in his life, it would be a lot fairer to his kids to just leave me a reasonable bequest in his will. Fort had made a new will by then.

It was pretty complicated, with trusts and so on, but the basic idea was he'd leave me half and them each a quarter. I told him I didn't want to make that kind of hard feeling, and he got so annoyed I had to drop the whole thing. I had to go to the bank with him a few times to see Mr. Andrus, the assistant trust officer, and sign things. He's very nice. I decided that after it was all over I could talk to him and see about some way of taking just what I'd need to get settled into a new life, and let his children have the rest of it. As it turned out, there was no problem."

"How do you mean?"

"He just didn't leave anybody anything. There wasn't anything left to leave."

"What do you mean? Had he been kidding people?"

"No. Starting about a year ago in July, he started changing things into cash. Mr. Andrus is going to bring the list around tomorrow. You see, he didn't have things actually put away in trust where he couldn't get at them. Mr. Andrus can explain all that. And his lawyers had no way of knowing what he was doing. He just . . . sold the stock and the bonds and everything and kept putting the money in checking accounts. Then he kept drawing cash. Nobody knows where it went. He mortgaged this house right to the hilt. He cashed in his insurance policies. All but one. I'm the beneficiary on that. And it pays me f-f-four hundred dollars a m-month as long as I . . . as long as I . . . l-l . . ."

"Whoa, girl."

She rubbed the corduroy sleeve across her eyes. "Damn! I'm not the crying kind. It's just that everybody has been so damned ugly to me."

"How much has disappeared?"

"A little over six hundred thousand dollars."

"In a little over a year!"

"He did it in such a way it wouldn't attract attention. He opened other checking accounts, and he'd make deposits to other banks by check and then draw the cash. There was enough for the funeral, and enough to run this house for . . . oh, until February or March. Roger and Heidi seem to think it's some kind of cute stunt I've pulled. They act as if I'd drugged him or hypnotized him or something. The Internal Revenue people and the state tax people started treating me like a criminal or something.

They came with a warrant and they searched every inch of this whole house and made inventories of everything. They kept coming back and asking the same questions. I told Mr. Andrus I couldn't stand it, and he took me right down to Fort's attorneys. Waldren, Farhauser and Schrant. Old Mr. Waldren kept asking me questions. He looked as if he was taking a nap all the time I was answering. But finally he said he would see that I was not bothered anymore, but I had better stay right here at the house, for the time being. I know I'm being watched. I think it's Roger or Heidi though, paying someone to keep an eye on me. I yelled help, Trav. I don't *want* the damned money. But I don't want people following me for the rest of my life trying to catch me with something I haven't got."

"Was there any change in Fort's attitude or manner?"

"When he started selling things? I didn't notice a thing different. He seemed happy. That's what I wanted. I mean we couldn't be all the way happy, knowing the time was growing short. But we could give it a good try. And we did. That's another thing. I don't think he was trying to cheat on estate taxes or anything like that. I don't think he wanted to cash in those things. So somebody was making him do it somehow. And so that *was* making him unhappy, but he kept it from me. He hid it from me. And I would like to get my hands on somebody who'd do that to him when he had so little time left, damn them."

"Would the illness affect his mind in any way?"

"Absolutely not!"

"Could he have been planning some . . . easier way of handling his estate and died before he had a chance to tell you?"

"They kept asking me that, sort of. No. Those last days before he went into a coma, I sat by him all day long. Held his hand. We'd talk. He'd nap and we'd talk more. He had a chance to say everything to me. He knew he was going. And . . . God, how he hated to leave me. He wasn't afraid of death. He was a man. It was the same way he used to hate to leave me when he had to go to a meeting. That's all. How much in love do you have to be before people believe it? I would have burned every inch of all that money to give him one more day."

She stopped looking fierce and glanced at her watch.

"Medium rare? Butter on the baked? Garlic dressing?"

"Your memory is still working, kid."

She trotted out toward the back of the house to tell Anna to serve as soon as it was ready. When she came back I asked her how well-fixed Fort's children were. She said that Heidi seemed to be doing just fine. She was twenty-five—married at twenty-two and divorced at twenty-four. It had been a second marriage for her husband, Gadge Trumbill, usually referred to in the society pages as a prominent sportsman. When Heidi had tired of Gadge's fun and games on the side, it was rumored that she employed people thorough enough to make an iron-clad list of positives which had included eleven wives of fellow members of the Harbour Yacht Club, but that the generous settlement and alimony had been the result of the respondent's unfortunate carelessness in not hiding more successfully his occasional penchant for willowy young men. Heidi Trumbill was living in a studio apartment at 180 East Burton Place, was busily painting very large abstracts, and was showing and selling them at a gallery four blocks away on East Scott Street called Tempo East. Gossip of the more rancid variety pointed out that her partner in the gallery operation, Mark Avanyan, was one of those who had made Gadge's second divorce considerably more expensive than his first. It made for interesting speculation.

"She is one very icy dish indeed," said Glory. "Take Grace Kelly like ten years ago, and give her a little more height and heft, and put her in a part where she's a nun who has to dress in civilian clothes to smuggle the code to the French army, and you'd be close. She's really beautiful, but she's one of those people you can hardly believe they have even a digestive system. She's a lot brighter than Roger, I think. He lives in Evanston, where else? He'll be thirty soon. He works downtown in one of those big new office buildings. He's a specialist in the commodities market, and his father-in-law is very big in the commodities market. Jeanie, his wife, seems nice enough. She's one of those brown tennis-playing ones, and they have three kids, and they go to horse shows and eat off the tailgate and talk about hocks and fetlocks and all that.

"Neither of them are hurting a bit, but you'd think I'd pulled some tricky thing to get them tossed out naked into a blizzard. From everything Fort told me about Glenna, she must have been a doll. How could those two have such dreary people for their children?"

We ate busily and finally she looked over at me and said, "What I really had the most need of, Trav, was somebody to be my friend and take it for granted I haven't stolen money, and who'd know I didn't know anything about the money when I married Fort. I didn't make friends here. We wanted all our time together. There wasn't enough to share. But I thought, too, it *is* a lot of money and it *does* have to be somewhere. And I remembered the way you . . . make a living. Maybe I'm crazy to think you or anybody could ever find out where it went."

"It went somewhere. It's a nice jackpot. He had to have a good reason. Let's just say I don't have the feeling I'm wasting my time. If I can get some kind of line on what happened, then I'll see if my fee formula grabs Sonny and Sis. If the only way they can possibly get what they had coming is through me . . ."

"Expenses off the top and cut the rest down the middle. You know that is okay with me on my share, dear. When I think it even entered my mind to turn mine over to those two . . . I'd rather give it to a home for . . . old television comedians!" She looked so totally outraged and indignant I had to laugh. She put her plate aside and I saw she had not eaten much.

"Where's that wolf-like appetite I remember from old?"

"I don't know. It's fine for five minutes and then gaah. I guess I could have expected some kind of crazy thing happening, like the money. What is it, Travis? Why in the world should *my* life be some sort of continuous soap opera? I think I had six uneventful years. The first six. Gloria Anne Ridgen. Then all hell broke loose. Is there such a thing as drama-prone? You know, *you* go *hunting* for the action. My daddy bought me a ride on a merry-go-round, and that was the time the man running it had to be drunk and decided he wasn't going to stop it. When they died I had to live with my nutty old aunt, and if my astrology tables were wrong any given day, she wouldn't let me go to school. The boy I went with in high school was walking by a building and somebody dropped a can of paint, and when he woke up from the coma a year later, he had the mind of a two-year-old. In college my roommate was a secret klepto and hid the loot in my luggage and when they began to narrow it down, she turned me in, and six months later she got caught and they apologized and asked me to come back to school and the day I was due to leave I got infectious mononucleosis and my dog was run over. All I want is a plain, neat, ordinary, unexciting life. But what happens? In Buffalo one day I got off the bus downtown on a hot afternoon and the bus door closed on my wraparound skirt and drove off and left me spinning like a top in my little yellow briefs on the busiest corner in town. You know, I dream about that. There I am, and everybody is applauding and I can't stop twirling."

Anna Ottlo had gone to bed. We took the dishes out to the big bright kitchen and she rinsed them and put them in the dishwasher. I was aware of the wind, and of the emptiness of the stretch of dunes and winter beach outside, and of the comfort of the house.

"Was this whole thing in the news?" I asked her.

"No. From what John Andrus says, it isn't news until there's some kind of legal thing that goes on, the probate or something. He can explain."

I decided it would be better not to tell her what had entered my mind. If a man, before dying, had converted his holdings into over half a million in cash, there would be a certain number of dim minds in a city of this size who would be inspired to pay a night visit to the little woman and see if she could be persuaded in ugly ways to tell where the deceased had hidden it away. It would be a clumsier variation of Heidi's and Roger's incorrect suspicion.

She turned lights off, and when one was left, we said goodnight by the embers of the fire. "You're so good to come," she said softly, standing close, hands holding my wrists, head tilted back to look up into my eyes.

"Beach bums have to take care of each other, Glory."

"But it's never your turn."

We were smiling, and then there was that awkwardness born of a simultaneous remembering of a special closeness of long ago. Her gaze slid away, and I bent to her quick kiss, and we said goodnight. I took one glance back into the big room after she had turned the last light out,

and I could see her small brooding silhouette in front of
the ember glow.

three

There was a watery sunlight when I got up, and a diminish-
ing wind. I found the bright and cheerful breakfast alcove
off the kitchen. Anna said Miss Glory had gone walking
along the beach and should be back soon, and I should
eat.

"Eat like the bird, Miss Glory is. Too thin, ya?" Anna
said.

"She looks healthy."

"Need some fat. Better in the winter some fat."

When she brought my bacon and eggs to the breakfast
booth I asked her if she had worked long for Dr. Geis.

"From I was thirty only," she said proudly. "Refugee.
Only the German language I had. My little girl eleven.
Husband had one grandmother Jew. He got us out, was to
come later." She shrugged. "The Doctor Geis helped looking for him after the war. Never found. Then it was the
house in the city we were in, ya? Heidi has only one year
then and Roger has five years. All happy. Three years
I am here and the lady then has the bad sickness of the
heart. A very sad thing for the house. Weaker weaker
weaker, and the last year in bed. Nurses. Even such a
man like the Doctor Geis, he cannot the lady save." Her
broad heavy-featured face looked tragic, but then as she
looked beyond me out the window, she smiled suddenly,
"Here comes Miss Glory."

Gloria came striding through the loose sand and stamped
her feet when she reached the flagstone walk. She had on
wine-red wool slacks, a stocking cap with a red topknot,
her hands shoved deeply into the slash pockets of a short
leather coat. She smiled at me through the window, and
came in, yanking the stocking cap off, shaking her black

24

crisp hair out, shedding the leather coat. As she slid in opposite me, Anna brought her a steaming cup of coffee. Glory had red cheeks. She wore a black lightweight turtle-neck sweater. "My word! Can we afford to feed this creature, Anna?"

"Good to cook for a big stomach."

"Sleep well, Trav? It's going to be glorious later on. There's that feel in the air. It's going back up into the fifties, I bet."

She had a toasted English muffin, and we took our second coffees into the living room where she called John Andrus and told me he said he would try to get out to the house by ten-thirty.

"Who does he think I am?"

"Sort of an appointed big brother. An old friend. Some-body I trust. I told him I wanted him to explain the things I don't quite understand, so you can advise me and help me."

"What does he think I do for a living?"

"Well, I said you're in marine supplies. Okay?"

"It's nice to know what you said," I told her. "And after we get into it, could you sort of remember some-thing you have to go do?"

"Darling, it will be a pleasure. When he talks about that stuff, it makes my head hurt."

John Andrus was a likable guy in his late thirties. He was stocky, dark-haired, well-tailored, with the strong features of a character actor. We talked in Fort's study. Andrus had brought along the documents in a black dis-patch case.

"This report summarizes an awful lot of leg work," he said. "He had thirteen months of activity. It would average a little under fifty thousand a month converted into cash. He didn't want to attract attention, obviously. He opened up checking accounts in six other banks. He fed the money through the seven accounts. Apparently he also, in addition to cashing checks at the banks, cashed checks at clubs, restaurants, and hotels where he was well-known. He cashed in his securities holdings at at least four different brokerage houses. I think this summary by month of the assets converted to cash and the cash with-drawals through the checking accounts is very close to

25

actuality. See, here is the biggest month for sale of assets, over two hundred thousand. He converted seventy-two thousand into currency last January, and that was the biggest month. The smallest was last June. Twenty-one thousand. He was a very respected—and respectable—man, Mr. McGee."

"Strange behavior."

"We're a little dazed, frankly. We had the estate set up so beautifully. Residuary trusts, insurance trusts, beautifully drawn instruments. And when the time comes to put them into effect, we can't find anything except some very minor asset values. It wasn't really big money, of course. But it's enough to be worth handling properly. We've been through all his personal papers and records, and there isn't a clue. It's distressing."

"To you and the IRS too."

He frowned. "Unfortunately the man assigned to it was not too experienced. He got very agitated. He was going to attach everything in sight, the small equity left in the house, Mrs. Geis' insurance, the cars and so on. So we elected, as executor, to have the estate appraised one year from the date of death, as is our option. I imagine the IRS man thought it was some sort of attempt to evade estate taxes."

"But you don't."

He looked shocked. "Of course not! Fortner Geis was not a stupid man, and I think he was an honest man. I think he would . . . weigh all the alternatives, and do what he felt he had to do."

"Which one of us is going to say the nasty word, Mr. Andrus?"

He shrugged. "Okay. Blackmail. I investigated that possibility with Mrs. Geis, and with the daughter, Mrs. Trumbill, and with young Mr. Geis. I also checked with . . . some of the doctor's associates. It is a complete blank. Well, not exactly a complete blank. Mrs. Trumbill was very distressed when her father married a woman so much younger, and a woman . . . not quite on the social level of the Geis family, let us say. She suggested that her father might be paying out large sums to protect Mrs. Geis."

"From what?"

"When her father brought her back here, Mrs. Trumbill thought it would be wise to . . . have her stepmother investigated. She got a report on what had happened to Mrs. Geis' first husband and her two children in Buffalo over six years ago." He hesitated, looked troubled, and said, "I have a lot of respect for Gloria. I like her a great deal. And I do not like Heidi Geis Trumbill. Mrs. Trumbill suggested to me that perhaps Gloria in a jealous rage had killed her neighbor and her first husband, and the two children who witnessed it, and then someone who could prove that's what happened showed up and the doctor was paying that person to keep silent."

"Heidi seems to have a nasty mouth."

"She thinks Gloria had her father hypnotized. I felt duty-bound to check out her murder theory. Nonsense, of course. According to the Buffalo police reports, a neighbor saw Gloria turn into the driveway and get out of the car with a bag of groceries about two minutes after the woman had phoned the police about hearing the shots. When I told Mrs. Trumbill about that, she gave me a strange little smile and said perhaps if we kept on digging we'd probably find something sufficiently nasty in Gloria's background to account for where the money went. And, if not, it was obvious that she had talked the Doctor into putting his estate into cash and turning it over to her. How could we be sure, she asked, that Mrs. Geis hadn't already taken it out of the country?" He sighed. "I suppose I shouldn't let it bother me. Estate work gives you a chance to see people at their worst."

"How much would Heidi have gotten?"

"The way it was set up, and you must understand that there were insurance policies cashed which would have built the estate up to over seven hundred thousand. Once the estimated taxes and expenses were paid, Gloria would have gotten three hundred thousand, and his children a hundred and fifty thousand each. Three trust funds. Heidi's was the most restrictive. She was limited to the income only, say seventy-five hundred a year, and at the time of her death the principal amount was to be divided equally among her children, if any, and her brother's children. Roger was to be given the right to withdraw in any year up to ten per cent of the amount originally placed in trust for him. Gloria was to have the house and all physical property, and the right to withdraw all or any part of the monies in trust at any time. When he learned

27

of this provision, Roger said it proved that his father was not of sound mind at the time the instruments were drawn up, because it did not make sense to give a woman untrained in the handling of money complete freedom of access to three hundred thousand dollars, while restricting the son, who was in the business of handling money, access to not more than fifteen thousand a year of the principal amount."

"Great kids, those two."

"Unfortunately I'd say they're about average."

"If nobody ever finds out where the money went, what happens? Can Gloria lose that insurance money?"

"No. There'll be no estate taxes at all. The government can't merely assume she has the money, and procede against her on that basis. I imagine they'll keep careful track of her, and if she seems to be spending more than her income, they would ask awkward questions."

"She thinks she's being watched now."

"She might be. If it bothered her too much, I'd arrange to find out who is behind it. Oh, there was something else I discovered when I was asking Mrs. Geis about the possibility of blackmail. She said that there was a clumsy attempt to blackmail the Doctor over two years ago, nearly three years ago in fact."

"On what basis?"

He looked uncomfortable. "I think it would be more proper if Gloria told you about it."

"Sure. I understand."

"Mr. McGee, I think it would make sense if you would advise Mrs. Geis to close this house and let us put it on the market. I think we might be able to clear fifteen out of it, possibly a little more. I hate to see her run through what she has in her own checking account so quickly."

"She said Fort's attorney, Mr. Waldren, advised her to stay put."

"It was my impression he meant she should stay in the Chicago area. Well . . . I have other reports here, but they don't help us much. He died on October seventh. It wasn't until early November we began to realize most of the capital asset value had disappeared. By then the trail was cold. He'd wound it all up four months earlier, in July. If he was turning the money over to someone, we have no way of telling when or how or who."

"Gloria said he seemed happy that last year—as happy as you could expect a man to be under those circumstances."

"That's puzzling, Mr. McGee. He would have had to be under strain no matter what the reason behind it was."

"Strain," I said. "I guess it's relative. I remember a story about him in *Time* magazine. I can't remember the details. It must have been at least ten years ago. He flew over to some place in the Middle East and took a benign tumor out of some politician's brain. He operated for nine hours, and he could have lost the patient at any minute of those nine hours, and there was a chance that if he did lose him, some of the wild-eyed members of the party would have gunned him down when he left the hospital in spite of the troops they'd assigned to guard him. There was some background in the article on him too. In World War II in Europe he went AWOL from the General Hospital where he was on the neurosurgical team, and they found him at a field hospital trying out and getting good results with a nerve graft technique that had to be done as soon as possible after the wounds happened. He'd made his request through channels and nothing happened, so he reassigned himself. The only time I knew him was when he was in Florida and married Gloria. Okay, a very mild and gentle guy. But he had that look. The ones who get past the point of ever having to prove anything to themselves or anyone else have that look. We laid on the bachelor brawl bit for him. By two in the morning there were just the three of us left, Fort, a friend named Meyer, and me. Fort started telling doctor stories. He talked until dawn. Meyer said it had been a long time since he'd had anything shake him up that much, anything that started him thinking in a different kind of pattern. I have this feeling, Mr. Andrus. Anybody who tried to lean on that nice mild guy would do better trying to pat tigers, I think."

"So what did happen?"

"Somebody as essentially tough as Fortner Geis found some leverage that would work on Fortner Geis, and they were smart enough to stay back out of range while they squeezed him. And he was fatalist enough to adjust, to accept a lesser evil. Next step: accepting Fort as the kind of man he was, that leverage had to come from something in the past, some place where their lives crossed. Somebody has a very large and nervous amount of cash. If they were hard enough and smart enough to squeeze it out of Fort, they must have some very good idea of how to get the juice out of it without alerting the IRS computers."

John Andrus nodded slowly. "The more you have, the easier it is to add more without attracting attention."

"And if you can't do it that way, you have to have a lot of patience and control. You have to sit on it and then have some logical reason to pull up stakes and go elsewhere. Then, if you can get to Brazil or Turkey, and move very carefully, you can dig yourself in as a rich man without creating too much suspicion."

"Yes. It could be done," he said.

"Another thing interests me. The man applying the squeeze apparently knew or had some way of knowing how much Fort had. Otherwise I think Fort would have come up with, say, a quarter of a million and then made the squeezer believe he had it all."

Andrus began staring at me with a curious expression. "Mr. McGee, a lot of people have done a lot of wondering about this whole thing. And I've sat in on most of it. So you come along and for the first time I am beginning to get some kind of an image of what the person or persons had to be like. A very vague image, of course. But somehow . . . things seem to be narrowing down for the first time. Did Gloria tell me you're in the marine supply business?"

"Supply and salvage. Maybe I have a talent for larceny. A great parlor trick, thinking like a thief."

"Are you going to . . . pursue your theories?"

"I might look around a little, sure. Just as a favor for an old friend."

He put his papers away and snapped the catches on the dispatch case. "Is there any way I could make things easier for you? Unofficially."

"Did you have something in mind?"

"I don't think any friend of Mrs. Geis' is going to get any casual conversation out of Heidi Trumbill or Roger Geis." He took out two calling cards and with a slender gold pen wrote on the back of each, "Any cooperation you can give Mr. McGee will be appreciated—John Andrus."

"Thanks. Little talent for larceny yourself?"

"If there is, I hope to God they never notice it down at the Trust Department. Or run across one of those cards."

After we'd said good-bye to him, I went walking on the lake shore with Glory. She told me it was turning into a beautiful day. I told her that twenty-five more degrees would make a Floridian happier. Then I told her what John Andrus had said about cutting her expenses by giving up the house.

"Oh, I suppose that's very logical and bankerly," she said. "But Fort built it for us. The happiest time of my life was right here. Fort is here too, when I wake up, in those minutes before I remember he's gone. And he's in the next room, or around a corner, or on his way home. Those things hurt, Trav. They sting like mad. But when I leave here, then he's really gone forever. How else could I . . . buy the feel of having him near? The first insurance check came December third, last week. One every month for the rest of my life. Four hundred dollars. I'll put that into the kitty to hang onto the house a little longer. I'm not even going to think of what comes next, or plan anything, until I am all packed and on my way down the road. Don't expect me to be practical and logical, dear. Okay?"

"Okay. John Andrus seems fond of you."

"I know. In a very nice and special and, thank God, unsexy way. He has an adored wife and teen-age daughters. I think I was a refreshing experience to him because he finally realized I was absolutely sincere in not giving a dang about money, really. Oh, it's kind of delicious to have it. But too many of the things I like best don't cost a thing. At first poor John seemed to think I was trying to knock the Establishment. We were standing in the yard a month ago. One of the last leaves came off the maple. So I picked it up and made him look very closely and carefully at it. I made him *see* it. Then I asked him what it was worth, without cracking a smile. I could almost see the light bulb going on in the air over his head, like cartoons. Then, bless you, I fed him that speech you made a lifetime ago on Sanibel Island. If there was one sunset every twenty years, how would people react to them? If

31

there were ten seashells in all the world, what would they be worth? If people could make love just once a year, how carefully would they pick their mates? So now John thinks I am very nice in spite of being quite mad."

"I had to hold the world out to you the way you held the leaf out, Miss Glory, and make you look at it. Question. Does this hotel serve lunch?"

"Anna wouldn't miss the chance. She goes around smiling, she's so happy to have somebody around here who eats."

"What will happen to her when you close the house?"

"From what has happened so far, I imagine you will see the most noted socialite hostesses from the entire lake shore skulking around in the brush and crawling across the dunes, with money in one hand and leg irons in the other, wearing fixed glassy smiles. Anna Ottlo can name her own ticket."

It wasn't until cocktail time in front of the fireplace that I got around to the blackmail attempt John Andrus had thought more fitting for Glory to tell me.

"Heavens, he could have told you! He's really very circumspect. But . . . I'm glad he didn't, really. Because I think that you might not understand just how it happened. Fort, all his life, was very attractive to women. I guess he made every woman feel . . . valuable. He listened. He was interested. He liked them.

"Travis, I have to go way back to what life was like for him with Glenna, the things he told me about their marriage. They were very close. They were very important to each other. It was wretched timing for them that as soon as he got out of the army—he was about the same age then that Roger is now—and he and Glenna were just one month apart, they found out Glenna had congestive heart disease, and had maybe had it for some time without knowing it. Let me see now, Roger was eight and Heidi must have been four, because when she died three years later, Roger was eleven and Heidi was seven.

"Because Glenna had some money, they'd been able to marry and have children when Fort was going through the intern and resident thing, and they'd been able to have a nice home in the city, with Fort devoting more time, both before and after the war, to staff surgery and instruction

32

than to surgery for private fees. He came back to find that Anna Ottlo had become indispensable to Glenna, and that her daughter Gretchen, who was fourteen then, had become almost an older sister to Roger and Heidi."

She turned her glass slowly, then held it and looked at the firelight through what was left of her weak highball. She gave me a small and humble smile. "I'm not as objective as I sound, you know. I'm still jealous of Glenna for having so many more years of him than I did, and I resent her, sort of. That's kind of lousy, isn't it?"

"No. It's kind of nice. It's part of the human condition."

"The human condition isn't very logical. When Fort married Glenna, I was spilling pablum. Anyhoo, as more background, I have to give a little sex lecture. Sex and the doctor. It's something Fort explained to me. There are all those doctor-nurse stories, and there is a certain basis of truth in them, and here is one incident Fort told me about that explains that strange kind of truth. He said that when he was operating in the General Hospital, doing more operations in one day than he ever had before or ever would again, he had the luck to get hold of a great operating-room nurse, a big severe steady tireless girl named Fletcher. First Lieutenant Lois Fletcher. He said you have to acquire some kind of emotional immunity to all that terrible waste, all that young battletorn meat. He said you get a kind of black humor about it, and a good team, like he and Fletcher were, get in the habit of saying things to each other that would make a layman think they were heartless monsters. Fletcher's husband was a sergeant with the First Marine Division in the Pacific. He said that he and Fletcher were not promiscuous types, even in that permissive and demanding place. But one week they had, he said, a run on paraplegics. A terrible incidence of them, and not one of what he called the happy ones—where you could go in and take out a splinter of metal and relieve the pressure and know that the feeling would return to the lower body. After several days of that he said they finished one night, took off the bloody gowns, and went and sat in silence having coffee. They were both beat. Suddenly he said they were looking into each other's eyes, and they just got up without a word and went off to an empty room and closed the door and with a kind of terrible exhausted energy they made love. He said she clung to him and cried almost soundlessly, and they made love again and again. A despairing affirmation, he said. That was his phrase. And he said it was transcendent. That's the important idea, Trav, the one to remember. He said it was a way of turning the mind off, where all the horrible wheels are going around and around, and losing yourself in sensation for a little while. He said that was the only time for them, and the team was a little awkward the next day or so, getting signals slightly crossed, but from then on they were okay again, and they never spoke of it to each other."

She stopped and sat, scowling. "What's the matter?" I asked.

"I talk too much. Maybe now it's going to sound like a bigger deal than it was. Anyway, here's the scene. They have tried everything for Glenna. But the heart just does less and less of its job. She has been in bed for ten months. He has been back home for three years. Now it is suddenly necessary to have nurses around the clock. He does not know how long she will last. Actually, she lasted about six weeks more. She would not benefit by being put in a hospital to die. It would frighten her. Circulation is so bad the organs are not able to function properly. There is a danger of gangrene of her feet. But worst of all, because the brain is not properly supplied, her mind is failing. She moves from lucidity to fantasy and back, sometimes thinking he is her father. He is in hell. To provide better accommodations for the nurses, he moves to a small bedroom in the back of the house above the kitchen and pantry and service areas, the area where Anna and her daughter sleep. Both Anna and her daughter Gretchen are terribly worried about him. Their hearts go out to him. Anna cooks his favorite things so he will be tempted to eat. Gretchen's feeling toward the Doctor are complicated by two factors. First, she has such a fantastic crush on him, she can think of nothing else all day long. Second, she is not really very bright. She is not a retarded child. Just a little slow of wit, with a short attention span. She has romantic dreams of sacrifice, for the sake of love. She is seventeen, intensely physical, completely mature, and healthy as a plow horse. The doctor is thirty-five, suffering, miserable, wanting Glenna to die before she becomes a total vegetable, yet unable to comprehend how he can make a life without her.

"And now, Trav, the final little factors that made such a weird thing possible. An old house, thick walls, heavy doors. He has found that he can sleep if he drinks a great big slug of bourbon as he is going to bed. The infatuated girl is in the next room, her mother in the room beyond. Fort awakens, half-stoned, with the naked girl snuggled against him in darkness, hugging him, gasping into his throat, her body all hot velvet, smooth as a seal he said, her blonde hair long and perfumed, her hands damp and cold with nervousness. There is a perversity about the tempted animal, Fort explained to me. First you say you are imagining it or dreaming it, and then when it begins to become all too real, you tell yourself that in a moment you will wake up all the way, register shock, and end the self-indulgence before it goes too far."

"But there was the word you told me to remember. Transcendent."

"Yes. Turning off all the awful engines in the mind. He said that only when the child began orgasm did he suddenly realize what a shocking and fantastic and inexcusable thing had happened. Afterward he told her that he was as guilty as she, and they would talk to her mother about it the next day. She wept and begged him not to, and said she would never tell, and said she loved him, she would die for him, all she wanted was to please him a little, to make him happier, to make him forget a little bit.

"In the morning it seemed very unreal to him. And he could not imagine how in the world he'd tell Anna Ottlo that the master of the house had romped the housekeeper's more than willing daughter."

As she told what happened I could see just how he could have been in the emotional condition to get into such a bind. The girl had come sneaking back the next night, of course, and then he knew he couldn't tell Anna. He knew after it had happened again. He made her promise never to come back again, and never to tell. So she stayed away one night and then she came back saying she couldn't help herself, couldn't stay away from him, loved him and so on. Fort was, from my candid appraisal, a thoroughly masculine type. He was thirty-five, and he certainly hadn't had any sex in his marriage for a long time. From what Glory was telling me, I could see how it could happen even with a man like Geis, to whom you could apply the adjective good without feeling self-conscious about it.

The girl Gretchen, from Glory's second-hand description, was a sturdy fräulein, extremely blonde, big breasts, big hips, China-blue eyes, who'd blush so furiously every time she ran into Fort during the day he wondered how soon somebody would guess what was going on. So each day the beloved wife faded further toward death, and each night Fort would lose himself in that firm, eager, abundant young flesh. I could guess that she was not sensuously complex, just hearty and lusty, and it was very probable that as they became closely attuned, they would find the joining becoming almost ritualistic in its sameness, the hands, heads, mouths, legs always placed just so, the bodies becoming like one entity, so that no matter which one began the completion first, the laggard would be brought quickly along by the body's awareness of it being the time of climax. It would be ritualistic and hypnotic, and a man like Fort would feel guilt and shame, but it would be cushioned by his knowing that no matter how wretched the inevitable ending of it would be, the bad ending of marriage and the bad ending of his wife's life was just as inevitable. In such a situation there could be almost a compulsion to find a guilt-feeling. When the beloved is dying, we want to be blamed and punished. Without that there seems to be nothing left but an indifferent malevolence of fate.

She fixed new drinks, handed me mine and said, "Fort told me it all became unreal to him. And then Glenna died. He moved back to the bedroom where she had died. He'd become so . . . habituated to Gretchen he could not comprehend not wanting her. But suddenly he didn't. She couldn't risk sneaking through the house. Two days after the funeral she was waiting in the garage when he came home from the hospital. She told him she was pretty sure she was pregnant. He gave her a test. She was. She said there was no reason why he couldn't marry her. Now if Fort had been a weak, silly, sentimental man, he might have done just that. But he was always able to look at things objectively. A marriage that grotesque would have been as bad for her as for him. So he told her it was ridiculous to even think of such a thing. He came home in the middle of the morning the next day, when his kids were in school. He had told Gretchen to stay home from school. She was slow in school. She was in the tenth grade, and kept asking her mother to let her drop out. Fort brought Anna and her daughter into the living room and had them sit down and he told Anna what had happened and what the situation was.

"That must have been a dandy morning."

"Fort told me that it had to be done. When something has to be done, you do it. You have no choice. Gretchen tried to lie, and say that Fort had seduced her. Anna knew Fort better than that. She got in about three good whacks, and Gretchen, bawling, told the whole truth. Fort said Anna was very pale. She asked questions about exactly how the affair had begun, and then sent Gretchen off to her room. Fort said Anna was eminently practical. She blamed him only for not telling her the first time it happened. She said it was best to assume the girl had been impregnated that very first night. Then there was less guilt. A man was a man. The girl was very ripe and eager. But the girl's idea of marriage to Herr Doktor was, of course, impertinent. Arrangements could be made if it was known how much the Doctor would settle on the unborn child. She said that if Gretchen were a bright girl and doing well in school and deserved more education, perhaps an abortion would be best. But a girl like her daughter would be much better off married, and with children. Fort said that as soon as Glenna's estate was settled, he would arrange very quietly to buy a single payment annuity which would provide the child with approximately a hundred dollars a week for life, and in the interim, he would turn over a hundred dollars a week out of pocket to Anna to give to Gretchen. Anna said that was more than enough, much more. Fort said he would not feel right about making it any less. Two weeks later Gretchen was married to a twenty-year-old boy named Karl Kemmer. Karl's mother was, like Anna, a refugee, an older woman than Anna. She had lost two older sons in the war. She had gotten Karl out and into the States less than a year earlier. He was an apprentice, learning sheet-metal work. Fort said he seemed like a very decent kid. Gretchen gave birth to a girl. They named her Susan. Through his lawyer, a man who has since died, Fort arranged the annuity in the name of Susan Kemmer with the money to be paid monthly to her parent or guardian until she reached eighteen, and then paid directly to her."

"How did Gretchen react to that?"

"Not so great. She blamed her mother for not siding with her to get Fort to marry her. Fort said that while Anna and Gretchen were still getting along, Anna enjoyed being a grandmother. Then the marriage started to go bad. Maybe Karl Kemmer resented the bargain he made. Gretchen started going with other men. Fort said she and Anna had battles about it. When Susan was three, Gretchen had a little boy. When the little boy was a year old, Karl Kemmer was killed in an industrial accident. After another quarrel, Gretchen left town suddenly with a married man, taking both children with her. Fort said Anna was grim and remote and unapproachable for a time, and then she became herself again. But she would not mention Gretchen. She told Fort she did not have a daughter."

"So it had to be Gretchen who tried to shake Fort down a couple of years ago?"

"Three years ago next month. She waylaid him at the hospital. She said she didn't want to come here because she didn't want her mother to know she was back in Chicago. She'd been back three months. She didn't want her mother to know that things hadn't gone too well for her. Fort said she was heavy and coarsened, but sexy in a full-blown blowzy way. She said she was doing waitress work in a restaurant on West Lake Street, and living with her five kids in a fourth-floor walkup in the Maywood section. She had married somebody out West. I can't remember the name he told me. And she'd had three children by him and one had died, and she had married another man and had one child by him who was then three years old. I can't remember the third husband's name either, but she told Fort he was in prison. She said that even with the money coming in for Susan, she couldn't seem to make ends meet, so she'd come to tell him he had to start sending her another hundred a week."

"Just like that, eh?"

"It irritated Fort and it puzzled him that she should put

it in the form of a demand, and look so perfectly sure of herself. So he asked her why she thought he'd do that. So she said she'd found out he'd just moved into a fine new house and he had a new young wife and probably the new young wife thought she'd married a great man, but she wondered how the new young wife would react if Gretchen paid her a little visit and told her that while his first wife was on her death bed, the big famous Dr. Geis was busy knocking up a young dumb kid, his housekeeper's daughter, right in the same house, every night for weeks. Fort said he wasn't irritated anymore. Just sad. So he told her about how he and I had no secrets, and he had told me the whole thing, so there wasn't any way she could put that kind of pressure on him. Then in that gentle way of his he asked her why she would try such a thing, and why she would make what had happened between them, foolish as it might have been, sound so much dirtier than it had actually been. So she began to cry and she told him that her husband had told her to try it. He realized that she was basically unchanged. She was still a slow-minded, amiable, romantic kind of person. He said he would look into her situation and see if he could give her some help if she really needed it."

"I would guess she did."

She explained that Fort hired investigators to make a full report, and asked them to go into detail about the daughter Susan, age fourteen then. He showed Glory the report. It said she had been the common-law wife of the man out West and she was the common-law wife of the man in prison in Wisconsin. She was a sloven, but good with her kids, affectionate with them like a mother bear, hugging them and whacking them. But not much sense of responsibility. She'd get off work and go to a beer joint, and Susan would be the sitter for the littler ones. She apparently could be picked up without too much trouble, but she never took men back to her place. Susan sounded pretty special. Bright and blonde and pretty, and very earnest about seeing that the kids got proper food and were dressed adequately. And she kept the apartment clean. It looked as if they could get along on the four hundred from the annuity and the two hundred and fifty or so that Gretchen was making in wages and tips, but Gretchen liked to play the numbers and the horses too well. If there was more money, she'd just bet more.

"Fort and I talked over what if anything he ought to do. In the end he got in touch with Gretchen and told her that if she stopped gambling, all her kids would be better off, and he had no intention of giving her any money. Then he had the same investigators get word to Susan that if any emergency ever came up that she couldn't handle, she was to contact them, but it would be best not to tell her mother about it. We wondered what we should try to do when Susan became eighteen and began getting her own money directly. We talked about it as if . . . Fort would still be around. She'll be eighteen next year. We wanted to make sure she'd go to college and not get cheated out of it by having to look after the other kids. She certainly wasn't any threat—Gretchen wasn't—to Fort. It was just sort of dreary and sad. I'd half decided that after Fort died, I'd go to Susan and explain everything and see if I could sort of . . . look after her. After all, I guess I'm only a couple of years too young to be her mother. So that's all it was. Look how long it took me to tell it. That's what comes from living alone. Dinner now?"

"Unless you want to see a grown man cry."

When we were eating I asked her if Anna knew about Gretchen's attempted shakedown. She said Fort hadn't told Anna about it, but he had told her about Gretchen being in town with five children. At first Anna hadn't wanted to do anything about it, but Fort had sensed it was pride and bull-headedness. She had visited once when Gretchen was there and it had ended very badly, so from then on she had visited when she knew the kids would be there and Gretchen would be working.

"Did you go see Susan yourself?"

"I waited too long. I had . . . a sentimental idea, Trav. I thought I would find out very carefully if she knew Fort was her father. If she did, I wanted to find out if she had any bad feeling about him. If she did, I was going to try to make her see how it was, how it happened, how Fort had done what he could, and then, if she was willing, bring her out here to see him. I know he wanted to see her. I mean from the report I guess he had the feeling he had fathered at least one pretty good kid. But he had felt reluctant to upset whatever adjustment the girl had made. I went there in September and they were gone. They'd been gone a couple of weeks. I asked Anna about it. She looked pretty bleak. She said that if she'd known I was going there, she would have told me they were gone. She said it was her idea Gretchen didn't want Anna buttering up the kids, so she just moved, maybe somewhere else in the city, maybe out of town. No forwarding address. Probably some new man, Anna said, looking as if she wanted to spit."

"Glory, have you got that investigator's report?"

"No. I thought they'd find it when they went through everything. But I guess Fort destroyed it."

"I wonder why he'd do that?"

"I guess he had a good reason. Trav, Fort had a lot of . . . wisdom. I guess that's the word. He thought things out and did what he felt would be best for everyone. Like when . . ."

"When what?"

"Nothing."

"From the expression on your face when you stopped yourself it wasn't exactly nothing, girl."

"It was just a personal thing, between Fort and me."

"And has nothing to do with anything else?"

"Nothing."

But I knew she was troubled, and so I decided not to take her off the hook. Again I went to the kitchen with her while she stowed the dishes. Again we had a nightcap by the last small tongues of flame in the glowing bed of embers. She talked trivia, and kept lapsing into silence, and finally out of a silence she said a bad word.

"Hmmm?" I said.

"Okay, okay, okay. That personal thing. Maybe it does have somethng to do with something. Trav, Fort and I had kind of let ourselves drift into a fool's paradise. We'd begun to believe it wouldn't end, and then the pains began. And when they did, neither of us were as good about it as we thought we were going to be. We disappointed ourselves. Depression and irritability and restlessness. It looked as if it was going to be totally lousy from then on in. We just didn't seem to be able to handle it . . . and get any good out of the time we had left. So Fort got something from a friend of his. Dr. Hayes Wyatt. He'd told Fort one time about the good results he'd been having with terminal patients using psychedelics. As Fort explained it to me, when there is pain, after a while the patients begin to identify the pain with death. Then the pain becomes like something that's after them, trying to take them away, and that makes the pain worse because there's fear there too. So he talked our problem over with Hayes Wyatt and Hayes thought it would be a good idea for both of us and told Fort what kind of a procedure might work best, and gave Fort a tiny little vial of it. LSD-25. Do you know about it?"

I did not tell her how it could still give me the night sweats to remember one Doctor Varn and the Toll Valley Hospital where they had varied the basic compound and boosted the dosage to where they could not only guarantee you a bad trip, they could pop you permanently loose from reality if you had any potential fracture line anywhere in your psyche. As a part of mending the damage they did to me, a bright doctor gave me some good trips and had given me in that special way the ability to comprehend what had happened in my head during the bad ones.

"I've been there," I told her.

She lighted up. "Then you *know*! You can't tell anybody what it's like."

"I haven't taken the social trips with a batch of acid heads who want to freak around. It was a medical thing, controlled."

"Oh, it has to be!" she said. "Fort measured the dosages onto little wads of surgical cotton. He gave me four hundred micrograms the first time, and stayed with me. It took about eight hours before it began to wear off. I watched over him after he took five hundred micrograms. It's spooky, you know. It was much too much to get the kind of good out of it we wanted. It took us too far to let us make any good bridge between here and there. But then we knew. And then, twice, we took a little less than a hundred micrograms at the same time. We could talk. We could talk with a closeness we never had before, and we'd thought we were as close as two people could get. What you learn is that you are . . . just one part of the whole human experience, part of a great rhythm of life and death, and when you have that insight, there's no fear. I knew the ways we would always be together, and I knew the ways we would have to part and I could accept that. Twice was all we needed. It gave us peace. It gave us a special happiness, not *more* than we had before, but different. It made us able to understand and accept . . . our identities."

"And you found out why you were so badly racked up when I found you on the beach?"

"Of course! Because I was wishing he'd die without letting myself know I was wishing it. And when he died and the kids died with him so horribly, losing the kids was the penalty I had to pay for wishing him dead. And Fort, to his utter astonishment, found out that he had secretly resented Glenna. She was one of those terribly terribly sweet women who never raise their voices, and who are fantastically strong and tough and aggressive underneath. He discovered that he had pretended love and created a myth-woman to fit that love, and that underneath she was maybe not a nice person at all. So he could not ever let himself comprehend he was glad she was dying. Accepting Gretchen's silliness gave him a guilt he *could* admit."

"So after the LSD, you both could handle the situation."

"He died damned well, and I helped him die well, and . . . those insights are still with me, Trav, still helping me. But I had never thought of how . . . it could relate to the money. Psychedelics give you an acceptance of inevitable things. Sort of—'so be it.' It would have given him the chance to weigh the difference in importance between death and money, and money is so . . . kind of insipid compared to true identity. Without that experience, Trav, I couldn't stay here. It would smash me to stay here. Now I wouldn't want to be anywhere else."

There is, I thought, almost no useful thing the human animal will not in his eternal perversity misuse, whether it be alcohol, gasoline, gunpowder, aspirin, chocolate fudge, mescaline, or LSD.

I once helped a baffled father get his daughter out of an acid party in downtown Miami. She went from the party directly into a private sanitarium. She had been a mildly disturbed personality before she got into that cult group. There were nine kids in that small room, aged eighteen, nineteen, and twenty. They had taken the trip together and they were about three hours into it, and had taken a heavy dose, so heavy there was no relating or identity between any of them. They brooded over the infinite in separate silences, isolated, somnambulistic, while the record-player needle made a hissing sound where, at the beginning of a record, it was trapped in a locked groove. Only two of them were having a bad trip. One boy sat in yoga position in a corner, facing into the corner, beating wearily at the side of his head with his fist and weeping hopelessly. The girl we were after was on her belly, creeping slowly backward, her shift hiked high above her waist by the friction, her eyes full of terror. The kids had not picked anyone to be the gooney —that wingless bird which never flies—to see that no one took a bad trip and harmed himself. The girl we took out of there had chewed her fingers to bloody ragged ruin. The others dreamed, swayed, smiled—and we left them there.

four

The next day was Saturday, and after breakfast I had Glory drive me into town and drop me. I told her I would poke around and be in touch. It was another one of those days Chicagoans have no right to expect in December, bright and balmy. My topcoat was more than adequate. I decided a large impersonal commercial hotel would make sense, so I took a cab to the Drake, checked into a single, found Mrs. Heidi Trumbill in the book at the 180 East Burton address, and phoned her. It was ten-fifteen.

After four rings a female voice said with considerable impatience and exasperation, "Yes? Yes?"

"Mrs. Trumbill, my name is McGee and . . ."

"*Please* try again at eleven-thirty, will you? I'm working with some acrylic paints, and they're drying so fast I'll lose what I'm after if I keep answering this goddam phone!" She hung up. Forcefully.

I went out and walked south on Michigan Avenue. In nice weekend weather it is one of the specialties of the house. Chicago is a strange one. It is not on my list of favorite places. Insofar as restaurants and lounges and hotels are concerned it is strictly hinterland, strictly hick. And as you go down the scale it becomes more shabby and shoddy than rough. I do not know why anyone should expect anything special in that line from a place where the Hefner Empire seems to represent some sort of acme of sophistication, based as it is upon fantastic centerfold mammalians for the pimpled self-lovers, upon a chain of bunny-warrens styled to make the middle-class sales manager feel like a member of an in-group, and upon a laborious philosophical discourse which runs interminably in the ad-happy magazine and in the polysyllabic style of the pseudo-educated, carrying the deathless message that it is healthy to screw and run if everybody is terribly sincere about it.

A great university they have indeed, but if you take a train there from the center of the city, you pass through whole areas of the South Side which make the worst of Harlem look like Scarsdale. It is a gigantic shameful tinderbox everybody is trying not to notice. If you are a stranger and want to leave the university area after dark, they insist on getting you a cab.

The best of Chicago, I think, must go on quite privately, and it must be very fine indeed. Private homes and private clubs, and a lot of insulation and discretion, because as I hiked along Michigan I saw and admired what I had come to see, strolling, window-shopping flocks of women of that inimitable smartness, style, loveliness, assurance, and aroma of money which will make headwaiters and captains all over the Western world leap, beaming, to unhook their velvet ropes before they even hear the name. I feel that they live in Chicago in very much the same spirit the early settlers lived in the wilderness full of Indians. They keep the big gates closed. They consort with each other, and they import those specialties their rude environment cannot supply, and when they need relief from that nerve-twanging combination of unending drabness and glittering boosterism, they take their ease at

45

the truly smart spots of the world and, when asked where they are from, tell the truth with that mocking inverted pride of the fellow pinned to the sod with a spear who said it only hurt when he laughed.

Statistically it is probably the one city in the world where the most people have been killed in arguments over professional athletes. The middle of the city, where nine bridges cross a large sewage canal called the Chicago River, is beginning to look as if Martians had designed it. For untold years the city has limped along under what might well be the most arrogant, ruthless, and total political control in the country. In a kind of constant hysterical spasm of self-distaste, the city uglifies itself further each year by chopping away more trees and paving more areas for all those thousands of drivers who seem to have learned their art at Daytona.

So I walked in the sunlight, and appreciated all the lovely ladies, and looked at the rich goods in the rich store windows. They had strung their Christmas lights, thousands and thousands of tiny white transparent bulbs festooning the bare branches of the trees which, by some oversight, still remain standing along Michigan Avenue. At the corner of Huron something that was entirely girl came swinging along, and wrapped the whole thing up for me. Nearly six lithe feet of her, and unmistakably great handloomed tweeds in conservative cut, lizard purse and walking shoes and hair chestnut-brown and gleaming with health, styled with no trickery, bobbing to her resolute stride, and one gloved finger hooked through the string of a parcel wrapped in gold foil paper, and on her mouth a lovely secret smile, perhaps part memory, part anticipation, and part appreciation of the day and of the good feel of taking long strides, and part being lovely and young. There is something about seeing one like that which tries to break your heart. You will never know her, but you want it all to be great for her, all the parts of it, the wine, the weather, the food, the people, the beds, the kids, the love, and the being old.

I walked all the way down to Monroe and then over to Wabash and into one of the great pipe stores of the Western world, Iwan Reis, across from the old Palmer House, and celebrated my luck at having seen so marvelous a girl at so marvelous a moment by gifting myself with a pale Ropp with a birds-eye grain, comfortable bite, and generous bowl.

Then I took a cab back out to East Burton, to a quainty old pile of red stone squatting close to the narrow sidewalk. There were four mailboxes and push buttons in the small foyer. Over the tube when I gave her my name, her voice, reduced to a frail buzzing sound, demanded to know what I wanted. So I said I had a note from John Andrus. She said she was on the second floor in the back and the door catch made a sound like a rattlesnake as she pressed the release.

Her heavy door was Chinese red, and when she pulled it open I saw how accurate Gloria's description of her had been. She was a tall slender golden-blonde, features so coin-cut, so classic and clear she had an ice-maiden look.

She looked at Andrus' card, front and back, handed it back, and said, "You're not exactly my picture of a banking type, Mr. McGee. Come in, please."

I followed her into a high-ceilinged living room. She wore white canvas coveralls, too big for her, man-size, the pant cuffs turned up. She had fashioned a belt out of a red scarf rolled to narrow width, and cinched the baggy garment around the narrowness of her waist. She had appraised me with blue-gray eyes which told me nothing, merely looked at me and made a record and filed it under McGee. Minimum makeup, no jewelry of any kind. She had that rare and contradictory look of being both slender and substantial, a look which I suspect comes from a certain breadth of shoulder, fruitful width of pelvic structure. Though the coveralls were spotted with stains of paint old and new, she looked groomed and immaculate.

She turned and leaned against a table edge, crossed her ankles, crossed her arms under her breasts and said, "So?"

Personal chemistries have not yet been isolated and analyzed by the physiologists. Here was a specimen in her twenty-five-year-old prime, in full bloom. Certainly the female of my species, beyond question. She had walked with a promising curl of power in the haunch. Her arms were crossed under a hammocked roundness of breast, and her mouth was of an understated sensuality in shape and dimension.

But we were saying no to each other without any words.

In my out-sized, wind-weathered, semi-battered, loose-jointed way I seem to get the right responses for my full and fair share of the fair ones, but I could not see any signs of impact, or experience any. Maybe Old Lady Nature sets up some kind of overriding counterirritant when the genetics are a bad match. I knew this could be a heady package for somebody, but not for the McGee. I had caught the smiling eye of the girl at the corner of Huron for a half-second, and it had been a resounding yes, both ways. A conditional yes. Yes, if it wasn't too late for us by the time we met. Yes, but I'm sorry it can't be.

I wondered about the No which Heidi Geis Trumbill and I were saying to each other. I know when you can hear that large No: when they are too wrapped up in exactly the right guy to even be aware you are alive, when they are one of the cool voyagers from the Isle of Lesbos, and when they are seriously thinking of killing you. I could not fit Heidi into any pattern.

"Sometimes," I said, "the banking types get some help from non-banking types."

"Let me say I think they need it. Talk about impartial. Hah! It's perfectly obvious John Andrus has let that sweet demure elfin little bitch sell him down the river. Any slight suggestion that she might not be a hundred and ten per cent perfection, and he gets furious."

"Kind of a strange marriage, I guess."

Suddenly she approved of me. "Do take off your coat, Mr. McGee. Care for a drink?"

As she went and fixed herself a beaker of dry sherry and some gin over ice for me, I wandered over and looked through a wide arched doorway into her studio. It had a lot of tall windows for good north light, and it was painted a good off-white. It had at least the look of a working artist's studio—work tables, easels, bouquets of worn-out brushes in old paint pots, new work on easels and on the walls, deep painting racks, scabs of paint on the floor, stacks of paintings leaning against the walls.

She came up and handed me my drink and stood beside me looking into the studio. "Please don't ask me to explain my work."

She had a rare talent for irritating me. So I said, "I doubt if you could, Mrs. Trumbill."

With a cold smile as she turned toward me, she said, "And what is that supposed to mean?"

"Sorry. I don't think you know what you're doing."

"My dear man, abstract expressionism has been around so long that it . . ."

"That it gets imitated too much. You've got some color sense. You go too far in setting up weird composition. But that doesn't mean you are setting problems or trying to solve them. It's glib stuff, Heidi. It hasn't got any bones. It hasn't got any symbol values, any underlying feeling of weight or inevitability. It's just sort of shock-pretty, and you certainly get some satisfaction out of doing it, but just don't start taking it or yourself too seriously."

Fury drained the color out of her face. She went striding away, whirled so quickly she slopped some of her sherry onto the living-room rug. "Just who the hell are you? My work *sells*! I've been in damned good juried shows. I've had some fantastic reviews."

"I'm just a guy who buys a painting once in a while."

"Then what could you possibly know about it? You jackasses learn a couple of stock words and voila! you're a critic yet."

"There's nothing wrong with decoration, Heidi."

"You will call me Mrs. Trumbill if you don't mind."

"I mind, Heidi. Your stuff will melt right into the wall after a week. Nobody will see it. That's no disgrace. It's decorative, but it ain't art."

"Get *out* of here!"

"You can call me Trav, or Travis." There was a piece of paper on a table beside a lamp. I saw a pencil on the coffee table. I took the blank paper over and put it beside the pencil. "Just make me a sketch of that lamp and the window beyond it, girl, and I'll go quietly."

"Oh, you mean draw you a cow that looks like a cow?" she said with a poisonous and knowing smile.

"Go ahead. Funny, but everybody I can think of right off the top of the head could sure God draw a fat realistic cow if they ever happened to want to. Hans Hoffman, Kline, Marca-Relli, Guston, Solomon, Rivers, Picasso, Kandinsky, Motherwell, Pollock. And you know it, baby. If you can't stand the heat, stay out of the kitchen. You dabblers bug me. You want the applause without all the thousands of hours of labor learning how to draw, how to make brush strokes, learning all the things that give painting some bite and bones even when you don't use any part of it. Go ahead, draw the lamp. Quick sketch. Prove I'm a jackass."

She trotted over, flounced down, took the pencil and made some quick lines, then stuck her tongue tip out of the corner of her mouth and drew a more careful line, then she got up and threw the pencil at the paper. It went bouncing under a chair. "Shit!" she said. "So I fake it. Everybody does. And I get away with it."

"Suddenly I think I like you a little better, Mrs. Trumbill."

Her smile was wan and strained. "I'm underwhelmed, Mr. McGee. People don't talk to me like that often."

"Drenches out the glands, they say."

She studied me. "I suppose it's an approach, actually. You get nasty to a girl and it shocks her so she gets hung up. Nice try."

I gave her my most amiable grin. "Miss Pussycat, I have the feeling if some jolly experimental giant crammed us both buck naked into a one-man sleeping bag, we'd apologize to each other, get back to back, and try to get a little sleep."

"And that too is an absolutely transparent pass, damn you."

"Try me. You turn on my lights not at all, Miss Heidi."

"I damned well could if I should ever develop a taste for huge dull muscular men, but I'm afraid I put all that behind me when I reached sixteen. Can't we please finish whatever it is you came for and break this off?"

"Pleasure. We're checking out Gloria Doyle Geis very carefully."

"It's about time, wouldn't you say?"

"I know you made some suggestions to Andrus."

She sat on the couch again. "But he won't really see what a cheap little adventurer she is. I think I've figured it all out. Of *course* there isn't anything on her record. I think she had an accomplice. They worked out some kind of a story about something she was supposed to have done, and then the accomplice blackmailed all that money out of my poor sick confused father. She had him on drugs, you know. I think that could be proved in court. Now all she has to do is just sit tight and pretend she doesn't know a thing. Believe me, that money is hidden in some safe place and when the fuss dies down, she and her unwashed friend will disappear with it."

"Makes sense, I guess."

"You *know* it does. My God, he denied his own children, his flesh and blood, by leaving that grubby little waitress a whole half of his money anyway. But oh no, that wasn't enough for her. There's no limit to the greed of that kind of person."

"Pretty tough to prove that was the way he was cheated."

"You people should track down all her old boy friends, and you can tell just by looking at her that there are plenty of them and they weren't very carefully selected either. Did you know she knew Daddy was dying when she married him? What kind of a person would be so eager to marry a dying man who was pretty well-off? Ask yourself that."

"I guess she didn't get a very warm welcome from the family when he brought her back here from Florida."

"You can say we made it very clear to her how we felt." She shook her head, slowly. "And to think that Roger and I used to think what a shame it would be if Stanyard's husband died and Daddy made an honest woman of her. But we would certainly have settled for Stanyard a dozen times over rather than darling Gloria."

"Stanyard?"

"Chief OR nurse on neurosurgery at Methodist Hospital where Daddy did most of his operations. Her husband was hurt about the same time Mommy passed away. It was a fishing accident and they resuscitated him, but he'd been out too long and because of no oxygen going to the brain, there was a lot of damage. I guess he's sort of half in a coma. He's in an institution near Elgin. He sort of wanders around, I understand, and he can say a few words, and he seems glad to see her in a vague way. They had a little boy and he drowned when the boat was swamped. Stanyard has some kind of a thing about getting an annulment or a divorce. She was at the funeral. I hadn't seen her in years and years. I don't know when she and Daddy started having a thing. Probably not a very long time after Mommy died. I'm not censuring them, you understand. Two lonely people with the same interests. She's still fairly attractive—as nurse types go. And they did make a big effort to be discreet, at least. But the summer I was twelve, one evening after dark she drove him home because his car was being fixed, and I looked through the hedge and saw them kissing. You know how kids are. It made me feel quite ill and wretched and confused. I told Roger and he said to keep my mouth shut. He said he'd known it for a year at least. I guess it really must have shaken her up when he married that Doyle person. Poor thing. When he had to go off on trips to do special operations he'd arrange to have Stanyard go along as OR nurse. She was—is—very good, I guess. I mean nobody would question his wanting her right there for tricky operations. But I guess it was . . . quite a handy arrangement for them."

I said nothing. She realized how patronizing she had sounded. She colored slightly. "I'm not really a prude, Mr. McGee. When it's your own father . . . somehow it's more tawdry. You expect more. Mommy was such an absolute angel. I guess I should realize that Daddy was a man, with a man's . . . requirements. But it seems like such an insult to my mother's memory, the affair with Stanyard and then marrying the Doyle person. I guess that because a man is famous in his field, it doesn't mean he can't be foolish and gullible about women. Of course, I didn't exactly make one of the world's best marriages."

"Better luck next time."

Her smile was cold. "No need for a next time, thank you."

At that moment the red door swung open and a young man came hurrying in, saying, "*Really,* it's too *much*! Darling, that wretched Kirstarian is absolutely *intent* on ruining the entire exhibition, and I just . . ."

He stopped and stared at me, eyebrows arching in surprise. "Well, excuse *me*! I didn't know anyone was . . ."

"Mark," she said wearily, "you've promised and promised not to come charging in here. If you ever do it again, I'm going to make you give me that downstairs key back."

"I was just terribly excited, Heidi. This is really a *crisis*! Wait until you *hear*! But shouldn't you introduce us?"

"Mr. Travis McGee. Mark Avanyan. Mark and I run a little gallery on East Scott Street."

"The Tempo East," he said. He wore a shaggy green

turtleneck and skinny jeans in an almost white denim. He had the build of a good welterweight in peak condition. His hair was a half-inch length of dense black pelt that began about an inch and a half above his dark heavy brows. He smiled approvingly at me. "It's so marvelous to see somebody who looks really *outdoors*." He sat on a bright blue hassock and tucked his sneakers under him and scowled and said, "Kirstarian is absolutely *adamant*, darling. He brought in a new piece and he says it goes in the show or there won't be any show. And I can't *endure* it. It is absolutely *ghastly*."

He turned to me and explained, "Kirstarian calls his latest work Stappenings. For static happenings. He makes these marvelous life-size wire armatures of people and objects and wraps them with muslin and then sprays them with some sort of hardener. They have tremendous *presence,* they really do. And I have been working myself into exhaustion since dawn, practically, making the most effective arrangements, and then he comes in with his . . . impossible *thing*."

"What is it, dear?" she asked.

"It's two large dogs—uh—copulating like mad. They are sort of vaguely dogs, you know. Kirstarian just *stands* there, saying it is one of the statements he wishes to make in this show, and he is not going to let anyone censor his work. And there are those fat white terrible beasts, and it is the *only* thing people are going to look at, and it seems like some sort of terrible vulgar joke he's trying to play on us. Actually, he *hates* me. I'm just becoming aware of it. Heidi, darling, we're not *ready* to show something like that. I mean you could say that *Chicago* isn't ready. And the preview is *tomorrow*. And we've *publicized* it. Darling, you have to *do* something."

"He's *your* friend, dear."

"Not any longer, believe me."

"Run along, Mark, dear. Run on back and tell him to wait and I'll be by in a little while to take a look."

As he started to leave he looked into the studio at the new painting on the easel. "Heidi!" he cried. "It's *stunning*. And I believe it's transitional. Your work is getting so *strong*!"

After saying he hoped we'd meet again, he went hurrying off.

"Poor Mark," she said. "Everything is always a crisis. But he does work very hard. Had we finished?"

"There's a couple of questions. I'd like to get a look at those problem dogs. If you want to change, I could ask the questions on the way."

She changed to a gray flannel suit worn over a pale green sweater, and agreed it would be pleasant to walk the four blocks or so to the Tempo East Gallery. I did not have to shorten my normal stride very much to stay in step with her. I said, "Did you have any idea the bulk of the estate had been liquidated before the bank told you?"

"I had no idea! Roger and I knew he'd changed his will and was cutting us each from a half to a quarter. Roger even had his attorney look into it, but there was nothing we could do. I suppose we could have guessed the woman might be capable of some sort of trickery."

"How was your relationship with your father the last year of his life?"

"Unfortunate. The Doyle person poisoned his mind against his own children. We saw him a few times, of course. He seemed pleasant but . . . remote. Not terribly interested in what we were doing. Oh, he was a lot of help to me with the wedding, and later with the divorce from Gadge. Actually, Jeanie—Roger's wife—seemed to get along with him better than we did. She'd stop with the kids. Daddy enjoyed seeing his grandchildren."

"Gloria Geis claims that all she gets from the estate is the insurance policy that brings her in less than five thousand a year."

"A lovely smokescreen. That's what I think."

"Maybe that nurse blackmailed your father."

"Stanyard? Janice Stanyard? Nonsense!"

"Actually, since you couldn't have touched the principal, your inheritance would have been just the seventy-five hundred a year, right?"

"Meaning I shouldn't care so much about it? Mr. McGee, I do not like to be cheated. The amount is not the point at issue. I *can* get along without it, of course. My alimony is four times that, and I do sell many of my paintings, regardless of your opinion of my work."

"And there's an income from the gallery?"

"A small one. My divorce was final about . . . fourteen months ago. There was a settlement and the alimony agreement, and at Daddy's suggestion John Andrus advised me on handling the settlement money. I bought the building where my apartment is, and I bought some good blue-chip stocks, invested in the gallery, and put what was left in a savings account. I can get along nicely, thank you. But why should that make me feel indifferent about someone else having something Daddy intended I should have?"

"Is Roger doing as well?"

"Better, if anything. Jeanie has her own money. And Roger is very good with money, very shrewd. But he doesn't like being cheated any better than I do. Here we are."

The sign on the door said the gallery was closed. As she was looking for the key in her purse Mark Avanyan opened the door for us. When we went in, he gestured toward the dog tableau, gave a loud theatrical sigh, and turned away. Though small, the gallery was well-lighted, attractive, pleasantly designed not to detract from any work being shown. Kirstarian stood with his back toward us, arms folded, and he was as motionless as all his white muslin people. They made an eerie effect, white mummies frozen at some moment of action. The form was entirely derivative, of course. A movable spot on one of the ceiling tracks shone down upon the large dogs. Mark had not reported inaccurately.

Kirstarian turned very slowly to face us. I was astonished to see how young his face and his eyes were in that small area not obscured by the huge, untrimmed black beard. He wore the kind of black suit favored by European intellectuals, and I had thought from the shape of him that he was at least middle-aged. But he was merely a plump young man with bad posture.

"Avanyan," he said in a slow and heavy voice, "is incurably middle-class. He is a silly little tradesman and this is his silly little shop. Perhaps, Mrs. Trumbill, you have more integrity."

Heidi stared at the muslin sculpture, fists on her hips. "This is a necessary statement?" she asked.

"An expression of eternal relationships. Yes."

55

"Dear Jesus," whispered Mark Avanyan, rolling his eyes toward the ceiling.

I broke the impasse by saying, "I think it's fabulous, Mr. Kirstarian." I caught his hand and pumped it.

"Thank you, sir. But, please, not mister. Just Kirstarian."

"Let me give you my card," I said. I had managed to turn him in and position him perfectly. I fumbled in my wallet and dropped several cards. "Oops!" said I, and ducked for them as they were still fluttering down, and put my right foot crosswise, an inch behind the heels of his shabby black shoes. As I straightened up, I managed to nudge him in the chest with my shoulder. He teetered, waved his arms wildly, then sat solidly upon his dogs. As I had dared hope, the hardening agent made the structures brittle. Muslin love ended in a huge Nabisco crunching, a spanging of wires, a rattle of dog-fragments across the floor.

With loud sounds of apology and dismay, I lifted him up out of the unidentifiable ruin. As he sputtered I turned him and heartily whacked all the white powder off the back of his shiny black suit. He was in despair at the tragic accident. He kept picking up parts and dropping them. We all tried to comfort him. He said he hadn't even photographed it. He went trudging sadly off, a blackness marching through the brightness of the Saturday midday.

At one point during the helpless laughter I learned something about Miss Heidi. She clung to me, tears rolling down her face, and then suddenly became aware of my hands on her waist. She froze at once, and turned rigidly away, taking a tissue from her purse and dabbing at her eyes. She said she had some errands, and left so abruptly it was very much like flight.

After she left, when Mark wanted to know how I knew Heidi, I explained that I was investigating the disappearance of Fortner Geis' estate. He had no ideas. He wanted to be helpful, because I had extricated the gallery from an idiotic impasse. There is a delicate protocol in such relationships. He was carefully flirtatious, looking for any subtle encouragement. So I managed to drop into the conversation quite casually those clues which turned him off for good. His acceptance of the inevitable was philosophic.

I am always skeptical of the male who makes a big

public deal out of how he hates fairies, how they turn his stomach, how he'd like to beat hell out of them. The queens are certainly distasteful, but the average homosexual in the visual and performing arts is usually a human being a little bit brighter and more perceptive than most. I've had the opinion for a long time that the creative work of the homosexuals tends to be so glossy and clever and glib that it has a curious shallowness about it, as though the inability to share the most common human experience of all makes it all surface and no guts, and when there is an impression of guts it is usually just another clever imitation.

But once he knows that it is absolutely no dice, there is no persistence. They know how to keep their worlds separated. And most of them are wryly aware of the ugly fact that the overly male type who thinks he hates them so thoroughly is the man who is,' deep in his heart, unsure of his own masculinity. The man who knows that his preferences are solidly heterosexual has no need to go about thumping everybody who lisps.

That outraged and muscular attitude always reminds me of a curious aspect of the Negro problem in the South. It is something seldom if ever touched upon in learned surveys of the situation, but the intelligent Negroes have been sourly amused by it for many years. When you see photographs of violence directed against Negro civil rights workers, photographs in newspapers and magazines and on the television screen, it is inevitable that among the most hate-filled and violent faces on the whites you will spot an interesting incidence of a touch of the tar brush a few generations ago. Through ugliness and violence they are trying to overcompensate for that inner awareness of an ancestor who studied himself in the mirror one day and decided he could pass and get away with it, and who—young man or young woman—went underground and reappeared a hundred or five hundred miles away as a white, married white, and prayed to God almighty that every baby would be fair enough. And, because the dark skin of the Negro is genetically a recessive characteristic, the babies were fair—unless, of course, by cruel chance both parents carried the recessive gene. Other characteristics of race are there, exposed these days by the impartial lens.

So, sitting in the back of the gallery, drinking cold beer from a small refrigerator, I asked him what made Heidi tick. I knew that in the close associations of work they would have been like girls together, exchanging confidences.

"Poor Heidi," he said. "She's blocked. She's all tied in knots. She can't make out. Gadge had sort of a snow-maiden complex, I guess. But the kiss didn't awaken the virgin, the way it says in the books. To her it was just a lot of terrible senseless nastiness. *Heavens,* Gadge Trumbill would have been one of the *least* likely anyway. He's a possessor. He's a brutalizer. *Horribly* demanding. I met him through Heidi, of course. And I rue the day. I suppose it does give Heidi and me some kind of sick something in common. Disaster victims. A dear friend of mine, Anna VanMaller, the cellist, you must have heard of her, took a great interest in Heidi last spring, but poor Heidi can't go either way. She sublimates every bit of sexual drive into her work, and she uses the most *fantastically* subtle erotic symbolism without even *realizing* it. I keep telling her psychiatry might help, but she says she is perfectly happy the way things are. I think it is some sort of a father thing. When she was little, she adored him. Once I tried to tell her that she married an older man because the father had betrayed her by marrying the Doyle woman, and I *actually* thought she was going to scratch out my eyes. I will tell you this, though. It is a damned good thing Dr. Geis brought some good tough lawyers into that divorce action last year. I think Heidi would have settled for peanuts, just to get out of Gadge's bed forever. Funny, though, if Heidi had turned into what Gadge thought she might become, he wouldn't have had to go catting around after everybody in sight."

As I trudged back to the hotel for a late lunch, I decided there was no point in trying to sort out the fragments of inference and information until I had more.

In many ways life is less random than we think. In your past and mine, there have been times when we have, on some lonely trail, constructed a device aimed into our future. Perhaps nothing ever comes along to trigger it. We live through the safe years. But, for some people, something moves on the half-forgotten path, and something arches out of the past and explodes in the here and now. These are emotional intersections, when lives cross, diverge, then meet again.

Rational examination of the specifics, like Janice Stanyard, Gretchen's disappearance, Heidi's coldness, Anna's denial of her daughter, would do me no good, not yet. I had to get more of the feel of Fortner Geis' life before I could understand how he could accept so blandly a condition which caused him to steal the inheritance his heirs expected and then die without leaving any explanation, though he knew that it would create a curious kind of emotional and legal chaos. It is almost impossible to bully a dying man, particularly one with the inner strength of Fortner Geis.

five

After lunch I rode up to my floor in an elevator-load of very noisy jolly fellows wearing nickname badges and smelling of sour mash.

I sat on my bed and checked the big phone directory and found several Stanyards. One was Mrs. Charles Stanyard. The others were male. It was a number on Greenwood. I had picked up a city map. Apparently the address would be reasonably handy to Methodist Hospital. Glory had given me Roger Geis' address in the Evanston area off Glenview. I wasn't interested in Roger. If there was anything he could add, Heidi would have known it. I was more curious about his wife, Jeanie, who'd gotten along well with Fort. Most of all I wanted to talk to Gretchen, to Susan, and again to Anna Ottlo.

I arranged for a rental Ford and drove out to the Roger Geis home, red brick with stubby white pillars, some fine old trees. I got there a little after three. The maid was there alone with the youngest child. She wouldn't take the chain off the door, and told me through the opening that the mister was playing golf, and that Mrs. Geis was at the Countryside Tennis Club with the two older children. When I asked her how to find it, she closed the door.

I got my directions at a gas station. The day was turning colder, but most of the dozen courts were in use. In a large play area noisy platoons of small children were keeping two young girls very busy. I asked a big winded lady carrying three rackets if Jeanie Geis was on the courts, and between pantings, she pointed to a game of mixed doubles and told me she was the girl on the far court. I moved over and watched them. Jeanie was a sturdy woman nearing thirty, not tall, a bit heavy in the leg. Brown legs, arms, face, hair. The heavy legs were the hard, muscular, springy legs of the athlete. She covered more than her share of the court. Her partner was a spry old man with white hair. They were playing a boy and girl in their early twenties. It was very respectable tennis, craftiness against power. Jeanie's little white pleated skirt whipped around as she twisted, cut back, dashed to the net. They weren't jolly about saves and misses. It was a blood game. On set point, Jeanie banged a cross-court shot to the young girl's backhand, and the girl took a nasty fall trying to get to it, but missed it. They gathered around her. She had taken some hide off her arm. She said she was all right.

As they all started back toward the small clubhouse, I asked Mrs. Geis if I could have a word with her. The others went ahead.

"Yes? What about?" She had that husky semi-drawl of the better finishing schools, an effective delivery styled to give equal and additional impact to witticism, cattiness, or love words.

"Excuse the expression—money," I said. And there, for a few moments, was the jackpot, and I couldn't bet my hand because I didn't know what cards I was holding. Jackpot in the sudden draining of all blood and color from under the tan, in a sudden sickness of pleasant green eyes and in the shape of the mouth, and in a rigid kind of stillness. These are the parts of a terror almost animal in its intensity, when the body aches to spin and run blindly. But before I could find any way to make any use of it, I saw the swift return of control. It seemed almost as if control had returned through an exercise of logic. She had looked more carefully at me and had decided I did not fit into the pattern of fear, and so it had to be a misunderstanding on her part.

"Pretty broad topic to discuss, Mr. . . ."

"McGee. Travis McGee."

"I've heard that name before. Where? I have a fantastic memory for names. Faces mean nothing. Could we move along? I don't want to get chilled." As I began walking beside her she said, "Got it! Daddy Fort and Gloria were talking about you . . . oh, at least three years ago. I'd taken the kids by. He was kidding her, in a nice way. Something about her Florida boyfriend. You? The tan would fit."

"Old friend, yes."

"Wait just a moment, please." She went quickly over to the playground. As she was speaking to one of the girls in charge, two kids, a boy and girl perhaps seven and five, came running to her. She squatted and gave them a simultaneous hug. They went racing back to their group and she spoke to the girl again and then came back to where I waited. "I had to make sure we had the signals right. The sitter is going to pick them up here and take them home. And I go from here to join Roger at a cocktail thing. We'll have time to talk after I shower and change. You go through that door and turn left for the lounge. You could wait for me there. Order yourself a drink, please."

The lounge was comfortable. The healthy tennis set was noisily taking on a small Saturday night load before heading off to do the serious drinking elsewhere. The lounge had seen a lot of hard use, and the drinks were substantial. I picked a corner table where there seemed the most chance of privacy. After a half-hour Jeanie Geis joined me, looking more elegant in dark green cocktail dress, high heels, mink over her arm, than I'd expected. As I was seating her, the bar man brought her a Gibson, straight up. "Thank you, Jimmy, and another whatever he's having for my guest, Mr. McGee. How's Skippy making it?"

"You know. Drifting and dreaming. Twenty times maybe she's tried on the wedding dress, her mother telling her she's going to wear it out."

"She's a dear doll and she's getting a nice guy."

When he was out of earshot she looked speculatively at

61

me and said, "As a friend of Glory's, it has to be Daddy
Fort's money you wanted to talk about. But why me?"

"I talked to Heidi. I don't think your husband could
add anything. Incidentally, Heidi doesn't know I'm
Glory's friend."

"How could I add anything Roger couldn't? I mean it
is all terribly mysterious, and Heidi and Roger are furious,
and it puts Gloria in a very odd position. But if she asked
you for help, if she asked you to come and see if you can
find out what *did* happen, I can understand but I don't
have to approve."

She hesitated as Jimmy put the new drink in front of
me, continuing as he moved away. "It's over, isn't it? If
Fort thought anything should be explained to the family,
he would have. And maybe you should explain why you
came to me? Are you implying I'd keep anything from
my husband?"

"I am not concerned exclusively with what people know
they know, Mrs. Geis. From what Heidi told me, you were
getting along with the Doctor better than his own children.
So you saw him oftener. So you could have pertinent
knowledge you don't realize *is* pertinent."

"Are you some kind of a detective?"

"Me? No. Just a friend of Glory's. You come in from
the outside, sometimes it's easier to see the shape of things.
You must have had some guess as to why Fort did what
he did."

Her mouth firmed up. "Mr. McGee, the only thing I
can tell you is what I have told my husband. And though
I do not think it good taste to tell this to a stranger, Roger
and I have come closer to . . . very real trouble in our
marriage over this than anything. Heidi is in no financial
pain. Neither are we. Gloria is the worst off, but if people
would just leave her alone, I think she'd be quite content.
We're not close friends. We don't have enough in common.
But I realize how good she was for Fort. And certainly
she'll marry again, and she should be able to marry quite
well. She has a special style of her own, and a capacity
for loyalty, and a very personal kind of warmth, and the
urge to take care of a man and please him. I have told
Roger that I think it is shameful and vulgar and disgrace-
ful to keep prodding at this whole thing. It isn't a financial
motive at all, really. It took me a long time to understand

it. Fortner Geis was a very strong personality. When his wife died, he lost himself in his work. Roger and Heidi thought he was rejecting them. It turned them into emotionally insecure people. Heidi is a crashing neurotic. I've had to work twice as hard as anybody knows to make this marriage of mine work. I think that all the time they hoped that one day he would . . . accept and cherish them. What happened? An affair with a nurse that lasted for years. That was a rejection. Then, after they learned he had a fatal illness, he came back here from vacation with a bride. That hurt them. It was a symbolic rejection when he changed his estate arrangements in her favor. They hate her. The final rejection was to find that he had somehow arranged to leave them nothing. They talk about money but they are really looking for some proof of love. Heidi is far worse than Roger, God knows why. I feel this way. Fortner Geis must have had a very sound and good reason for not telling Gloria and Heidi and Roger what he was doing and why he was doing it. To me that means that if they do ever find out, it might be worse than not ever knowing. They should trust him, accept it, forget it."

Had I not seen the earlier and more extreme reaction, I might have missed this one. It was just a hair too much intensity, too much edge in that hoarse social voice.

"Did you make any guesses why he did it?"

"It doesn't matter to me why he did it."

"You liked him?"

"I think . . . he was the finest man I've ever known."

"But he fouled up his kids, didn't he?"

"Did he? Maybe their mother did. They were eleven and seven when she died. She had enough time. And, believe me, I have heard far too much talk from Heidi and Roger about how sweet and brave and noble she was. She's assumed the stature of a mythological being, Mr. McGee. She's hard to believe in."

"Mrs. Geis, I'm a little puzzled by one thing. Who did you think I was when I stopped you and said I wanted to talk about money?"

"I had no idea who you were."

"Then why were you terrified?"

She frowned and smiled at the same time. "Terrified? Oh come now, really! Why should I . . . Oh!"

"Oh what?"

The green dress made her fine green eyes greener. Though they had shifted about during all the previous conversation, now they were very steady on mine, and she had widened them a little bit. "They kept us on the run for two long sets, trying to wear the old man down. When I stopped to talk to you, I suddenly felt quite faint. The world had a swimmy look and my ears were ringing, and then it went away, or I would have had to sit down right in the middle of the walk."

"Son of a gun!" I said. "That must have been it." It was more gallant than telling the lady she was a lousy liar. "I guess I should tell Gloria she shouldn't let all this bother her so much. Having Fort's children hate and resent her so much confuses her. She's one of those people without malice. Did you ever tell her your rejection theory?"

"Yes. She seemed to understand how it could be that way."

Night had come. The lights were on. She craned her neck to look at the clock over the bar. I walked her out to the parking lot to her car. After she got in, she looked out at me and said, "I think it would do Gloria a lot of good to get away now. Maybe she could go back to Florida with you, Mr. McGee. You'd be doing her more good that way than by . . . trying to find out why the Doctor did what he did."

"It's an idea," I said.

I found my way, after several wrong turns, to Lake Pointe, the handsome house, snap and hiss of logs aflame, chunky glass in my hand, Glory Doyle Geis in wine slacks and white sweater sitting on a cushion on the raised hearth, dainty, bitter-sweet, semi-sad in the firelight.

"Not so good of a day for me," she said, "and I don't really know why. I couldn't settle down to anything. Kept roaming. I'm supposed to be inventorying the books. They go to the university library. What did you do? Who did you talk to?"

"Heidi. And Mark Avanyan. And a fat boy named Kirstarian. Jeanie Geis. I saw the happiest girl in Chicago, but I didn't meet her. I busted hell out of some very advanced sculpture. I nearly ran over a black cat wearing a red collar."

"Tell me all!" she cried, her face lighting up.

"First you tell me about Janice Stanyard."

She studied me for a few moments. "You mean you're annoyed I didn't tell you about her before?"

"Didn't you think it was pertinent?"

"Not particularly."

"You sound as frosty as Miss Heidi."

She looked dismayed, then grinned. "I didn't know I could. Anyway, when I tell you you'll understand. Fort told me about her while we were still on our wedding trip, before we came back to Chicago. We were talking about different kinds of love. And he just sort of casually mentioned he'd had a long affair with a nurse. He said it started a year after his wife died. And it ended two years before he met me. When I realized that was nearly eleven years, I was *furious*! And he laughed at me. He didn't explain for a while because he said he wanted to prolong the pleasure of having me so jealous of another woman. He said it was marvelously flattering at his age. But when he saw I was really getting upset, he told me just how it was."

"About her husband's accident and the little boy drowning?"

"Yes. He said she had worked with him long enough by that time so that she was like an extension of himself, like having another pair of hands. She knew his procedures, knew the instruments he would want at each stage, and also knew what to have ready to hand him when things went wrong this way or that way. She did not disturb his concentration the way other surgical nurses did. He said she seemed glad to share the enormous work load he had shouldered after Glenna died. After a year had gone by he knew he was changing in some way he did not like. He was thirty-six. He had not been with a woman for a year. He was putting so much of his total energy into his work he did not feel any particular tension because of physical desire. As a doctor he knew that continence does an adult no particular physical harm. He told me that the idea of regular sex as a necessity for health is something young men use as part of their persuasion technique. Fort told me he began to feel remote. He said that was the best word for it. He had less feeling of involvement with his patients, less triumph when things went well, less regret when they didn't. He couldn't chew out people who made foolish errors the way he used to. It didn't seem worth the effort somehow. And he knew his praise was becoming half-hearted, which is worse than no praise at all.

"So he went to his friend Doctor Hayes Wyatt with the problem. Dr. Wyatt gave him a complete physical, and then listened to Fort describe the remoteness. Then he told Fort that no matter how much he might try to deny it or ignore it, he was still a mammal. By questioning him, Dr. Wyatt showed how much warmth there had been in Fort's childhood. He'd been breast-fed, hugged, patted, cuddled, kissed, spanked. People with austere childhoods could adjust to the life Fort was living. But for Fort, some essential assurance-area was being starved. He felt remote because his body, untouched, was beginning to doubt the reality of its own existence. Hayes Wyatt told Fort that casual sex relationships would not do very much to help him. He said Fort should marry an affectionate and demonstrative woman."

"Like Glory Doyle."

"Sure. What was I then? About fifteen? Great. Fort didn't want marriage, not then. For weeks he wondered what he was supposed to do, what would be best for him. One day, after they scrubbed, there was a long delay in setting up the proper anaesthesia for a complicated spinal disc operation, and he realized that Janice Stanyard was once again talking about her two Siamese cats, and it was a little bit too much like the way people talk about their children. He watched her and thought about her for days. He knew she admired and respected him, and he knew they liked each other. She was twenty-seven, nearly twenty-eight. He said he would like to meet those most unusual cats. He went to her apartment a few times. One night, like a fatuous pretentious damned fool—Fort said— he asked her what she thought about the sort of 'arrangement' he had in mind.

"She was puzzled, hurt, offended. She still loved Charles and always would. It was ugly to think they could enter into that kind of thing without love. It would not hurt anybody else, she agreed, but it would cheapen both of them. A month later they were in Atlanta on an emergency, a small-caliber bullet lodged in the frontal lobe of a young girl, pressing against the optic nerve. It was long and precarious, and it went well. They had dinner together at their hotel, with wine, feeling good about the day's work. He seduced her that evening in her room. He spent the night in her bed. When he awoke in the morning he found himself looking into her sleeping face not a foot away. Her arm rested on him. Her round knee was against his thigh. Fort said he had a terrible sinking of heart, a dread about the inevitable scene when she awakened. He remembered all the tears, the protestations, and even, after she had been at last aroused, the small dead voice in which she had begged him not to. He said her face looked as calm and unreadable as the face of a statue. Her slow warm exhalations brushed against his lips. At last she stirred and her eyes opened. At first they were blank and unfocused. Then they focused on him and she gave a great start and pulled her arm back. She looked into his eyes, half-frowning, and he told her that it was a mistake, all a mistake, and he was sorry. He said the corners of her mouth turned up, she stretched and yawned, then put her arm around him, hitched close, put her face in his throat, made kind of a little purring sound of contentment and in moments went back to sleep. Fort said it was a kind of love, always gentle, always placid, always kind. He said that the sexual release was less important to them than the nearness of someone, the warm flesh and the breathing and the beating of the nearby heart when you woke up in the night. Once it had begun, he said she accepted it undemandingly, and with the enormous practicality of which most women seem capable. He said they tried to be discreet, taking the chances which came along rather than trying to make chances. Remoteness went away. As a team they functioned as perfectly as before, no better and no worse. He said that once again his work came alive, and the intense involvement with it returned. So, I'm grateful to her, Trav. She kept him whole and alive for all those middle years of his life. He said there wasn't any decision to end it. They just seemed to need each other less often and finally not at all, without jealousy or suspicion or regret. He said that it was an affair without the words people say during affairs. When they were together, when they talked, it was not about their work, or about Glenna or his children, or her husband. It was easy, homely talk, he said, about the cafeteria coffee, and if it was the right time for her to trade her car, and what the cleaner was doing to his suits, and how she had liked Kup's show the other night, and who to vote for this time, and how the weather was hotter or colder than usual. That's what it was, Trav. An arrangement. It was a good thing for them. Heidi told you about her?"

"To say it would have been bad enough if he'd married that nurse person, but it would have been better than marrying you."

"What a disastrous marriage!" she said bitterly. "I made the poor man so miserable. *Damn* her!"

"Don't let it get to you. She isn't worth it. Did you ever meet Janice Stanyard?"

"Oh yes. While Fort was still operating. She must be about forty-five now. She is . . . attractive in her own way. You don't see it at first. She grows on you, sort of. You see, she knew Fort's bad prognosis before his children did. He handed her the results of the tests moments after he read them. Then when he came back from Florida married to me, the first time I met her was in the staff lounge at Methodist. Fort introduced us and then made out like there was something he had to go and do. She wasn't antagonistic, just very curious about me, about what sort of person I am. Finally she decided in my favor. We were sitting on a couch. She took hold of my hand and held it so tightly it went numb. She told me to help him. I knew what she meant. She said he was great and good, but he might be scared. I said I loved him with all my heart. And so we sat there with goofy smiles and the tears running down our faces. She's nice, Trav. She came here a few times toward the end. She was at the funeral. We had a few minutes alone, afterward. She hugged me and said nothing better could have happened to him than me. I haven't seen her since."

"And it didn't occur to you, Glory, that if he had a very tough decision to make, if he was in a real bind, he might go to the person he had worked with for years, whom he liked and respected and trusted, and to whom in a strange way he had been in effect married."

After a few moments of round eyes and parted lips, she said, "But he was closer to me!"

"Which could have been his reason for not bringing you into it."

"What do you mean by that?"

"I don't know yet. Maybe he said nothing to her. Maybe she knows the whole thing. I have to talk to her."

"Of course."

"So call her and I'll get on an extension."

But when nine rings brought no answer, as we went back to our places by the hearth, Anna came in and said proudly that the kidney mutton chops she had were so thick, maybe she should start them now. I knew that with absolutely no trouble at all, Anna could balloon me up to a mighty two fifty, and it would take me months to fit back into my clothes. When I said I hadn't planned to stay to dinner, she said with a kind of contemptuous sadness that if I hadn't stopped by, Miss Glory would have insisted on some cold cereal and a piece of dry toast.

With icy gin replenished I told Glory about the rest of my day. I pointed out the significance of learning that Fort had taken direct steps to improve the terms of Heidi's divorce. "He'd already started liquidating the previous July. He knew Roger was pretty well set. He knew then he wasn't going to be able to leave them anything, so he made sure Heidi got some security out of Trumbill's money."

"Which didn't exactly pinch Gadge Trumbill," Glory said. "He had an ancestor who homesteaded two hundred and forty acres. The Chicago Civic Center is right smack in the middle of it, and the old boy believed in leasing instead of selling."

"Next item. Neither Heidi nor Jeanie brought up the Gretchen thing. And they had their chance."

"They never knew about that."

"Now to get back to Jeanie Geis. She was terrified, and then she lied about it. Why?"

"I think I can answer that, Trav." She explained that nearly two years back, when their eldest child was five, there had been an attempt to kidnap him. The boy, Branton Fortner Geis, named after both grandfathers, had actually been taken, but the kidnapper had evidently lost his nerve because after he had driven the boy all the way into the city, he had abandoned him in Grant Park near the fountain. The boy had been driven around for some time, because it gave his parents about three hours of terror before a park policeman took him in and he was identified.

"Since then it has been a thing with Jeanie. She takes the kids wherever she can, and doesn't let them out of her sight. She even got a pistol permit, and she spent hours and hours on the police range, and she's an expert now. Their home has all kinds of burglar alarms and flood-lights, and their sitter is a retired cop. He has a license to carry a gun too, and he takes them back and forth to school. I think she goes a little too far. I don't think it's what you could call a normal childhood for them. Roger is just sort of . . . tolerant of Jeanie's precautions. I guess you can't blame her too much. But it's such a twitch with her, I guess that's the first thing that would enter her mind if you walked up to her and said you wanted to talk about money. You aren't exactly a clerical type, Mister McGee. You are huge and it is obvious you have been whacked upon, and you look as though you damn well en-joyed returning the favor."

"An obvious criminal type?"

"To Jeanie, for a couple of seconds. Until her mind went to work on it, and she got a better look at you. Nobody would walk up to her in broad daylight with all those people around and say, Lady, I got one of your kids."

"So why did she lie later?"

"A white lie, dear, to avoid telling you what she thought you were. It wouldn't be terribly flattering. Besides, she's a little punchy about the precautions. She gets a certain amount of snide comment from the other mothers."

"It explains why the maid wouldn't unchain the door or answer questions. But, baby, it does not explain her earnest sales talk about let's all forget the whole thing. Why don't you take Glory to Florida, and so forth and so forth."

"How do you explain it then?"

"I don't know. When I get reactions I don't understand it's like an itch I can't reach. I have to make the logical or illogical connection between six hundred thousand gone into thin air and somebody being kidnapped. When did the boy get grabbed?"

"Let me think. I have to remember what we were . . . oh, we'd just come back from New York. Fort read a paper at a medical convention. It was quite warm. . . . May. That was it. A year ago last May."

"Two months later Fort started cashing in his securities. What about this? Suppose somebody got a message to Jeanie. Come up with lots of cash or we'll take one of your kids. So she comes running to Fort. And . . . No, there's two big holes in that."

"Like what?"

"One. She'd tell Roger. He'd know that's where the money went, and he wouldn't be making such a jackass of himself about it. Two. Fort was certainly smart enough to know it would be an awful lot cheaper to get Jeanie and the kids out of reach. Fly them to Switzerland for example, and put the cops to work on the problem. I suppose the kid was too little to give any description of the person or persons who took him riding, or the car they took him in."

"Branty said it was a nice man who sang a lot."

"That doesn't sound like a nervous type."

"Somebody saw the car driving away. They said it was a blue Dodge. I think it was about a week later they found what could have been the same car, but they couldn't be sure. It had been stolen from a shopping center the morning of the day the boy was taken, and they found it in a big used-car lot out near Midway Airport with no plates on it, and no fingerprints or anything. Nobody could say how long it had been there."

"It doesn't fit."

"What doesn't?"

"The car is clouted in a very professional way, from the kind of place where the pros work, and it is unloaded in a very professional way, as if it had been iron they'd used in a bank job. But the man gets nervous and changes his mind and leaves the kid off. It couldn't have been the same car, Glory. That's the only thing that makes any sense."

Her mouth trembled for a moment and then she smiled. Her eyes were shiny. "We better face it, McGee. Nothing about this whole thing is ever going to make any sense,

71

and for the rest of my life people are going to keep an eye on me, just in case."

At quarter to ten after Glory had stashed the dishes, we tried Janice Stanyard again. She picked up the phone on the first ring.

"Janice? This is Gloria Geis."

"Hello! I've been wondering about you, dear. I was wondering if I should ask you to come in and have lunch with me some day."

"I'd like that, I really would. I tried to get you earlier."

"Today? I was over in Elgin."

"How is he?"

"Fine. He had a bad cold but it's nearly gone now. What did you call me about, dear?"

"Well . . . I want to introduce you to a friend of mine from Florida. He's on the line too. Travis McGee. Janice Stanyard."

"Hello, Mrs. Stanyard."

"How do you do, Mr. McGee." Her voice sounded puzzled. It was a good voice, a firm and nicely articulated contralto.

"Trav would like to come and talk to you, Janice."

"He would? What about?"

Gloria started to explain, but I broke in and said, "It's just a little confusion about Doctor Geis' estate, and Glory thinks you might have some answers."

"But I wouldn't know a *thing* about that!"

"Sometimes the way these things work out, Mrs. Stanyard, you can help out without realizing you can. I'd just like to drop by anytime tomorrow at your convenience for a few minutes."

"But . . ."

"We'd both be very grateful to you."

"Well . . . would three tomorrow afternoon be all right?"

"Just fine."

"Will you come too, Gloria?" she asked.

"Just me," I said quickly, "and now I'll hang up and let you people fix up that lunch date."

As I was leaving, I remembered my other question. I asked Glory who had done the investigation work for

Fort when Gretchen had asked him for more money. "He dealt with a Mr. Smith. But I don't know the name of the company." We went to his study and looked up Smith in his address book and found a Francisco Smith, hyphen, Allied Services, in the Monadnock Block on West Jackson. I checked the yellow pages and found Allied Services under Investigators.

A funny thing happened to me on the way to the hotel room. I was a long way from the elevators. When I approached the last right-angle turn before my room, I came upon a couple standing and talking in low tones. I heard her say in wheedling tones, "Whey-ya yuh room key, honeh? It hey-yuv the nummah onto it."

He peered at me and said, in surprisingly articulate tones, slightly Bostonian, "Sir, I have a distressing concept worthy of scholarly research, and it should appeal to anyone of conjectural turn of mind. Have you a moment?"

I stopped and said, "Conjecture away, friend."

"Is there a sense of entrapment in being locked into your own century without chance of escape? What is the effect on the psyche? Those of us born in the first two decades of this century are subliminally aware, my good sir, of that marker on the grave which will say nineteen hundred and this to nineteen hundred and that. Do you follow me?"

He was fifty-something, excellent suit, topcoat, shoes, hat, shirt. But the hat was dented and sat askew, stubble on the jowls, necktie awry. His face had the slack sweatiness of heavy drinking, and he had trouble focusing his eyes on me.

And he was being tugged this way and that way by the girl who was going through his pockets with great energy, muttering about the room key and saying, "You wah somepin, honeh. Somepin for shu-wah."

"I follow you," I said.

"But this lovely child is going to break through into the next century, at exactly the age I am now, and the prospect makes me desperately envious. You, sir, could well manage it too, I suspect, but in the fullness of your years and with dimming . . ."

With a little squeal of satisfaction she yanked the key out of one of his pockets, stared at the tag, then looked at

73

the nearby room numbers. She wore a bright red cloth coat over a very short white dress that was cleft almost to the navel. Her pouty, saucy, cheap little face peeked out from between the two heavy wings of white-blonde hair that hung straight from center part to collarbone.

In the corridor light I noticed their hands were dirty. It is impossible to drink all evening without ending up with dirty hands. It is one of the unsolved mysteries of our age.

"Raht they-yahs youwah nummer, sweetsie pah!"

He put a soiled hand against the wall. "I don't believe I . . . I think I'm going to . . ." He slid slowly and fell on his side with a small thudding sound against the carpeting.

I offered to help her with him. She refused so very sweetly. She couldn't trouble me none. She said she could manage all raht. So I went around the corner and began humming just loudly enough so my voice would carry to where she was. I unlocked my door and opened it and then closed it again without going in, closing it audibly and cutting off the little tune just as it clacked shut.

I went back to the corner and put one eye around carefully. His topcoat was pulled out of the way. She was kneeling, just pulling his wallet out of his inside jacket pocket. Her thick white hair hung forward as she bent over him. Her underlip had fallen away from her teeth and I could hear how her excitement and fear was making her breath fast and audible. She kept snapping her head around to look the other way, toward the elevators. She shoved the currency into the slash pocket of her red coat, put the wallet back in his inside pocket. She picked his arm up and started to take the wristwatch, hesitated, let the arm fall. She picked the key off the carpeting, stood up, and, biting her lip, looked at him and at the door to his room. I could guess what she was thinking of. Would it be worthwhile to unlock the door, drag him in, and go through his belongings? She stood crouched, fingers hooked, her stance ugly. It was a posture feral as any carnivore. It was the hunting stance, and it made me think of Fortner Geis' money, and the far cleverer beast who had gone after it and taken it from him.

I saw her decide to settle for what she had, and cut her risk by getting away quickly. She straightened, shook her hair back, and I pulled back and flattened against the wall, realizing she would come my way, heading for the fire stairs.

The only sound she made was the quick whisking of fabric. She came around the corner in a hurry, saw me out of the corner of her eye, gasped, tried to run, but I caught her from behind, my left arm around her waist, right hand snaking into the right pocket of the coat and coming out with the folded wad of bills as I released her.

She spun, felt in the pocket, came cautiously toward me. "Hay-yuff, huh?" she said in a husky whisper. "Gimme hay-yuff."

"Give you nothing, dear girl."

"Oney a feeyiffteh then, huh? Pitcher a Gen'l Grant for lil ol' Cinny Lee?"

She spread her coat, wet her mouth, arched her back. "You room raht close by, innit? Less you'n me tote that ole man inna his room so as nobody gets agitated bout him lyin inna hall, then it give me time, I go inna your room, given you a ride like you never hay-yud afore, worthen at fifty plusen a tee-yup for sure, lahk to pleasure me a big size may-yun all the whole naht long, honeh pah."

"Run on back to your cotton patch, corn pone."

She had the heels of her hands on her hipbones, fingers spread on her thighs, pointing to the floor. I saw the hemline of the narrow skirt of her white dress climbing as she stealthily worked it up with her fingertips. I knew what she was going to try. If the kick had landed where she wanted it to, she could have plucked the cash out of my nerveless hand and gone tripping happily down the stairs, leaving me there making goldfish mouths, and sweating into the carpet. When it came I turned sharply and, as she missed, got my palm under the back of her ankle and gave the kick a lot more elevation than she wanted. The skirt ripped up the side and she went tumbling back, rolling up onto her shoulders, legs scissoring. I noticed with academic appraisal that she wore nothing under the dress, that she was an unpleasant soft white, almost blue-white, and that she was by no means a natural blonde.

"And the accent is fake too," I said.

She sprang up, looked as though she might try for the eyes, and thought better of it. And in the brisk and nasal flatness of the pure Midwest accent, the kind you hear in the small towns of Indiana and Iowa, she suggested I perform an anatomical impossibility, and categorized me as an indulger in several of those specific practices most frowned upon in our culture. Somebody behind one of the closed doors yelled to knock it off for chrissake, and she stopped abruptly, ran to the stairway door, yanked it open, and disappeared.

I found the key on the carpet beside sweetsie pah, unlocked his door, scooped him up, carried him in, and dumped him on his bed. I went out and got his hat and brought it in, closing the door behind me. Turned a light on, worked him out of topcoat and suit coat. Hung them in the closet. Put money in billfold, billfold in suit coat. Loosened tie, belt, removed shoes. Turned out light. Stood for a moment looking down at him, hearing his steady snore. Poor honeh had slipped through the fangs of the cat, and he wasn't the type to give them a chance at him again. I had fanned the currency before putting it back where it belonged, didn't make an exact count, but saw it was over four hundred. We were both locked into this single century. As Fortner Geis had been. So help the fellow traveler, McGee. The Cinny Lees spring at you every chance they get.

If this man could be a four-hundred-dollar fool, Fort could have been one too—at fifteen hundred times the cost. I set his night latch and closed the door behind me and went back to my own leased cave.

After my light was out I made a better identification of Cinny Lee's emotional climate after she knew she'd lost it all. Outraged indignation. She had invested time, training, and experience, had cut him out of the pack, softened him perfectly, had slipped by the hotel security patrol, and had gotten the chloral hydrate into him at just the right moment. If he had not gone into that talking jag, if he'd had the room key in his hand instead of an inside pocket, if the big stranger hadn't come along, she would have gotten inside the room with him minutes before it hit him and knocked him out. Then, in privacy and safety she could have plucked him clean of every valuable from his gold wedding ring and cuff links to the change on his bureau. Then, if she was the cool hardened operator I guessed she was, she would sneak out with his key, stash the loot, sneak back into the room, strip him to the buff, take all her clothes off, rip the cheap dress in strategic places, tip a chair and a lamp over—quietly—and get into bed with him and get some sleep and be ready, when he awakened with a savage and blinding headache and total loss of memory, to be crying hopelessly and pitifully. She had no idea where his money was. He could search her if he thought she had it. All she knew was he had forced her. He had torn her pretty new dress, see? Her father and her brothers would be frantic. She'd never been away from home all night before. She was really only fifteen. He'd been like some kind of crazy horrible animal. Oh, oh, what was she going to do. Oh boo hoo wah haw hoo, oh God. She'd better k-k-k-kill herself. Th-Throw herself out the windowwwwwww . . .

The timing would give her all day Sunday to work on his fears, with the Do Not Disturb sign on the room door, food and drink ordered up, and she would hide in the bathroom when it was brought in. She would have learned every scrap of usable information about him from what she could find in his billfold and elsewhere in the room and in his pockets. He could cash checks, couldn't he? He could have his bank wire money, couldn't he? She would have to leave town. She would remember a girlfriend in New Orleans. Monday morning he could go out and buy her some clothes and luggage for the trip, and get the money in cash. She would have to have money to live on until she could get a job. At least fifteen hundred over the airline fare to feel really safe. If he dragged his feet she could wonder out loud if maybe she ought to go back to Boston with him and see if his wife could help her get a job. Her name is Frances, isn't it, honeh? Once he agreed, she would become very happy and excited and affectionate, and with any luck she could seduce him, a shameful confirmation of his guilt, and good for at least five hundred more for the poor dear girl. It wouldn't work on a man who had been down the mean streets and seen the dark places. It would work on just such a man as honeh—bright, good, and decent, and, in this first and last wild oat, gullible as the youngest sailor in the Navy.

It made me realize with what exquisite care, caution, and patience Fortner Geis had been cleaned. A man will let his money be taken only when the alternative is something he cannot endure.

What was it Fort could not face? And how much more

dangerous was the predator who hunted him down than was this faked-up Cinny Lee?

six

Nurse Janice Stanyard lived on Greenwood in one of those standard six-story apartment houses of yellow brick which were built in such profusion after World War II. They were planned to do an adequate and durable job of housing people, and were designed with the idea of minimum maintenance and upkeep, and with all the grace and warmth of the Berlin Wall.

She was on the fifth floor toward the rear, with windows that looked out over a tarred roof of a neighboring building to the Sunday emptiness of the broad asphalt parking area of a shopping plaza a half block away, the gray paving marked in the yellow herringbone pattern of the parking slots.

I had not known quite what to expect. My first impression as she let me in was certainly not of a femme fatale. She was a sturdy woman with a big-boned look, a broad and pallid face without animation, dark brown hair turning gray. She wore scuffed loafers, white ankle sox, a baggy herringbone tweed skirt, a loose-fitting brown cardigan. The impression was that of an enduring and stolid woman with no interest in self-adornment. The furniture was plain, heavy, and not new. But it looked comfortable. The decor was a monotone of grays and browns without pattern or touches of color except for the dust jackets of hundreds of books in long low shelves, and the covers of the magazines in racks and stacks.

"Do sit down, Mr. McGee. I'm afraid I'm not going to be much help to you." She sat at the corner of a couch and I sat in a facing armchair. I suspect that it was the quality of her voice, the earthy richness of the contralto modulation that made me look at her more closely. Her hands were large, and beautifully formed. Her throat was long and solid and graceful. Her eyes were particularly lovely—large, the iris a deep clear blue, the lashes naturally dense and long. Once I had seen that much, I could then see the gentle contours of her mouth, and the rich curve of the strong calves.

What had seemed drabness, both in her and in the room became merely understatement. I had the feeling this would be a comfortable room to be in, a comfortable woman to be with. She had the indefinable quality of restfulness, of making no trivial demands upon others or upon herself.

"You worked with Fort a long time and knew him well. I need to know more about him, and maybe then I can figure out why he did what he did."

"Did you know the Doctor well enough to call him Fort?" There was cool surprise in her tone.

"Well enough so he asked me to. In Florida. I stood up with Fort and Glory when they were married. I didn't know him long. I liked him. I was supposed to come visit them here after the house was built. It didn't work out. I wish it had."

"He was a good man," she said. "I miss him. But why did you sound as if he did some inexplicable thing? Fort usually had reasons for what he did."

"Would you have any idea about what sort of estate he left? The size of it?"

"I wouldn't know, really. When Glenna died he got her money. I don't think it was really a lot. I think he used it on Heidi and Roger. They seemed to get anything they wanted at least, cars and sailboats and trips to Europe. Money wasn't particularly important to Fort. I don't mean he was indifferent to it. He would bill a patient according to what the patient could afford. From ten dollars to ten thousand. He didn't spend much on himself. It wasn't because he was stingy. He just didn't have expensive hobbies. He invested his money after taxes and living expenses into good stocks mostly, I think. If I was forced to guess, I'd say he probably was worth half a million dollars when he died. Another man with the same ability and reputation could have been worth . . . three or four times that, possibly."

"When was the last time you saw him?"

"Ten days before he died."

"When was the last time you worked with him?"

"Last January, almost a year ago. The last operation he did. Craniotomy for a neurofibroma, extensive. He started it but he didn't finish it. By then he had good people backing him up every time. His fingertips went numb. He couldn't get the feeling back into them. It's one of the symptoms of what he had. So he turned it over to his assistant. He stood by and watched. It went well. Outside, afterward, he told me that was the last he'd try. He thanked me for putting up with him in all those hundreds and hundreds of operations. At least I held the tears back until I was alone. Everybody who ever worked with him felt the same way."

"Did you have any kind of contact with him between that time and when you visited him at his house?"

There was a little flicker behind the blue of her eyes, a half-second delay. "No. Why?"

I wondered if with a wicked needle I could penetrate that placid manner. "I suppose like all the rest of them, the reputation was a little larger than the man."

Her eyes narrowed. "What is that supposed to mean?"

"There can be twenty or fifty men with the same ability, and one seems to get the good publicity."

"You don't seem to know what the hell you're talking about!"

"Cutting is cutting, no?"

"And some of them are so concerned about setting records they go in there like a whirlwind, and some of them are so picky and cautious the patient is under for six hours when it could be done in four. Then there are people like Fortner Geis who are as quick as they should be and as careful as they should be, but there's something else too, something that isn't in the books, and you can't describe what it is, and damned few surgeons in any generation have it. It's an instinct for the living flesh under the knife. Two surgeons can make two cuts that look identical, and one will bleed like a pig and the other will be almost dry. One surgeon can cut to where something is supposed to be, and it isn't there, and another will somehow guess that the patient doesn't quite match the anatomy lessons and, without knowing how he does it or what clued him, go right to where he wants to be. Surgeons who worked beside Fort have a right to make comments about his ability. You don't!"

She sat glaring at me. I smiled and said, "I gave you a cheap opportunity to put the knock on him, Mrs. Stanyard. Just checking."

Anger changed to a puzzled indignation. "Why do that? What's the point?"

"I guess the point is that he would have left around seven hundred thousand and something, but he canceled out his insurance for the cash value, and he cashed in everything else too, except a small equity in the house and a life annuity option policy for Gloria that'll bring her ninety something a week. It took him thirteen months. He finished the job last July. He did it on the sly and covered his tracks. The money is gone and everybody is upset, each one for his own reasons. So when I find out that the Doctor and his favorite nurse had an affair going for ten or eleven years and then he married somebody else, I want to see if there is enough hate left for the nurse to leap at the chance to lay a little bad-mouth on the famous surgeon."

"She told you about Fort and me?"

"She did."

"She had no right!"

"Heidi mentioned it first. I think she said she was twelve years old when she saw you and the Doctor necking. And just how much poking around would I have to do, amid the medical brotherhood and sisterhood, before somebody mentioned old times?"

"You make it sound dirty!"

"Do you know how it sounds to me?"

"I can't imagine caring."

"It sounds as if it was a very good thing for two lonely people to have. I think you are much woman, Mrs. Stanyard. I know where your husband is. I know Gloria *thinks* the affair ended a year or two before she met Fort. If he could change six hundred thousand in assets into cash and put the cash where nobody can find it, keeping you on the string would be no special problem."

"He wasn't that kind of man. I'm not that kind of woman. I didn't even know if he told her about me. But from the way I acted toward her when they came back from Florida, she certainly would have had to guess something. I like her *very* much."

"He told her. In detail."

"And she told you. I don't think I care at all for her telling you."

"After what Heidi said, she had to tell me something. And the detail was so I'd understand. She was anxious to make sure I didn't think less of Fort or of you. Of course, I go around making these moral judgments all the time. Meaningful relationship. That phrase has sure God been worked to death. Like constructive and sincere. What it is, Janice, it's a curious, confusing bitch of a world, and you don't get a very long ride on it, and it is hard to get through to anybody merely by making mouth-sounds. So we all do some taking, up to the point where we don't gag on it. And we all do some giving, because taking doesn't taste right without it. With any luck we can sneak through without crapping up too many other lives, and with a little more luck we can make things shine for somebody sometime."

As she was staring at me, a chunky Siamese cat, a pale one like tea with cream, came in through the door that probably led to the bedroom. He stretched each hind leg separately, gave me casual inspection with eyes as blue as his mistresses', though slightly crossed, came over and snuffed at my shoes, and went on out to the kitchen, indolently purposeful.

"Who *are* you?" Janice asked me.

"T. McGee. T for Travis. Friend of Glory." I motioned toward the kitchen. "Who was that who went through?"

"Ralph. Maybe I made things shine for Fort. My husband will be a four-year-old child as long as he lives. There was that much damage. I visit Charlie every week. I'm a quiet person. I don't require much of life. After Fort and I became lovers, I couldn't understand why I'd put up such a desperate fight for my so-called honor. Maybe I thought that if someone made love to me, I'd start to resent Charlie. I didn't want that. Fort needed me. My God, there was a man I would have crawled through broken glass for, jumped out windows for. And I couldn't willingly give him something ... nobody was using and Charlie wouldn't miss. But Fort made it happen anyway, bless him. And then all of a sudden it was just something two people could have. Closeness and pleasure, and all the ordinary little things. Socks and shaving and reminding him of haircuts, and waking up and hearing somebody breathing beside you, feeling the warmth of their body near you. When he wanted me, I wanted him *because* he wanted me. It was like a voyage, I guess. We traveled from one place in our lives to another, and then what we needed from each other was over. I never made any demand on him after it was over. Sometimes I would wish he was with me so I could tell him some dumb thing, like how my alarm clock finally quit—he hated it. It had a terrible ring. I'm a heavy sleeper. Once, after he was married, I *did* ask him to come here. He came as soon as he could. He knew it wasn't . . . what some small-minded man might have guessed it could be. It was a year ago last May. On Memorial Day. I didn't know if I should report it, or what I should do."

"Report what?"

"I went to see Charlie and I got back at ten-thirty at night. When I went into the kitchen there was my poor old Ethel cat dead in the middle of the floor. She was Ralph's mother. Somebody had put a big meat skewer out of the drawer right through her, just behind the shoulder, right through her heart, and left it in her. It was such a horrid, pointless thing to do. A very sick mind, certainly. There was still some warmth in her body, and all the blood was not clotted on the tile floor. I'd left a kitchen light on, knowing it would be after dark when I got back, and they like a light to eat by when they get hungry. Ralph is like Ethel was. They leave a little in their dish and go back and have a little snack every now and then. There's a ladder that is fastened to the outside of the building and it passes right by the kitchen window. The weather forecast said no rain, so I'd left the bottom sash all the way open. Somebody had kicked the screen out and come in through the window in the night. It wouldn't be hard to do. Poor Ralph was all scrunched down in the back of my closet on my shoes, still growling, and terrified. Fort answered the phone and he got here at eleven-thirty. I was a mess, of course. It upset him terribly too. Ethel had been very fond of him."

"Did you report it?"

"We decided not to. I'm not a sissy usually, but I was

83

all shaken up. I packed an overnight bag and Fort dropped me at a hotel. He had wrapped poor Ethel up in an old sheet. I couldn't find any damage beyond the broken screen, and nothing seemed to be missing. He put Ethel in the trunk of his car, and the next day we buried her at a place down on Marley Creek where we used to have picnics sometimes. I had the super come and look at the broken screen. He was upset. But he wasn't going to do anything about it. I had people come and put steel mesh on that window and I told the other people who had windows close to that ladder what had happened and what I'd done about it, and what it had cost."

She stopped, frowned at me, shook her head. "What in the world could the Doctor have done with six hundred thousand dollars in cash? It wouldn't be like him to do something like that."

"Could his illness affect his mind?"

"Oh no. And the few times I saw him, toward the end, he was perfectly all right. He knew he'd never get out of that bed. The pain was bad and getting worse, but he decided he'd rather fight it than be so drugged he couldn't communicate with anyone."

"And he was an honest man?"

"Certainly. Oh, he didn't make a big thing of it, and go around glowing with righteousness—you know the type."

"Mrs. Stanyard? Janice?"

"Janice is fine."

"You didn't know a thing about the missing money. But you can count on other people getting around to you before very long."

"I don't understand."

"Excuse the bluntness, but when the wife and children get dealt out, they dig up the past, and you are the ex-mistress, the trite old triangle of doctor, wife, and nurse."

"But it . . ."

"I know it wasn't like that. But for seven of the thirteen months he was cashing things in, you were working with him."

"Not anything like the way we used to work, though. No routine things at all, no matter how intricate. He was sort of . . . wrapping up what he knew and what he was still learning. His post-operative dictation was about twice as long as it had ever been, because he was making suggestions about alternative techniques he knew he was never going to have time to attempt. He wanted to leave something other surgeons could use. And he wanted to spend as much time as he could with Gloria and his grand-children."

"Do you remember anything at all strange during those seven months? Any mysterious letters or visits or phone calls? Did he seem troubled?"

"No. But he didn't trouble easily, you know. He had his own philosophy about worry. He always told me that people spend so much time fretting about what they did yesterday and dreading what might happen tomorrow, they miss out on all of their todays. He said that when you realize you can't change the past or predict the future, then you come alive for the first time, like waking up from half-sleep."

"You might be questioned by people who are better at it than I am, and a lot more merciless."

"Why do you say that?"

"They'll catch you up a lot quicker when you lie about having no contact with Fort from January to when you visited him at his home."

"Lie! I swear to you I did not see him once during that time."

"That isn't what I said. A contact is not necessarily a confrontation."

"I don't have to take this, you know."

"Phone? Letter?"

"*Damn* you!" She stood up and went to the windows, stood there with her back to the room. Her anger made a pink tint on the pallor of her neck below the graying hair. I went over and stood behind her and to her left. The sky above the distant parking plaza was as gray as the asphalt. Three kids were running diagonally across the lot, a big yellow dog loping along with them.

"Use your head, Janice. If you don't know how to handle it with me, how can you expect to handle it when the cold winds really start to blow?"

"He had reasons for everything he did."

"And never miscalculated? Never made an error? Do you really believe that he *wanted* Gloria to be persecuted, treated as a suspicious person and watched and followed the rest of her life?"

She turned and stared up into my eyes. "Will it be like that?"

"Not if it was six thousand or sixty thousand. It's six hundred thousand. It hasn't hit the news yet. The bank and the lawyers and the tax people have kept the lid on it. Fort's mind was clouded in one way. I can draw pictures for you. There have been people killed in this happy village for forty cents. No matter how carefully the missing money is reported, there are going to be some types sitting around wondering which way and how soon they'll pick up the bride and take her to a cozy place and treat her pretty little feet with lighter fluid. They'll think that either she knows or she doesn't, but that much cash is worth the try. She'll end up in the river wrapped in scrap iron either way."

Her eyes widened and her throat bulged as she dry-swallowed twice, and, with her color going bad, she braced a hand against the window frame and closed her eyes for a moment. I asked her if she was going to faint.

"No. I don't faint. It was just the idea anybody . . . could do that to Gloria Geis."

"And if she doesn't know, there's always Heidi and then Roger and then you. It's big loot, and it is in the handiest form loot comes in. You don't have to fence it."

Her color was better. She swallowed again. "I . . . I guess I do have some of it. Not here. It's in my box at the bank. The letter is here. But I don't think it will mean anything, and it says not to tell anybody. But, as you say, I don't think he realized what could happen . . . Excuse me."

She went over to a desk and opened a drawer and sorted through a half-box of new stationery, riffling it with her thumb until she came to the letter. She looked at it before she handed it to me. She shook her head. "I hate what happened to his muscular control. His hands were so good."

It was small, shaky, uncertain writing, but reasonably legible. It was dated the previous August eleventh.

Janice, dear,
Put this in your lock box at your bank.
I have gotten word to someone to come to you in
case of emergency. You will find out what might

*have to be done. Use the money for that purpose.
You will understand why I couldn't ask G for this
kind of help. If no one comes to you within a year of
my death, please get the money to G. I would write
more, but it is hard to write. I know I impose. Thanks
for many things, and thanks for this.*

Fortner

"It's ten thousand dollars," she said. "In hundred-dollar
bills, mostly. It was in a manila envelope wrapped with
rubber bands inside another manila envelope. I think he
thought it was ten thousand even, but it was a hundred
dollars short. It came in the regular mail."

"You saw him after that. Did you mention the note and
the money?"

"When I started to, he closed his eyes and shook his
head. Gloria was out of the room just then."

I read it once more and gave it back to her to put away.
"Not a clue," I said. "Some unknown person may or may
not come to you for help, and if they come, they'll tell
you what kind of help they need. Isn't that just dandy?
Only five hundred and ninety thousand to go."

"I wish I could help. I really do."

She meant it. Sincerity and conviction, and a great di-
rectness. But I had to come to the usual screeching halt. I
didn't have her lashed up to a polygraph with a good man
watching the styluses or styli or whatever the hell the
proper plural might be. Pen points, maybe. And I didn't
know if she was one of the small percentage who can fool
the polygraph every time. In a world of plausible scoun-
drels and psychopathic liars, hunch can take you only so
far.

I have to keep remembering at all times that sweet
little old lady on the veranda in Charleston, South Caro-
lina, the one who told me the story of her life in a sighing
little voice, a story so sad that my eyes were misty and my
voice thick by the time she shot at me with the Luger
she was holding in her lap under the corner of her shawl.
The slug took a little bite out of the side of the collar
of my white shirt and exposed a dime-sized piece of blue
necktie.

"Maybe," I said, "the money's for Gretchen."

"For who?"

"For Gretchen. I guess you could call her an indiscretion. Long ago. Way back when Glenna was dying."

She looked puzzled. "I don't know anything about that. It doesn't sound right, somehow. He worshipped his first wife."

"At least he always thought he did. Until he took a little acid LSD, provided by a buddy."

"Dr. Wyatt? Hayes Wyatt?"

"Glory took the trip too. I guess they were both getting a bad hang-up on his situation being terminal."

She nodded. "Dr. Wyatt has had a lot of success with it with terminal cases, where the pain is bad and they're terribly frightened, or terribly depressed. It's disassociative, you know. It gives them a breathing space to kind of sort out what it all means."

"And he sorted Glenna out and found out he didn't like her at all. Glory says it surprised him."

"Who was Gretchen?"

There was no reason not to tell her. There was even the chance it might knock loose some useful memory. But I told her and it didn't. The tale intrigued her. It gave another dimension to her hero, Fort Geis. But at the same time it diminished her. She had thought of herself as one third of the women in Geis' maturity—Glenna-Janice-Gloria. News of hearty little Gretch made it a foursome. It complicated her mental biography of the great man. It put two little vertical lines between her eyebrows, and I no longer had her full attention.

So, with promises to get in touch if either of us learned anything, I went back out into the last gray fading of the daylight in the damp and windy streets. I knew the sun was still shining way down there at Bahia Mar in the bottom right corner of the map, and *The Busted Flush* would be creaking and sighing when the dying wash from the incoming charterboats got to her. The sandy little brown broads would be ornamenting the sunset beach, casting the swift sidelong glance, trying not to blow their cool with the slightest trace of smile, and other kids would be playing the big game of pretending to be surfers, as they rode their bright boards in the gigantic, savage, towering breakers—two feet high that break for twenty feet and six whole seconds sometimes.

[Surfers of the World, save your money and dream long

dreams of getting to that one unspoiled beach that makes both California and Hawaii look like a sometime thing. Two whole miles of ocean straight out from the beach, six feet deep on the median tide, all sand, and flat as pool tables. On the prevailing wind out of the southwest, girls and boys, those rollers start to build way down by Mozambique and Madagascar, and have a two-thousand mile run across the Indian Ocean before they crest white two miles off the great beach at Galle, Ceylon, and run all the way in with such a perfect symmetry and geometry that when you look down on it from twenty thousand feet it is like looking at a swatch of fabric, a pure pinstripe white on a pale tan-green background. As a special added convenience, just a bit south, toward Dondra Head, the deeps are close to the beach, so that after you get beyond the first few, you have nothing to fight on the way out.]

But I was too far from a softer sunset and a better beach. I knew that with a little luck I could either get part of my path smoothed for me, or find out something that would convince me it would make a lot more sense to head south right away. In the premature fading of daylight, I drove my rental car back through the damp and windy streets to the hotel and went up to the room, practicing a glassy smile to see if it would help lift me out of a mood turning as gray as day's end. See, brain-pan? The mouth is smiling. Feel the smile muscles? Hi ho, hi ho. The eyes are squinching too. McGee is one happy fella. Right?

I think I was trying too hard with the smile. When the elevator door opened at my floor, a substantial matron in a fur hat was waiting to board. When she glimpsed me, she sprang back a good distance and then waited until I was four strides away before scuttling into the Otis-Box.

I turned on the lights in the room and emptied all the cards out of my wallet on the bed. You may charge me, dear people, with being a Card-Carrying American. I find these little tickets to perpetual consumption distasteful. I do not like to see my name on them, deeply embossed into everlasting plastic. They make me feel as if I should wear a leather collar and hang them all thereon. When there is a mistake in the billing on any of them, if you persist, you can fight your way past the icy and patronizing indifference of the electronic computers and reach a semi-human who can straighten things out. It only takes a year or so.

Yet in our times the thick wad of credit cards is a cachet of respectability, something more useful to me than any questionable convenience. When a cop lays upon you the white eye, and you stand there hunting for a driver's license as identification, and he watches you fumble through AmEx, Diners, Carte Blanche, Air Travel, Sheraton, Shell, Gulf, Phillips, Standard, Avis, and Texaco before you find it, he is reassured. You may have thirty-seven cents and a dirty shirt, but you are completely on record and in good standing with the Establishment. If all you have is the license and a bale of vulgar cash money, it piques his curiosity. Who is this bum who can't get credit cards like honest people?

I found Maurie Ragna's personal card among the seldom used credit cards tucked into a side pocket of the wallet. He had written his unlisted phone number on the back of it. An East Chicago number, over the line in Lake County, Indiana, where as I understood it, the authorities were still as cooperative and hospitable to Ragna and his playmates as they had once been in Calumet City and Cicero. The Outfit, as it is known along the lake, had responded to the roust by moving over the line into Gary and East Chicago.

I had come along once at the right time and, down in the Keys, had pried Maurie out of an exceptionally ugly situation, wherein he had no future at all to speak of. Grateful as he was, he was astonished any bystander would voluntarily involve himself. As it was, he couldn't put any weight at all on his feet for days, and walked in a very tender way for much longer. But that is an old and complex story, and he had tried to show appreciation by gifting me with cars, broads, and vacations on the cuff, but I had settled for a dozen mohair cardigans and passed along eleven of the twelve to friends. So this was the first time I was making a call on an old obligation, and if he was not yet buried out in the desert near Vegas, or chained to the bottom of lake or river, it might hearten him.

The number answered. A skeptical fellow who spoke in grunts took my name and where I could be reached and said if Ragna never got back to me he was maybe out of town or something.

It took an hour and a half. He was bursting with hospitality. He offered a car and driver, a choice of any kind of action I felt like, a certified stupendous broad, baby, name the age you like, the size, the build, the color, Swede, Jap, Spic, Polski, call it, McGee baby.

His voice sagged when I said maybe later, that right now I wanted information. When I said important information he brightened. I went into the indirect and elliptical phraseology of those whose lines are ninety per cent certain of being permanently bugged.

"You are so right," he said. "It hasn't come to my ear but it can be checked. If say some associate of some associate built the action on the Doc, then you scuffle around too much, I got enough going here and there you should get maybe only roughed up some, a three-day rest with nice nurses. But you could not clout any of it back, so scuffling would be a waste, right? Now on the little guy Smith, I will find out who owns how much of him. Hang easy, Mister M. Give me one hour, two tops."

I ordered up some ice. Long long ago a lass had gifted me with a solitary drinker's kit. It is a squatty pewter flagon, cylindrical and with a king-sized old-fashioned-shaped drinking cup in pewter which fits upside down over the flagon with threads at the midway point of the flagon, so that assembled it is a perfect cylinder. With a nice regard for the emotional climate of the man who, when it is necessary, can drink alone without feeling degenerate, she'd had a single word engraved upon both flagon and glass: Mine. I had thought it all too elfin, thanked her too effusively, and put it away in a locker, and had come across it when packing for this trip and suddenly realized her instincts had been better than mine. It was not elfin. It was factual, and a derisive comment on all the His and Hers items in this chummy civilization. So I had filled it with Plymouth and brought it along, and it was indeed Mine.

I lounged and brooded and sipped and awaited Maurie Ragna's report. Sober sociological evaluations of the genus Hoodlumae americanus leave out their capacity for compulsive friendship. Once one accepts you he will lay gifts upon you like a potty rich uncle. You can do no wrong. You are forever his big great friend and buddy and chum and pal. If you get big-mouth disease, it is to him a disease, and he will have you gunned down, and he will cry, and send a whole truck of flowers. There are various levels of ethical values within the genus. I knew Ragna had a high contempt for those who deal in hash and grass, or schoolgirl recruitment, or housewife call circuits. He concentrates on such moral areas as bootlegging liquor and cigarettes, setting up casinos, operating resort properties here and there where he can supply a complete line of wheels, booze, hookers, and blue entertainment, as well as the more mundane items—such as vending machines, kitchen equipment, bed vibrators, and intercom equipment.

At last the call came back. "Took me too long, buddy boy, on account of a party I had to be sure of, he's at Acapulco and the call didn't go through so easy. It is no part of our action in any way, and though attractive, we stay off it, so go ahead and scuffle and stay lucky, you bum. I don't want you dead. About this Franky, he is owned like up to the throat and the word has gone to him to bust his ass doing any small thing anybody with your name wants done."

"It is a big help and a load off my mind, friend."

"Some phone calls, some lousy sweaters. Ask for something big so I can get even, will you?"

"When I need it, I'll holler."

After I'd said good-bye and hung up, I thought of a possibility which this contact with Ragna had suggested. The gambling itch was in many cases like other forms of addiction, a search for an excitement which turns the mind off. Maybe Geis had found a poker table. A big game would know just how high they would let the Doctor go on markers, and it was possible to lose six very big ones. It has been done before and will happen again. In some London clubs the biggest chip in play is worth twenty-eight thousand, and there are some in play every night. And if Geis had been expertly plucked, they would collect on the markers ruthlessly.

But I had to give that up. If the score had been made that way, Maurie would have come up with the information.

I rubbed a thumb across misted pewter and read the name again. Mine. That was the name of the problem. All mine.

seven

Francisco Smith cut me off when I tried to tell him over the phone what I wanted from him. The agency offices were in the Monadnock Block on West Jackson. He named a lunchroom a block and a half away. I said I was six four, Florida tan, gray topcoat, no hat.

I got there within the half-hour, and had a six-minute wait over bad coffee before he arrived at quarter to ten, came directly to the booth, and sat opposite me.

"Smith," he said to me. "Coffee black," he said to the chubby waitress. When she went away he said, "With everything in the shop bugged every way those sons of bitches can dream up, I couldn't take a chance you might say too much about what you want."

He was on the short side of medium height, stocky, balding, mottled red face, rimless glasses with gold bows and nosepiece, and lenses strong enough to magnify the size of his weak-looking blue eyes. Medium blue suit, dark blue topcoat, light gray felt hat. He talked with very little lip movement, rather like an unskilled ventriloquist. You would have to glance at him a dozen times in a dozen places in one day before you'd begin to wonder if you had ever seen him before. All the cities of the world are stocked with innumerable replicas of Frankie Smith. They are clerks, fry cooks, building inspectors, watch repairmen, camera salesmen, estimators, adjustors, civil servants, church wardens, florists.

"I want to know all about the job you did for Dr. Fortner Geis."

He looked puzzled. "Keeping an eye on that Gretchen Gorba and her kids? It went on quite a while. Better than two and a half years. Just a spot check to see how they were making it. He pulled us off it last summer. Early

July? No. Early August. He died a couple of months later. Big play in the papers."

"He was a big man."

Smith studied me. He nodded abruptly. "I think I get the picture. The contract with us would be sort of proof the kid was his. Susan. The oldest. Hell, copies of all the reports are in the dead file. The court can make us turn them over if it comes to that. There could be a nice piece of change in it for an eighteen-year-old kid, enough to split it a lot of ways."

"Did he tell you Susan was his daughter?"

"Hell no. Look, if you tell us to run a complete check on Joe Blow, we'll do it. But to keep our own noses clean, we'll want to find out why you're so interested in Joe. We got the contract three years ago next month. Gretchen Gorba is a big good-natured slob. She likes the horses and draft beer and shacking up, in any order they happen to come along. So I put a big old boy in our shop onto it. He's the kind women tell things to. He took a furnished room in a handy neighborhood, and as soon as he started laying her, she started telling her sad story, about how she was the housekeeper's daughter, and when the Doctor's wife was dying, the Doc knocked her up when she was just a dumb kid, and the Doc and her mother arranged to marry her off to somebody, and the Doc set up a lifetime annuity of a hundred a week for the kid named Susan. Gretchen whined to our boy that she had braced the Doc to improve the income, on account of having five kids, and her husband in prison, but he didn't scare and he didn't give. But from talking to him, I got the idea that if we'd reported they were having a hard time, he would have done something. She was making between sixty-five and seventy-five a week depending on the tips, and averaging maybe thirty a week to the bookies, so that if she was getting more, the bookies would get more. She bets the doubles and the parlays, a guaranteed way to stay busted."

"So Doctor Geis asked you to keep checking?"

"To keep an eye on them. I would have thought that Gretchen's mother, Mrs. Ottlo, could have done it just as well and saved him the fees. But I guess Mrs. Ottlo wasn't getting along so good with her daughter. She'd pick times to visit when Gretchen was working and the kids would be there. She'd bring food and presents. It could have been that the Doc was afraid Mrs. Ottlo would be too proud to let him know if Gretchen and the kids were having a hard time. After about five or six months he asked me to set something up with Susan. I handled it myself. Fifteen years old. Hell of a good kid. Smart. I gave her a phone number she could call day or night in case of any trouble where she needed help. She agreed to keep it from her mother. But she wanted to know who had this big interest in her family. I found out she had the idea she was adopted. Kids get that idea. Mama had gotten slopped a few times and said just enough so Susan thought the annuity was probably from her real parents. So I didn't say yes and I didn't say no. I left it the way I found it. Once it was set up that way, the Doc was able to cut down the expense of our checking them out so often. But I think it was the next January or February, two years ago minus a few weeks, he phoned me and said he'd heard through Mrs. Ottlo that Gretchen's husband had been released on parole and had rejoined the family, and he wanted to know what effect that would have on Susan. So I had a friend pull the file on Saul Gorba and give me a nice long look at it."

Smith had a good memory for details. Gorba had served over four and a half years of a six-year sentence in Wisconsin. Gretchen had lined up a job for him in a body and fender shop through the shop foreman who was a friend and a regular customer at the restaurant where she was working. Through a reciprocal arrangement on parole supervision, a duplicate file was sent along to the Cook County authorities, and that was the one Smith had examined. Gorba had been just past thirty when he had been tried, convicted, and sentenced. He and Gretchen had been living as common-law man and wife in Milwaukee. She claimed that during the two years they had been together, she had thought he was a salesman. They rented a small frame house in a quiet lower-middle-class area. She thought he sold novelties and specialty items and office supplies. He had a small hand press in the basement and he told her it was for sample letterheads. He had a large supply of the different colors of safety paper used for bank checks, and he had a perforator, cutting board, several styles of check-writers, several typewriters.

His business trips lasted a week or two, and he would take a week off between each trip. His trips took him into Iowa, Minnesota, and Illinois. His procedure was to acquire legitimate checks made out for commercial payroll purposes, or for payment on small accounts. One source was through mail order, where he would, using a false name and a post office box, send in an overpayment by money order and get a company check back representing his refund.

Once he had acquired, for example, a check from the XYZ Company in Madison, Wisconsin, he would take it home and, in his basement shop, make a dozen acceptable duplicates of it, in size, paper stock, imprint, check-writer patterns, typing, carefully traced signatures, and even to the careful duplication in India ink of the magnetic ink symbols used by the automated sorting equipment in the banks. With the dozen checks made out in varying and plausible amounts, usually in odd dollars and cents between one hundred and two hundred dollars, he would hit Madison with them, using a falsified driver's license as identification, and cash them without great difficulty as payroll in a dozen different places, clearing up to two thousand dollars. He was neat, personable, and careful to make significant alterations in his appearance for each job.

Shortly before he was arrested, he had told Gretchen that he was getting a chance at a better territory soon, and they would probably be moving to eastern Ohio.

An alert supermarket manager in Racine thought the check he had just cashed did not look quite right somehow. He compared it with another payroll check from the same company and discovered that the check paper was a slightly different shade of green, and that the check-writer numerals were larger. He ran out and caught Gorba as he was getting into his car. After he grabbed Gorba, the next thirty seconds cost the manager over three weeks in the hospital. An off-duty cop was trundling a wire basket of weekend groceries out to his car, and it took him a long and painful time to subdue the suspect.

Smith said, "A loner. A real weird. They confiscated twenty-eight grand he had squirreled away in hidey-holes in that basement. Previous arrests and convictions were not in any kind of pattern like you expect. Assault with a deadly weapon. Conspiracy to defraud. Impersonating an officer. Attempted rape. In and out of four colleges. An IQ like practically a genius. Emotionally unstable, they said. She had the youngest by him after they put him away. Tommy."

"He doesn't sound like the kind who'd be attracted to Gretchen."

"Why not? Those jumpy ones, sometimes what suits them best is some big dumb happy broad. No demands. No arguments. And also you have to figure it made a nice cover for him for those two years, the wife and family, quiet neighborhood, just another salesman. Anyway, I had to report to the Doc on how it was going to work out, and it didn't look so great to me. But it was the longest stretch he'd pulled, and it settled him down, apparently. His record on the inside was good. The parole officer said his attitude was good. Gretchen was clam-happy to have him back, and at the suggestion of the parole officer, they made it legal. The foreman was satisfied with him. He kept to himself but he did his work at the shop. Gretchen kept on with the waitress work. With more pay coming in, they got an apartment in the same building but down on the second floor, with one more bedroom, three instead of two. I wouldn't say the relationship with the kids was real close, but it was workable. And I guess Mrs. Ottlo, the kids' grandma, approved, maybe because it was legal. I guess she started getting along better with her daughter, because she took to going there Sunday afternoons when everybody was home, having dinner with them."

"And now she has no idea where they went. No forwarding address."

He stared at me. "You kidding?"

"They moved out last August, apparently."

Frowning, he counted slowly on his fingers, lips moving. "He was going to be on parole sixteen months, so it would run out last August, about. Maybe the brightest ones are the biggest damned fools. Maybe he kept his head down until he had his clean bill, then headed for someplace where he could go back into business for himself. Want me to try to trace them for you?"

"What are the rates?"

"Very funny! Expenses only, and on my own time, as you damn well know. And no written reports."

"Just checking," I said,

"Nothing has changed, and never will." He took his glasses off and wiped them on a paper napkin.

I wondered what hold they had on him. He apparently thought I knew about it. "See what you can do," I said. "I'm in 944 at the Drake. Meanwhile, I'd like some specific information out of your records on Susan and her brothers and sisters."

He returned in less than half an hour, sat across from me, and said, "Had to wait until the file girl went for her coffee break. Want to write this down? Susan Kemmer will be eighteen on January fourth. Gretchen had one kid by Kemmer. Freddy. He's fifteen. She had a common-law set-up out in California with somebody named Budrow. She had two by him. Julian is twelve and Freda is ten. The last one, Tommy, was by Gorba, and the kid is six now. The annuity is with Great Lakes Casualty Mutual. Their Chicago office is in the National Republic Bank Building on South La Salle."

"What happened to Budrow?"

"Just took off, I guess."

"Can you get on this right away, Smith?"

"All I can tell you is I'll do the best I can. It shouldn't be hard. I'll see what I can turn up at the places they worked, and see what happened with the kids' school records, and see where the annuity checks are going. Saul Gorba is maybe foxy enough to slip out of sight if he was by himself. A whole family is something else. I could get shot with luck and hit it the first try and know by tonight. Or it could take a week of leg work."

"Find out if they left owing."

He looked slightly contemptuous. "The *first* thing I would do is check the Credit Bureau. There could be a tracer request and the new address already."

It took me four dimes to track down Martin Hollinder Trumbill the Fourth. In a brassy bass rumble he said he was too damned busy getting ready for a trip to see anybody about anything. I pulled a gentle con on him by saying that if he could see me, then maybe I wouldn't have to spoil his trip. After we went around and around on that for several minutes, he asked me to meet him at twelve-thirty at the bar of the Norway Club atop the Lakeway Tower.

I was five minutes late and he was ten minutes late. He didn't come in from outside. He came in from some nearby area where the club members evidently worked out. His hair was damp and he had the glow of sauna and sunlamp. He was fifty, bronzed, about five nine, with most of his hair, a ruggedly handsome face, a body like a bull ape, as broad and thick through the shoulder as any NFL tackle. Arrogant little simian eyes stared out at me from under great grizzled black tangles of eyebrow. Tufts of black hair grew out of nostrils and ears, and his big hands had a heavy pelt on the backs and on the backs of the fingers down to the middle knuckle. A shetland sport jacket, perfectly tailored to his broad, long-armed, bandy-legged build, softened somewhat the brute impact of him. But I wondered what he was trying to prove by making his barber leave the nostril and ear hair alone.

An attendant had pointed me out to him as the man who was waiting for him. A drink appeared on the bar and he took it and walked away toward the view windows. A powder snow was falling, and the wind whipped it against the curved glass. I followed him as he expected I would.

"In thirty seconds make me believe you could spoil anything for me, or I'll have you thrown out." He spoke without turning to look at me.

I said, "Golly, sir, gee whiz, now you've got me so terrified I can't hardly think straight."

He pivoted and stared at me. "What the hell *is* this?"

I smiled upon him. "I guess I don't like jackasses. I guess I don't like rich jackasses. I guess I don't like rich, rude, double-gaited jackasses. Now would you like to try again? You got off on the wrong foot, Gadgey."

I didn't realize he could get those eyebrows so high. "Who the hell do you think you *are!*"

"T. for Travis McGee. I know. You'll buy the ground I'm standing on and have me torn down. I am an old buddy of the Widow Geis. Doctor Fort shoved the first legal team into the fray and Miss Heidi got very well. Am I getting past that hair in your ears? I wouldn't want you to leave town without answering a question. Are you a

99

miserable enough bastard to have found a way to gouge Heidi's winnings back out of her poor old dad's hide?"

"Gouge? Gouge?"

"There's no estate left."

"I know."

"Now how would you know, Gadgey?"

"Her brother Roger was wringing his hands about it. He's a goddam stuffed shirt and . . . What gives you the right to ask me questions anyway?"

"Because I am helping the Widow Geis find out where all the money went."

"*All* the money? For God's sake, McGee, sure Heidi took a pretty good cut. I've still got eleven million in tax-exempt municipals, if you can comprehend what I'm talking about."

"You're talking about at least three hundred and thirty thousand a year you don't even have to report on the good old ten forty. Cut the shit, Trumbill. If it was a hundred and ten million, you still couldn't impress me. You can afford to buy me a drink in your own club, can't you? A double Plymouth gin on ice, plain. I'll wait right here while you go make the arrangements."

I watched him head for the bar and I wondered how far he could be pushed. He did not lumber. He had a springy and youthful stride. As he approached bearing my drink, I heard him chuckling. He handed it to me, bowed, and said, "Golly, sir, gee whiz, now you've got me so terrified I can't think straight."

"Thank you for the drink, Mr. Trumbill."

"My pleasure, Mr. McGee," he said. "Let's sit in the lounge and get acquainted. There's no particular reason why I give a goddam about your opinion about anything, but there's one thing that needs correcting."

I followed him to two wingback chairs with a small table between them, angled to look out at the scenery and provide privacy for conversation. "You have met Heidi?" he asked.

"Yes."

"The ice queen. The snow maiden. But when you look at her, everything points the other way. When I married her three years ago, I thought I had the optimum solution. McGee, I am not a locker-room sex hero. I just happened to be born with a hell of a lot of sexual drive and capacity. Sleeping around is a damned bore. Everything about her looks as if she was made for it. Fantastic body. Healthy as a field hand. The way she walks, the timbre of her voice, the shape of her hands, it's all provocative and invitational. I thought to myself, hell, Gadge, there's the answer. She was twenty-two and I was forty-eight. She'd be thirty-five when I was sixty-one, and she'd be getting ready to slow down a little when I damn well had to. But finding out she was a twenty-two-year-old virgin should have told me something. Let me tell you, I worked like a slave on that damned girl. The harder I tried, the nastier she thought it was. Finally I could practically see her flesh crawl when I touched her. The only response I ever got was a goddam martyred sigh. Sexual frustration is a hell of a sorry condition, McGee. So I went out to get what I couldn't get from her. I think I was a little out of my mind. I grabbed onto anything warm and breathing that came within reach. And a couple of times when I was pig-drunk it happened to be her willowy little art-class boyfriends who wanted a way to get a hand in the till. When I gave no big gifts of money, they went whimpering to her about her gross, horrible brute of a husband. Now I give her this. She knows she's frigid, and she knows that her condition had a lot to do with the situations I got into after I gave up with her. So she wasn't going to try for a big settlement and big alimony. But her darling daddy egged her on and got her some hot legal talent, and they gave me a pretty fair bruise. It could have been even bigger if she'd really wanted to take it all into court, but they still had enough pressure to extract a generous agreement. Those months were the only time I ever went the AC-DC route, and it isn't going to happen again because I'm never going to get into that kind of desperate mood again. So drop back on the double-gaited. I like girls. Always have. Always will. And I prefer girl-girls with all the girl-girl equipment to the girl-boys with the long locks and the squeaky voices. I don't know why I should give a goddam about your opinion . . ."

"You're repeating yourself. There's another question I want to . . ."

He looked at his watch. "Okay. Come down to the

apartment and ask it there. I'm expecting some people and I want to be there when they get there."

I got my coat from the attendant and we rode down to the sixteenth floor and got off. He explained that quite a few of the members kept an apartment in the building as a convenience, and if they were going to be away for six months or longer, the club management would arrange a sublet.

He unlocked it. It was as impersonal as a decorator's advertisement.

As soon as I had a chance I asked my question. "Mr. Trumbill, last year, in April or May or June, while you and Heidi were still together . . ."

"I moved out the last week in May."

"Okay. During those last two months did anything happen which seemed odd."

"Odd?"

"Any kind of accident which could have been dangerous, or any near-accident, where Heidi was involved?"

"Why?"

"It could be important and the reasons would take too long to explain."

"Important to whom, McGee?"

"Does it matter? Come on."

"There wasn't anything . . . unless you mean something like that damned candy."

"Candy?"

"Oh, there was a kind she was nuts about. Chocolate cherries. A lot of juice inside. She never bought them for herself. Her father would bring her a box or have them sent over on special occasions. Birthdays, anniversaries. Sometime in early May—we'd had a big scrap—I walked through the living room. She was watching the news on television. I was going out, and I knew she damned well wasn't going to say good-bye dear have a nice time. The way she ate them, she didn't nibble. She'd lift one out of the box, pop it into her mouth, and mash it. The box was half gone. She was down to the second layer. Suddenly she began making the damnedest noises, gasping and whoofing and spitting pieces of chocolate all over. She went to the kitchen on a dead run, scaring hell out of the maid. She kept rinsing her mouth in cold water. Her eyes were running and her nose was running. She couldn't say a word we could understand. Finally after she ate some crackers and rinsed her mouth out some more, she started chewing me out for pulling such a nasty trick. I finally convinced her I didn't know what the hell she was talking about. She had gotten a chocolate that instead of having a cherry and cherry juice inside had apparently been filled with about a quarter ounce of straight Tabasco. She was furious. I was running late, so I left."

"How did it happen?"

"She never found out. She opened all the ones left in the box. They were all perfect. She phoned her father and told him about it. He said it must have happened after the box was opened, because he had bought it one day, and brought it over to our place the next day in person, and the shop was certainly reliable. He said maybe it was some friend of mine who knew her habits. I guess you could classify that as an accident. It made her very uncomfortable, but I guess there are things you could put in candy that would do more than . . ."

The phone rang and he answered it, then hung up and told me his people were on the way up. I thanked him and said I'd run along. He said, "Meet the group, McGee. Highly talented people. We're going to Gúadeloupe and make a motion picture. Highly unusual script. Be released in France. Some of the crew is there now, picking locations."

There was a brisk rap on the door, and he went and let four of them in, two young women, two young men. They were laughing and gay and all a little tight. One was a Limey lass, the height of mod exhibitionism, her little-girl skirt a good four inches above the knee, and a metallic golden serpent wrapped around her left leg just below the knee. While she was saying, with little chopping motions of her hands, "What a fantastically gawstly city, Gadge darling, ectually!" he was introducing her as Pansy Perkins, certainly I'd heard of her.

"Certainly I haven't, sorry," I said. "I live a quiet life."

With a speculative glint she started appraising me, but Trumbill put a huge paw on her slender shoulder, and as he introduced a busty Italian girl whose name *was* vaguely familiar (she took a slender cigar out of the center of her considerable mouth to acknowledge the introduction) and then a Pierre something, talented director, all in black, even to little black onyx buttons in his pierced ears, and a Willy something, fat, pasty, scruffy, with too blatant an Irish accent, Gadge was at the same time stroking the throat of his Pansy with a spatulate thumb, an attention which unfocused her eyes, loosened her mouth, and sagged her head like a wilting poppy.

"We are going to go down there and do something true," Trumbill said. "We are going to work hard and we are going to work well, and get it all down the way it happens."

Suddenly I realized who he was trying to be. "For God's sake, Papa, don't forget the wineskins. Catch a brave and true marlin. But if this curious quartet has conned you into backing some feelthy movies, why bother trying to snow me? I don't care who reels you in, Pansy or Pierre. Papa never had that kind of problem."

Pierre hissed like a pooty tat, and the Italian gave an evil grin around her cigar, and Irish belched loudly, and Pansy murmured a few gutter words. Martin Hollinder Trumbill the Fourth gave a tight grin and rolled his big shoulders, clapped his hands like a gunshot, and came at me very Black Belt, springing and landing this way and that, paws in chopping position as he yelled, "Huhh!" and "Haaah!"

His quartet backed out of the way, looking expectant. Their imitation Papa would defend the honor of the group and throw Bigmouth all over the place. I pointed beyond him at Pierre and yelled, "No knives, you!"

Gadge turned quickly to see the imaginary knife, and opened up his left side just enough. I screwed my heels down into his gunmetal carpeting, pivoted hips and shoulders like Palmer needing an eagle on a par five, and bombed him on the left side, just above the belt, slightly around to the rear, straight punch, hooking slightly at impact, good snap, lots of follow-through.

He groaned, arched, grabbed at the impact point with both hands, and stood with his face screwed up like a little brave boy on the playground trying not to cry.

As I headed for the door I said, "Get it looked at before you leave, Trumbill. I may have tore up that kidney some."

The four rushed to him with little coos and murmurings and cries of compassion. I left as they were leading him to a chair. As I was going down in the elevator I realized that my appraisal of the relationship was not quite accurate. Those four might be under the impression they had a captive placid beast and if they kept scratching it behind the ears, it would moo with joy and give milk indefinitely.

They would discover eventually that it was much more like the relationship of shark and remora fish. The four remora fish would suck hold of the shark for the ride. Sharks are messy eaters. Remora are sustained by the bits of torn meat afloat when the shark feeds. But when any remora becomes too greedy and a little careless, he becomes a part of the very meal he is trying to share, an accident seldom noticed by the shark.

I did know that I wanted no judo or karate games. The expert can whip you with no fuss, and the amateur can kill you without meaning to, if you give them a chance to play their Asiatic game. The mystique of judo is based upon an irrationality. It supposes that the opponent is going to play by their rules. The way to meet it is with a hefty glass ashtray smacko in the chops, or knocking a kneecap loose with a leg off a chair or coffee table, or faking them out and giving them enough bright and sudden pain they forget their trick art. The gutsy dramas on the mass media tend to make us forget that the average urban male is so unaccustomed to sudden pain that if you mash his nose flat, he'll be nauseated for hours, spend two days in bed, and be shaky for the rest of the week.

The temperature had dropped. Snow was bounding like wedding rice off the pavements. It stung my tropical nose, and the wind yanked at my topcoat, congealed my blood, and made my bones feel like old icicles wrapped in freezer bags. Santas dingle-jangled their street-corner appeals, hopping from foot to foot, changing the bell from hand to hand, saying thank you sir with a huff of frosty breath, and the department stores sang "Ave Maria" in stereo high-fidelity while stocky ladies whomped each other with purses and elbows as they competed for Bargain Gifts Galore, and the stone-faced virgins who staff the toy areas drove away the urchins who had come to play with the trains.

I found a warm and tranquil place where they put beef in the beef stew, and ground their own Colombian coffee beans, and even had a waiter who expressed a certain tender anxiety that I should be content with what he brought me. In the darkness of the afternoon when I left the car lights were on, the snow was horizontal, the girls hugged and scuttled, and I couldn't get my rental car started.

eight

The phone was ringing when I unlocked my room door at the Drake. It was Maurie Ragna phoning to see if I had talked to Smith and if he had been cooperative.

"I'd say he was very anxious to please, Maurie."

"Good. Good. Kid, what I wanted to tell you, I suddenly have to make a little business trip. Three days, four days. But what I am going to do, I'm going to have somebody stand by this number with the word if you call for any help, you get it."

"Don't go to all that trouble."

"Right now I'd be dead a long time and he talks about trouble! Look, I worry about you. It's a big piece of money you're working on, sweetie. I can give you some top-quality walkaround muscle for as long as you want. Looks like a bond salesman. Drives like Phil Hill. Knows the fastest route from anywhere to anywhere. Licensed to carry. Quick as a cat, with a left hook you got to see to believe. Kid, I would feel a lot better about you, and I swear to God, which you should know anyway, it isn't a way of moving in on your action."

I assured him that such a thought would never enter my mind, and I managed to refuse the offer without hurting his feelings too much.

My full and rightful share of Chicago's pollution had fallen onto me all day, a Monday fallout, rimming my collar with gray. It was four in the afternoon, but from my hotel window it looked like midnight. I ordered up a jug of ice, broke out my travel-keg of Plymouth, and built a tall one. I showered first, then drew a tub as hot as I could stand it, and once I had made a gingerly descent into it, I reached and gathered up the icy glass and took one long draw upon it and put it back, away from the steam.

Some of the small sybaritic enhancements of life are worth far more than they cost, and one of them is the very hot tub combined with a sup of dry and icy gin which goes freezing down the throat, bombs the gut, then spreads its inside warmth in pleasant counterpoint to the tub water. To hell with all their hot rocks, whipping each other with greenery and diving into snowbanks. McGee will take a hot hotel tub and a very cold gin.

This is when the mind works. There is a hairy chimp caged in the back of the mind. The bananas hang out of reach. If you can make him stop leaping and chittering and clacking his angry teeth, make him settle down and look around the cage, usually he can find some boxes which he can pile on top of each other, and some sticks, and some string to tie the sticks together. Then he can climb onto the top box and knock down some bananas.

The biggest box in my cage was the concept of how very busy that month of May had been, nineteen months ago. A singing fellow had snatched Branton Fortner Geis and let him go loose in a downtown park. Ethel the Cat had been skewered by a prowler and left in her blood puddle on the nurse's kitchen floor. Heidi, the snow virgin, had chomped tabasco candy and sprung into considerable activity.

Symbols of violence. Demonstration. Kindly note, Dr. Geis, that I could have strangled the kid instead of letting him loose. I could have skewered the nurse instead of the cat. The candy could have had the bland and deadly flavor of almonds instead of the heat of tabasco. So let us start negotiations, Doctor, sir, and you can give me six hundred thousand arguments as to why I should not ugly up your last year or so of life.

So I sipped of coolness again, and became Fort Geis. Okay, I have dealt in the very basic life-and-death business for many years. I have stuck my fingers into the brain-meat after lifting off the sawed lid of bone and laying it aside. Had I been hooked on money, I would have laid away a lot more. Now here is a crazy who wants to take away what I *have* put aside. Pay off, Doc, or you'll die absolutely alone, because everyone who loves you and whom you love will go first. I'll wear you out with funerals, man. Dying alone is a dreary bit.

But, I say, as the Doctor, how did *you* know I was dying? And, second question, how do *you* know how much I can come up with?

Drop that for the moment, chimp. It won't hold your weight.

So as the good Doctor Geis, I look around. Nurse Stanyard can make it. Heidi is married to a lot of tax-free municipals. Roger is doing well. But what about the new wife? So negotiations are in order. Look here, old chap, I can't leave Glory without a bean. You'll have to cut the demand a bit so that I can leave some of the insurance intact so she'll have an income. Money is not important to her. It doesn't have to be much. A little security for the girl.

Then, as I have begun the payoff routine, I find my daughter Heidi is divorcing Trumbill. She will need money. She depends upon it. I find out she is going to let Gadge off lightly. But if she can't get it from me, she better get it from him, so I run in a legal team to pluck him pretty well.

So why did I send ten thousand to Janice Stanyard with such a vague note? Why did I refuse to talk about it to her when she came to the side of the deathbed? Who has Janice's name and address to use in case of emergency? The signs pointed to Susan, the daughter he had fathered by the housekeeper's daughter during his first wife's final fatal illness. Susan had been given a place to turn, but that had ended when the Doctor had canceled his arrangement with Francisco Smith and Allied Services.

But why Susan? Why would *anyone* be in danger if Geis was paying off like a good pigeon? I might guess that the insurance saved for Glory was by arrangement, but that the ten thousand for Susan—if it was Susan—had been palmed and tucked aside, without permission of the fellow turning the thumbscrew. Again, a box that would crumple if I put any weight upon it.

So let us see how well Saul Gorba fits. A very meticulous, sly, clever, unbalanced fellow. Arrives in the city four or five months before Geis begins the thirteen-month span of Operation Payoff. Leaves a month after the payoff ends. A nice stick, but too flimsy to whack loose any of the bananas tied to the top of the cage.

Last sip of the ice-diluted gin. Cubes clicked against my teeth. I came sloshing and wallowing up out of water gone tepid, all long brown hide flawed by the healed places which marked old mistakes in judgment and reflexes, pelted moderately with sun-baked hair. Wiped misted mirror with the corner of a bath towel. Stared into my spit-pale gray eyes as I slowly dried myself. What are you doing here, laddy buck? This is a dirty one. Something is twisted. Something has gone bad. You are going to lift the wrong rock, and something is going to come out from under it as fast as a moray, aiming right for the jugular.

And, bless us every one, wouldn't *that* be a dingy way to die, in one of the greasy twilights of Chicago in December, a page 40 paragraph in the World's Greatest Newspaper.

Look, Maurie, old sweetie buddy of mine, you are so right about stumbling around alone, my solo gig, white knightism. The ladies have discovered that it stings too much to dangle the tresses down the tower wall for some idiot to use as a climbing rope.

And all the dragons go around looking just like anybody else.

On this kind of a Monday I know I'm going to get killed in this line of work. It should interest the statisticians. As I am the only fellow in my line of work, it would give it a rating of 100% mortality. Just as, until we lost an astronaut, travel in orbit was the safest travel man ever devised with 0% mortality for millions upon millions of passenger miles. Safer than wheelchairs.

Maurie, baby, make me the resident muscle at one of your island operations, with all the beach and broads and booze a man can use, and I shall have cradles built and the *Flush* deckloaded onto a freighter and let you guarantee all the rest of that retirement I am taking in installments every time I get well enough.

But in the cage the chimp was looking at the big box and scratching himself like a Red Sox outfielder. No bananas yet, so I called Glory Geis, who chortled happy welcome, and I fenderfought my way to the lake-shore fireside, where once again in the blue jump suit the graceful ragamuffin lady in her second widowhood plied me with a potion which sharpened the taste buds for what the kitchen would provide.

The snow had stopped. The wind still blew, whining around the house corners, intruding upon fire-crackle and music off the tape. When I asked my key question about accidents she looked blank. "Heavens, I can't think of anything like that. We had such a quiet life, Trav. Just being together. It was all we wanted or needed. No, there was nothing."

"Okay. Not here then. You went shopping and a truck nearly ran you down. Something fell off a high building and nearly hit you."

"Nothing like that! Really! What are you trying to get at? What does it mean?"

"Maybe nothing. I look for patterns. Did anybody bully you off the road in that hot little job Fort bought you?"

"No. I've never put a scratch on it. The only time it had to go in for repairs was when somebody played a joke."

"A joke?"

"Oh, one of those fool tricks that kids send away for. They put one on my dear little car. The yard man was edging the driveway and he came in to get the keys so he could move it. I left it in his way. Actually, I'd left it out all night. It was a Friday night, and I was going to go out again so I didn't put it away, and then I didn't go out and I forgot it and left it out and in his way. He used to come Saturdays. It was warm and the house was open, one of the first warm days, and Fort was here, and we heard this funny siren sound. It went up and up and up, and then there was a bang, and we went hurrying out and the yard man was standing about fifty feet from my car, staring at it with horror, and there was white smoke pouring out from the hood. You know those silly torpedo things they sell to play tricks on your friends. Some of the neighborhood teen-agers had put one on my little car."

"It damaged it?"

"It buckled the hood a little and blew some of the wiring loose. But that isn't the kind of thing you mean."

"No, it isn't," I said. Doc, I could have put the skewer

through the nurse, drowned the grandson, poisoned the candy, and wired the little Mercedes so it would blow her into the tops of several of your tall trees, a little here and a little there. "When did that happen?" I asked casually.

She scowled into her weak drink. "Hmm. Let me think. Memorial Day came on Sunday last year. So it was the following Saturday which would be . . ."

"June fifth."

"I remember he didn't expect to be home that morning. He had surgery scheduled. It was a primary cancer of the spine, which is very rare and supposed to be inoperable. It was a twenty-eight-year-old woman, and she seemed very strong, but they phoned from the hospital Friday and said she had died. Fort was depressed. The husband wouldn't give permission for an autopsy."

"So I suppose the smoke bomb was the final straw?"

"He was upset. Not too badly though. He went for a long walk down the beach. I remember I wanted to go with him, but he wanted to be alone that time. It wasn't like him. I was hurt, sort of. But I guess you aren't doing a husband any favors by smothering him, by hanging onto him every second."

"Glory, I know you kept pretty good tabs on him. When did he have a chance to pick up the cash and leave it somewhere?"

"It must have been done at the same time. That's the only thing I can figure out. When he got it at one bank or another, he must have gotten rid of it right away. He must have mailed it. Even if I had seen him mailing it, I wouldn't have paid any particular attention. He was always mailing things in heavy manila envelopes to doctors all over the world. Case histories, notes, things he was going to publish, film strips of operations. And the mail he got at the hospital was always full of things like that. Later that kind of mail came here."

In the artsy-fartsy tales of intrigue, the pigeon has to tote the bundle of bread to the city museum and stuff it under the tunic of the third mummy from the left, whistle the motif from "Lazy Bones," stick his right thumb in his left ear, and walk out sideways. A real live thief will go to the main post office, lay down cash, and rent a box under any name which happens to strike his fancy. If he does not want to take any chance on handwriting or latents, he will take the order form away and have somebody else fill it out for him, and bring it back in gloved hand. If it is a one-shot payoff, he will get a hungry bellhop to go open the box with the key, and then he will tail the kid through the streets until he is certain the kid is not under observation. If it is on the installment plan he is going to be certain enough that his pigeon will not get restless so that he can risk a bus ride to the main post office to clean out the box whenever it seems convenient. Otherwise the cleanest one I ever saw took place in a big busy New York restaurant during the lunch rush on a weekday. He was carrying the package as directed. He got a phone call. A muffled voice told him to take his package to the checkroom and ask the girl to put it with number 308, and go right from there to the men's room before returning to the dining room, and not to fake out because he was being watched. I got to the checkroom girls perhaps ten minutes after one of them had given the coat, hat, and parcel to number 308. They could not remember one single fragment of description. They were indignant to think I expected them to. Obviously he had checked his coat and hat, then used a pay booth to phone the restaurant number and have my pigeon paged. At Shor's you can see the check counter from the pay phones. He timed it right, when whole flocks of lookalikes were heading back from lunch to the Big Media. And he needed the money.

"Penny?" said Gloria Geis.

"Do you think you could make a chance for me to have a little chat with Anna Ottlo?"

"Why? What about?"

"Maybe I want to see if she'd like to cook aboard a houseboat for a single gentleman, quiet, respectable, appreciative."

"Oh, go to hell, McGee. Okay. I'll remember a phone call I have to make."

I went sauntering toward the good smells. Anna Ottlo looked anachronistic in that mechanized, stainless-steel kitchen. Broad, hefty, florid, with white hair and blue apron and twinkling eyes, she looked like a television commercial grandmaw who was going to tell me how to get the stains out of the sink, or grow coffee on mountains, or get rid of that oily taste. Real grandmothers don't look quite like that anymore. I think it is the water-skiing that keeps them firmed up.

"You like roast pork, sir? Yah?" she said beaming.

"I think you could make old floor mats taste good, Anna."

"To the big strong man, all taste vunderful the foods."

I leaned against a hotel-sized refrigerator, drink in hand. "Had any word yet from Gretchen?" I asked.

She stopped slicing a tomato, turned and stared at me, her smile still there, but without meaning.

"*Nein!*" she said. "Nothing. No Gott damn goot, that girl. Trink beer, throw away money, play with mens. Years I hear nothing. Not even how many babies. Gone off someplace. Some man, yah?"

"She's got a husband, hasn't she?"

"This Gorba? From jails? Hah! Best she can get. Another mans wink the eye, off she goes, babies and all. Now I forget. All done. Over. I said give me the babies. I can take care, raise goot. More time you have for beer and betting money and boyfriend. Big fight. No goot, my only child, that one. Bad life." She tapped her temple, shook her head sadly. "Not much bright."

After dinner Glory told me that she wouldn't be staying there as long as she had planned. "I'd be completely alone. Anna wants to leave, after Christmas."

"New job?"

"Not right away. Later, probably. She says she wants to go and visit an old friend. Mrs. Kemmer, the mother of the boy Gretchen married. She's somewhere in Florida, and Anna wants to spend the winter with her, and maybe stay down there if she can find work, after she's had a rest. All this hasn't been exactly easy on her either. I guess I'm going to have to find an apartment, and something to do. I'll have to stay in Chicago until . . . things are settled. But when I can leave, I'm never coming back. I don't think Heidi and Roger will miss me dreadfully, do you?"

"They'll brood about it."

"Trav? Are you finding out anything?"

"It's at that point where I don't really know. I don't want to talk about it until I have something worth telling you. Or asking you."

She tried to smile. It was a ghastly grimace. "I dreamed you were dead, Trav. It scared me."

"It scares me too, but nobody has figured out a good way to avoid it. The guy who does will clean up."

"Fort knew when. You and I don't. I guess that's the big difference. All we know is Sometime."

"That's what you know when you've grown up. The ones who never grow up keep thinking Never. Not me, boss. Take those others, but don't take me."

She hunched her shoulders. "Yesterday wasn't so great. I couldn't find any meaning in anything. I felt lost. I kept thinking I could find my way back if I took just a little more of that. But I didn't know how it would hit me. It might be too strange. I even thought of trying to get you to come out and be with me."

"Don't go freaking around alone, Glory. Ever. How much of that have you got left?"

"Just a little bottle. It's in a diluted form so that each drop out of a medicine dropper is fifty micrograms. If I had to guess I'd say there's a hundred drops in the bottle."

"Flush it down the toilet."

"Maybe I will. A little later. When I know I won't need it ever again."

"Why would you need it?"

"Because yesterday I thought it would be easier to be dead than be alive."

"I guess it would be a lot easier. No decisions. No headaches. No constipation."

"Sometimes you make me feel just as silly as I very probably am."

Fifteen minutes after I left to drive back to the city I felt as silly as a girl myself. It can happen when you get too cute. It can happen when you have a memory a little too fresh in your mind of disillusioning a muscular and hairy karate expert. I saw a movement in the bushes where there should have been no movement. I saw it in my side view mirror as I drove out of the driveway. So I drove briskly off into the curving maze of Lake Pointe, circled, left the car in a dark place near a house without lights, and went skulking back.

Bare-handed hero. But I cannot think of any kind of weapon small enough to lift that would have done me much good. I cased the empty bushes. I made a slow circle of the house. From out in the dunes I saw Glory move past an uncurtained window. I stood up and somebody hit my head on a line drive to third, where it was fielded on one hop and hurled across to force the base runner at second, but he came in spikes high to break up the double play, and the second baseman threw my head over the first baseman and smack into the wall in front of the box seats along the first base line. My head rolled dead, eyes turned completely around so that they looked back into the blackness of my brain where fireworks were on display.

Then I was in a pocket in the dunes with a mouth half full of damp cold sand, my hands fastened behind me with something, and with something tied around my eyes. Somebody of considerable muscular weight and with very hard knees knelt on my back. They put a hand on my forehead and lifted my face out of the sand. They lifted it too far. They lifted it until my neck creaked.

"Hey!" I said, and spat sand. "Wait!" I said and spat sand.

A whisper came from lips close to my ear. It seemed to be a whisper with an English accent. "If I tell him to snap your neck, he will snap your neck."

"I believe you."

"What is your interest in this, Mr. McGee?"

"Interest in what?"

"Are you trying to find out if I will actually tell him to pull your head back another . . ."

"No! I was visiting Mrs. Geis. I'm an old friend. I saw something move in the bushes when I drove out."

"You are a big man. You are in very good shape. You move very well through the night. With professional competence."

"They put me in a brown suit and taught me a lot of things like that. Could he ease the tension a little? I'd hate to go through life looking straight up."

"Terribly amusing," he said. He spoke in a language I could not identify. The fellow on my back lowered my forehead a generous inch and a quarter.

I said, "Did you fellows squeeze a lot of money out of Doctor Geis before he died?"

"No."

"Do you know who did?"

"It would be a matter of no interest to us."

"Gloria Geis asked me to come up from Florida and see if I could find out. It's sort of a hobby with me, helping my friends."

"A profitable hobby?"

"Once in a while. Not real often."

He was silent for a time. I listened to the surf. I ran my tongue over and around my teeth, collecting sand.

"I shall require you to accept certain assurances, Mr. McGee. We have no interest in any friends of yours, to do either good or harm. We are very careful people. You will gain nothing by reporting this to anyone. We examined everything you are carrying, and have replaced everything, exactly as we found it. If you had seemed overly nervous or hysterical about this, we would have been forced to execute you. In simplest terms, you go your way and we will go our way. Keep your mouth shut. We are not likely to meet one another again."

"I am glad to hear that."

They did not hang around to say good-bye and shake hands. A terse and guttural order was given. My face fell into the sand. The weight was lifted away, and a quick nip at my wrists freed them. I rolled over slowly and sat up. I worked at the small hard damp knot at the back of my head. My fingers were cold, and the tightness of the binding had numbed my fingers. When I at last uncovered my eyes, I was alone in the dunes. I was further from Gloria's house. Her house was completely dark. I massaged my neck and rolled my head around to loosen the kinked muscles. I found the strip of fabric which had been around my wrist, and put it with the fabric which had been tied around my eyes and stuffed them into my top-coat pocket. They were going to be very valuable clues. I found out later that one was my necktie and the other was the entire tail off my shirt.

I could find no specific impact point on my skull. The whole right side of it, from front to back, felt slightly tender.

The hideous and unspeakable bruise was upon my ego. I had been taken on open ground with a contemptuous efficiency, dropped, trussed, dragged, inspected, and dismissed. It had been done without giving me the slightest chance of any kind. Yet it was not because they thought me particularly dangerous, but because they were what the Limey whisper had described—"very careful people." And, I could add, very skilled people. Very well-trained and conditioned people.

They worked with military precision, spoke of execution as if it was their right by nature of their trade, and left me without a clue as to age, description, dress—or even how many there were.

At the end of a fifty-mile hike I got into the rental car, and as I started it up, I realized I was perfectly willing to take the word of the whisperer. They were not interested in Gloria Geis. Or in me. Or in the Doctor's money. On the drive back into the city I could come up with only one wild guess—that the piece of empty lake beach was some kind of rendezvous point for transshipment of something, import or export, by boat from beach to ship or ship to beach, or even beach to beach.

I knew one thing without having to guess. I did not want to try my luck against them in groups of two or more. Just as I had no interest in finding out if I had hands as fast as Cassius Clay, or if I could stop one James Taylor coming down the sidelines, all by myself.

There were two phone messages at the desk for me. A Mr. Smith had phoned, and would phone back in the morning before nine. A Mrs. Stanyard had called and left her number.

I got back to the room a little past eleven-thirty. I phoned Janice Stanyard immediately, and after it rang ten times I hung up. I showered again to get the sand and grit out of my scalp and limber up the muscles in my neck and shoulders. My head had begun to ache. It was that kind of dull traumatic throb which sets up echoes of queasiness in the gut and makes the eyes hypersensitive to light. And it makes you wonder if some little blood vessel in the brain might be ruptured and bleeding.

I sat on the bed and just as I reached toward the phone to try Nurse Stanyard again, it rang, startling me. It was Janice Stanyard.

"I called you back fifteen minutes ago, Janice, but there . . ."

"I'm not home. And . . . I need help." Her voice was very tense, very guarded.

"Help you get. Any flavor."

"Thank God! The person I'm supposed to help is with me. I have to get back to her. We're at the Oriental Theater. It's a movie house on West Randolph, just west of State. We're in the middle of the last row downstairs on the left. Please hurry."

I hurried. The box office was closed. I told the ancient ticket taker I wanted to catch the end of the feature. He pocketed my dollar, put a fist in front of a huge yawn, and waved me in. On the huge screen was an extreme closeup of a blonde singing about Troooo Laahv to an enchanted throng of about twenty-seven widely scattered customers, singing through a mouth big enough to park a pair of Hondas in. An usher bird-dogged me with wary flashlight until he heard Janice greet me, and then he moved away.

I sat beside Janice. A blonde sat on the other side of her, hunched and still, head bowed, hands covering her face. There was no other customer within fifty feet of us.

"She phoned me from the Trailways bus station. It's in the next block east. She said Doctor Geis had written her to contact me if she needed help."

"Susan Kemmer?"

"Yes. How did you . . ."

"Why wouldn't she go home with you?"

"She's afraid to. She's been terribly beaten. She won't tell me who did it. She seems . . . dazed. I phoned you before I left for the bus station. I've been phoning you from here. It seemed like . . . a good place to wait."

I got up and squeezed past them and sat on the other side of Susan. When I put my arm around her shoulders she flinched violently and moved one hand enough to peer at me. In the reflected light of the noisy movie I could see that her eye was puffed and discolored.

"I'm a friend," I said. "We want to help you, Susie. Doctor Geis told Mrs. Stanyard to give you any help you might need. Why won't you go to her apartment?"

"He'll look there," she said in a very small voice.

"If someone hurt you, we should report it to the police."

"No. Please. All I asked her for is some money, so I can go to a hotel. That's all. I can't stay with her."

"She shouldn't be alone," Janice said.

I thought of a wry possibility and said, "If she'll have

you, Susan, will you stay with a friend of mine, a woman who lives alone?"

"Who?" Janice asked.

"If she knows, I can't stay there," Susan said. "I've been telling Mrs. Stanyard. I don't want her to know where I'll be."

"Don't be idiotic!" Janice said crossly.

"He could make her tell," Susan said to me.

"Maybe it isn't exactly idiotic," I told Janice. "Sit tight. Let me check."

I found the phones and looked up the number. After the fifth ring, Heidi Trumbill answered in a blurred, irritable voice.

"Travis McGee, Heidi."

"Who? Who?"

"I saw you Saturday. John Andrus wrote a note to you about me on the back of his card."

"Oh. Yes, of course. How could I forget? Dear Mark has been babbling about you ever since. He was very taken." I heard her yawn, a very rich, gasping, jaw-creaking yawn. "This better not be a social call, McGee."

"It isn't. I'm making a little progress with our problem."

"Really!"

"And because what I am doing is in your interest, I have to ask you for a little help."

"Such as?"

"A young female is involved. She's been roughed up. She needs a safe place to hide out, to hole up and get some rest and recuperation. She has some information I want and I won't be able to get it out of her until she feels safe and unwinds a little. Miss X. No names. No questions. No answers. You have room for her there. Okay?"

"Are you drunk by any chance?"

"Not noticeably."

"What do you think I am? Some kind of rest camp? Some kind of a house mother?"

"Heidi, I think that in many respects you are a silly, arrogant, pretentious bitch. But I also think you are probably a patsy for starving kittens and busted birds."

"And painters who can't paint? And sculptors who can't sculpt? Say it all, McGee."

119

"If the spare bed isn't made up, make it up. We'll be along in a bit."

"You are so *sure* of yourself, damn your eyes. How soon?"

"Half an hour."

"See you," she said and hung up. I got back to the mouth of the aisle just as the marching-into-the-sunset music swelled strong, and the thin gray line of customers began getting up to walk through the spilled popcorn and paper cups toward their shrunken realities outside. My two females got up and we headed out of the palace. Susan was in a blue cloth coat and she kept her mouth and chin ducked down into a concealing billow of blue knit scarf, and kept her face turned away from the public as much as possible.

Before we went out into the icy night I stopped them and said, "You've got a car, Janice?"

"Yes."

"If you have any company, what happened was you got a call from the Trailways station. It was a girl. She told you Dr. Geis had said you would help her. She didn't give her name. You went there and she was gone. You waited around, then decided to see the movie. You thought she might be one of the Doctor's patients."

"Where will she be? Where are you taking her?"

"A safe place, where she'll get rest and care. I'll be in touch."

She hesitated, then touched the girl on the arm. "You can trust me, dear. I'll help you any way I can. And you can trust Mr. McGee. You have to tell someone what kind of trouble you're in." When Susan Kemmer did not answer, Janice gave a helpless little shrug and walked out. I gave her thirty seconds, then pushed the door open for the girl. I'd parked a block away. I held her upper arm, walked her into the wind. She was limping.

Heidi buzzed the downstairs door open, and when we got to the red door at the second-floor rear, she was standing in the open doorway, the lighted room behind her silhouetting her. She took Susan's coat and scarf and laid them aside. I had Susan sit in a chair and I said, "For reasons I won't go into, we'll keep this whole thing anonymous. Friends helping friends. Miss Brown, meet Mrs. Jones. Let's get a good look at you, dear."

I tilted the opaque lampshade to put the full light on her, and with my fingertips I lifted her reluctant chin. Heidi, looking in from the side, made a little whimper of concern. Young lips mashed, puffed, and scabbed. Nose intact. Eggplant bruises on the cheekbones, a quarter-inch slice of one blue eye visible between puffed flesh, and a slightly wider segment of the other. They looked out at us calmly enough. Left brow slightly split. Forehead bruise shaded with saffron.

"Yesterday?" I asked her.

She nodded. "Yesterday morning. Real early."

I put one hand behind her head and with the fingers of the other hand prodded at her cheekbones and at the brows to see if there was any give or shift of broken bone. She winced but endured.

"Double vision? Any nausea today?"

"No sir."

"Are you hungry?"

"I . . . don't know. My teeth are loose over on this side."

"Open wide."

I wiggled them with a fingertip. Four in a row on the lower jaw, right side. "You won't lose them. They'll tighten up again, kid."

Heidi said she had the ingredients for an eggnog, and she brought me some cotton pads and rubbing alcohol along with adhesive tape and scissors before she went to mix it. I had the girl stretch out on the couch and I knelt beside her. I loosened the caked blood on the split brow, wiped it clean, dried it, then used the strips of adhesive scissored to narrow widths to pull the split together. She sucked air a few times, but she was pleasantly stoical.

Heidi was able to produce a mild sedative. The girl took it with the tall eggnog. When I was able to look past the battered face I saw that she was practically type-cast, an almost perfect fräulein type, fair and blue-eyed, plump as a little pigeon, round sweet face. She should milk cows, and hop around in the Bavarian village festival in her dirndl to the accordion music while her boyfriend blew foam off his stein and slapped his leather pants and yodeled once in a while.

I decided it was no time to question her. Heidi took her in to bed her down and came back in about ten minutes. She wore a navy-blue floor-length flannel robe, starkly tailored. Again I wondered about that total lack of physical communication and awareness between us. It was incredible that a mouth curved thusly, eyes placed so, body with that look of slenderness and ripeness and power, hair and eyes gleaming with animal health, provocative grace in every movement—incredible that it could all add up to absolute neuter.

"I think she was asleep before I closed the door," Heidi said. "The child is exhausted in every way. Her body is terribly bruised. The worst bruise is on her thigh. It looks as if she was kicked. I asked her who did it and she just looked at me."

"No questions. Part of the deal. It's good of you to take her in. But what's with this child thing? How much older are you? Seven years?"

"Seven hundred. How long will she be here?"

"Two days, three, four. I don't know. Just don't let her take off before I get here in the morning. She might want to."

She drifted about, touching small things, straightening them. She turned and looked at me. "You're really strange, Travis McGee. You took it absolutely for granted I'd take her in. I just don't *do* things like that."

"Hardly ever. I know. How did the opening go yesterday?"

"As expected. Well, more people than I expected, actually. Poor Mark was darting about like a mother hen. One too many people compared Kirstarian to Segal, so he made a fantastic scene and stalked out. Mark sold three pieces, and it made him so happy he drank all the champagne we had left and I had to put him to bed." She sat on the arm of the couch and looked across at me. "It's so strange. That girl. I have the feeling I knew her long, long ago. But I couldn't have. She's too young for that. Who is she, Travis?"

The temptation was to drop the bomb and say it was her half-sister. But that wasn't going to do anyone any good. I said, "You don't know her. She very probably knows something about where your father's money went.

But she might not even know she knows. She is a good and staunch girl."

"I sensed that about her."

"The problem is the money."

"Oh yes, the money. And poor elfin little heartbroken Gloria, the waitress type, knows absolutely nothing about it. Right?"

"As far as anyone can tell."

"Well, she certainly fooled John Andrus without any trouble. And she sold my father a bill of goods. So I guess you don't present any special problem."

I smiled at her. "Heidi, she had to be lousy and crooked and dirty because she had the unholy impertinence to marry the daddy. She cast an ugly spell over him. She even seduced him physically, fornicated with him, and made him think he was enjoying it. What a degrading thing for the big wise important daddy to be doing! Didn't he know it made darling daughter feel actually ill to wake up in the night and think that right at that moment that woman was making him do that sick ugly animal thing?"

She turned ice-pale, jumped trembling to her feet and said, "Stop that! Stop it!"

"Where do you think you came from, Heidi? Did they find you out in the cabbage patch? There's only one known way he could get to *be* your father."

She wiped her mouth on the back of her hand. In a thin prim little voice she said, "It killed her. She died."

So I got out of there after suitable apologies. Two swings, two hits. Anybody who wanted to find a woman under that luscious structure was going to have to tear it down and start over. Marriage to her had been as exciting as two years of root canal treatments, on a dead fang.

I knew that Francisco Smith had better find me Mother Gretchen, and fast.

nine

Francisco Smith woke me up with his phone call at quarter past eight on Tuesday, that thirteenth day of December.

"Got something to write on?" he asked.

"Hold on," I said, and got set and told him to go ahead.

"Okay, here's the number of the annuity policy. GLC 085-14-0277. Four hundred thirty-three dollars and thirty-three cents gets mailed out the first of every month. The guy at Great Lakes is named Rainey. T. T. Rainey. The September check came back, addressee moved, no forwarding address. They tried a trace. The Gorba family left last August 22nd. A Sunday. The couple and the five kids, in a big gray Cadillac sedan, towing a U-Haul. License 397 110. Dropped the apartment keys in the super's box. Rent paid to the end of August and a month deposit in advance. Mrs. Gorba was paid by the week. She picked up her pay at the restaurant when she left work Friday evening. He was paid twice a month. His pay is still sitting there at the body shop. They left the apartment in good shape. They didn't pick up the utilities deposits. They left clean. At least there's no judgments filed against them."

"Is Great Lakes still trying to find them?"

"No. They tried it on the cheap and gave up quick. They weren't like somebody trying to collect. They sent out the check for a double payment October first and it came back too. So they put it and the November and December checks in an interest account. The January check will go in the same account, the one made out to her mother like the checks. But she turns eighteen in January, so if nobody shows up, they'll start a new interest account in the name of Susan Kemmer."

"Car payments?"

"No dice there. You see, it was a two-year-old Cad that the owner totaled, and the place Saul Gorba worked bid three-fifty for it. Then they found more wrong than the estimator thought there was. Gorba put down two

124

hundred on it and agreed they could take another two-fifty out of his pay. That was back in April, I think. It was with the idea he could work on it in his spare time when he'd put in his regular hours, and buy the parts from them at cost or scrounge them from the yards, and they'd let him use shop tools. A lot of those guys work it that way for a personal car. They don't like them trying to fix iron up for resale as it puts them in competition with the shops they're working for. But Gorba didn't have a car so it was okay with the boss. So for about nine hundred, plus all the hours he put into it, he came out of it with a pretty good automobile. I understand he's handy with tools and catches on fast."

"When did he finish it, Smith?"

"August sometime."

"What would be the chance of tracing them in a hurry?"

After a short silence he said, "I wouldn't say it was real great, not if Gorba doesn't want to be traced. School records, medical records, IRS refunds, Social Security—he'd be carefuler than most. He had to rent the trailer someplace and he had to turn it in someplace, but he could unload it, drive it three hundred miles empty, and turn it in. With the car registration, he could cover up best by unloading it on a cash deal and buying something else under another name. My hunch would be check close on the daughter's friends. You tear a seventeen-year-old kid away from all her friends, she is going to find some way to drop them a card. But I don't like the feel of it, not with those checks unclaimed. What is it now? Thirteen hundred bucks. Listen, they're going to keep me on the run all day. This evening I maybe get a chance to cover a couple of other angles. I'll be in touch."

The day was like a dirty galvanized bucket clapped down over the city. When you swallowed, you could taste the city. All the trees looked dead, and all the people looked like mourners. Happy Christmas. Bingle jells. Brace yourself for hate week.

Heidi opened the red door with a fractional smile of cool welcome. She was in one of her painting suits. This one was yellow, like shark repellent. It had forty-three pockets with flaps and zippers. "How's our patient?" I asked, very jolly.

"I made her go back to bed. She was shaky."

Heidi had a blue smudge on the back of one hand, two speckles of bright red on her chin. The door to her studio was open. She was dressed for air-sea rescue, visible at thirty miles.

I glanced through the doorway into her studio. She said, "Kindly do not express an interest in my work. I already know your opinion."

"Look, I did not mean to rawhide you last night. I'm sorry."

"It isn't something new, Mr. McGee. Men try to shake me up by saying ugly things. It's sort of an erotic compulsion, I guess."

"Maybe you're an example of conspicuous waste."

"Don't try to make phrases. You're not the type. She's in the second bedroom on the left."

Susan Kemmer was propped up on two pillows. Her face was turned toward the gray light at the window, and tracked silver with tears. She looked at me, dabbed in gingerly fashion at the tear marks with a tissue, snuffled, and hitched the pale blue blanket higher. The gestures had the flavor of bracing for ordeal. It looked to me as though some of the puffiness was gone. But the areas of discoloration were larger, and the hues more varied.

I pulled a chair over and sat by the foot of the bed, facing her. "Saul work you over?"

"I'm not going to answer questions, Mr. McGee."

"Why don't you just think the questions over, and answer the ones you feel like answering? I won't try to trick you. Take your time."

"Who are you?"

"A friend of yours. I might have some answers to some of your questions. If you have any."

"Why should I want to ask you anything?"

"You might want to know why Dr. Fortner Geis was anxious to help you. I guess he had the feeling you might get in a real jam. A ten-thousand-dollar jam, Susan. That's the amount of cash he sent Mrs. Stanyard."

"Ten . . . thousand . . . dollars!"

"If you didn't contact her in a year, then she was to give it to Mrs. Geis."

"But . . . wouldn't it be mine anyway?"

"How come?"

"I mean it would have been money he got from my . . ." She stopped abruptly. I could guess at what was going on in her mind. Storybook stuff. Afternoon soap opera. There could be a dozen versions. Famous surgeon has a friend who has a daughter dying of a brain tumor. She is pregnant. Unmarried. Influential family. They don't want a scandal. The Doctor keeps the girl alive long enough so that she can have her baby, and then he arranges with his housekeeper for the housekeeper's daughter and her young husband, Karl Kemmer, to raise the baby as their own. So the money that had always come every month came from the annuity her real mother's people had bought for her, and the ten thousand is some kind of emergency fund entrusted to the Doctor long ago. I did not want to reach into her head and wrench any of her dreams loose. They had sustained her. One day she would be able to jettison them herself, after they had served their long purpose. There was strength in this girl. But very strong people can break when there is too much all at once.

"How did Dr. Geis get word to you about contacting Mrs. Stanyard in case of trouble?"

"I don't want to answer questions."

"Take your time. See if there is any harm in answering that one, Susan."

"But if I don't want any help, why should I answer anything?"

"You have an orderly mind. But I gave you some help last night. You needed it and took it."

She thought that over. "He wrote me a letter last August. The writing was shaky. We knew from Grandma he was going to die. The Sunday before I got the letter she told us he was failing. It just said if I needed help I should go to Mrs. Stanyard. I was to write down her phone and address and destroy the letter, and not tell anybody. I thought it sounded sort of . . . crazy. He said Mrs. Stanyard was a nurse and a nice person and I could trust her. I did like he said in the letter even if I didn't expect anything to happen, and sort of forgot it until . . ."

"Until the day before yesterday."

"But you wouldn't go to her apartment with her because you said they'd look for you there. What did that mean?"

"Nothing."

"Okay. Now then. You're in some kind of a jam. You can call on me, and I can be just as rough as I have to be to get you out of it. And you've got ten thousand to finance the operation. I am yours to command, kid."

She turned her face toward the window. The tears started again. "But I can't do anything," she said hopelessly. "Nobody can do anything. She went away once in California and they put us in a place. There was just three of us then and we were little, and we almost didn't get Freddy back. The judge said he was disturbed."

"Gretchen has gone off someplace?"

Defiant eyes stared at me through the slits. "I don't know what you're talking about."

I stood up. "I'm going to leave you alone for a little while to think something over. Let me see if I have the names right. Freddy, Julian, Freda, and Tommy. Christmas vacation is coming up, Susan. I don't think it would be too difficult for an obviously respectable type like me to go gather up the kids. I know a crazy wonderful couple in Palm Beach. House as big as a hotel. Pots of money. Cook, maids, housekeeper, yard men. And scads of kids. They adopt them. Five more over Christmas would hardly be noticed. I could set it up with one phone call, and you've got the airplane money. Think it over."

I walked out without giving her a chance to respond. Heidi did not hear me. I leaned against the studio doorway. She was reworking the bottom corner of a big painting, standing bent over with her back to me. Her air-sea rescue costume was clinched tight around the slender waist, and stretched tightly across the pleasantly globular rear. I have always thought it fallacious to make an erotic specialty out of any particular portion of the form divine. When it is good it is all good, and some days some parts are a little better than others, but you need the entire creature to make any segment of it worthwhile. In three silent steps I could grab a double handful of all that and see if she could manage a standing high jump over the top of the painting.

"Ah Hem!" I said.

She straightened and whirled around. "Oh! Did you find out anything?"

First I broke it to her that her patient was Gretchen's kid, and was the eldest granddaughter of Anna, the housekeeper, and briefed her on Gretchen's home life, hubby and sudden departure.

She looked thoughtful and troubled instead of startled, and said that she guessed that subconsciously she must have had some hint. She had dreamed about Gretchen last night for the first time in years. So I went back to her specific question. Had I found out anything?

"Just enough to make some guesses, and they are probably wrong. She thinks any kind of help is going to make things worse. I have a hunch the Gorba family moved well out of town. Fifty miles, a hundred miles. Mama Gretchen missed the lights and the action, so she took off. So Saul Gorba took a little hack at the ripening daughter, maybe to get even with Gretch for taking off. I would think she'd put up a pretty good scramble, so maybe she got her nails into his chops, or a solid little knee into his underparts, and he lost his temper and hammered her. I think he would know she wouldn't blow the whistle on him. With his record they would tote him off gladly, and the social workers would, in the absence of the old lady, stuff the kids into the handiest institution. I think she is hooked on being the little mother hen to these other four. I think she is worried to death about them right now. If she goes back, the stepdaddy tries again. And if she stays away and Gretchen is away, who looks after the little ones? Not so terribly little, actually. Fifteen, twelve, ten, and six."

She nibbled the wood end of a paint brush, frowning. "That sounds so ugly, the whole situation. It's so strange, really. Roger has such clear memories of Gretchen when she lived with us. Of course he's four years older. But I must have been almost eight years old when Gretchen got married. I can remember a lot of things from a lot earlier than that. But Gretchen is sort of dim. I can't see her face at all, or remember her voice. Roger says she was good to us. He says she was good-natured and sort of dumb and sloppy. But would she just walk out on her kids?"

"Apparently she's done it before."

"Poor Anna. She deserves a more reliable daughter. Couldn't Anna take her own grandchildren for a while? Maybe not. Probably Lady Gloria wouldn't want brats from her own social level cluttering up her illusions of grandeur."

I started to speak and then let it stand. We could not

129

head in that direction and get anywhere. She was blocked. So I made some unimportant small talk and then went back in to catch Susan's reaction. It was a firm shake of the head—from side to side. No more questions and no more answers. She didn't want to be any trouble to anyone. She would leave as soon as she felt well enough. Thanks a lot.

I talked with Heidi again before leaving. She promised she wouldn't try to pump Susan Kemmer, but if the girl said anything useful, Heidi would get in touch with me right away.

I went to the nearby Ambassador for some midmorning coffee and some midmorning thought. A trio of high-fashion models, young ones, were gathered there for some do. They chittered and squeaked at each other. Their starved faces were painted to a silver pallor, their tresses shaped by men who hate women, using only soup bowls and hedge clippers, their clothing created by those daring little hanky-stompers who vie with each other in seeing how grotesque they can make their clients. It is an in-joke with them, and it gives them hysterics when they get together. They whinny, fall down, and spill their money. I think they would do a lot less harm sculpting pop-art dogs.

I ordered more coffee and went and phoned Janice Stanyard. No answer. I tried the hospital. She was in surgery, and scheduled through until at least four in the afternoon. I went back to my coffee and dug through the scrap paper in my side pocket and found the phone slip on Nurse Stanyard's call. It had come in at nine. So I went to the bus depot on East Randolph. It was to buses what Miami International is to airplanes. They had American, Continental, DeLuxe, Indiana, Santa Fe, Suburban, American Coach and so on—big inside ramps and stations, gates and callers.

In order to get anywhere I had to make certain assumptions. With her face in that condition, she wouldn't hang around waiting to make up her mind about calling Janice Stanyard. Give her ten minutes to get from the platform to a phone. Give Janice five minutes before calling me. So I was interested in anything arriving from, say, eighteen minutes before the hour to five minutes before the hour. After studying and cross-checking the printed schedules and the arrival boards, I came up with five possibles, all based on the assumption she came in from out of the city somewhere. My only prayer was her very memorable condition. When you see a young girl with the kind of a face Dick Tiger could give any contender back in his better days, it can stick in your mind. But I was at the wrong end of the day. Depot personnel on duty this Tuesday morning wouldn't have been around on Monday night at nine. If she was on one of the five arrivals, she would have used one of three gates to come into the terminal.

Mark time. Futz around. Scratch. Fret. Watch girls. Wonder what the hell you are doing in this huge damp cellar full of three or four million people. Between announcements the speaker system in the depot was telling everybody about we three kings of Orient are. Damn you, Fort Geis, why didn't you leave a message in a hollow tree? Why didn't you realize what a pot of trouble you were leaving behind? It was an example of the terrible innocence of men who are superb in their own fields. Einstein had some grotesque political opinions. Jack Paar knew how we should get rid of the Berlin Wall. Kurt Vonnegut keeps losing airplane tickets.

Fortner Geis had not the slightest idea that people representing a dozen different interests and points of view would compete for the chance to drag the widow into their particular cave and gnaw her bones clean. Six hundred big ones brightens the eyes, sharpens the taste, bulges the muscles. O speak to us from beyond, Great Surgeon.

I trudged out into a hooing of damp and grisly wind, into the kind of gunmetal day when you wear your headlights turned on, and think of a roaring fire, hot buttered rum, a Dynel tigerskin, and a brown agile lass from Papeete. I took my dismals to the Palmer House and traded them to a sad-smiling man for a C-cup of Plymouth. We stood on either side of the bar and sighed at each other in wistful awareness of our mutual mortality, and I left half the drink and went off and phoned Heidi.

When she answered I said, "Is the battered bird responding?"

"Not so that anyone could notice. She's taking a bath and washing her hair. If it's any use to you, her clothes are from a cheap chain with about ten thousand outlets in Chicago, and her shoes seem to be a very good grade of cardboard, and her total of wordly goods comes to four dimes and four pennies, a red comb, half a pink lipstick, and one wadded-up bus schedule."

"What bus line?"

"Hmm. Let me go look. She's still sloshing in there." She came back and said, "North Central. I looked to see if she'd marked anything on it. She hasn't."

"Thanks. It could be a help. You make a good secret agent."

"Secret agent hell, McGee. It's pure female nosiness."

I went back to my drink in better humor. I separated the North Central timetable from the others I had picked up. Bus Number 83 arrived every weekday night at 8:45, back at the point of origin from where it had left at 8:20 that morning. Elgin, Rockford, Freeport, Clinton, Moline, Galesburg, Peoria, Peru, Ottawa, Joliet, and home to the barn. I could guess the union wouldn't let them load that kind of a run on one man. Probably one man took it to some midway point, possibly Moline, and his relief brought it on in and took it out the next morning and traded off again at Moline.

So the driver who had brought her in Monday night would be bringing her in again on Wednesday night. The company ran shorter routes and longer routes, and the Chicago office address was printed on the timetable. I signaled for a refill, left money as my surety bond, and went off and called North Central.

"Give me somebody who knows your driver roster," I told the girl.

"Herbison speaking," a man said, moments later.

"State traffic control," I said. "Sergeant Ellis. Who brought your 83 in last night?"

"Anything wrong, Sergeant?"

"Just a routine check. Trying to pin down the time we lost some intersection lights."

"Oh. Hold on." It took him twenty seconds. "Daniel D. DuShane, Sergeant." He explained I could contact him after two o'clock at a Galesburg address. He gave me the phone number. He said DuShane would be in again on 83 tomorrow night, that he was a good man, held a schedule well, and would probably be able to help me.

I felt reasonably cheery through the first half of my second knock, then I began to realize how rickety was my

132

structure of hunch and logic. There were too many things wrong with it. If Gorba had cleaned out the Doctor's estate, and if he was as bright as Francisco Smith had reported, it seemed to me he would have done one of two things—either stayed put, kept his job, bided his time—or gone too far for the North Central Transportation Company to get anywhere near him. Also, if he had made that big a score, it didn't seem like a very good idea for Gretchen to go off rambling.

True, one of the kids was his, the youngest one, but it seemed out of character for a type who could score so cleverly to saddle himself with even one, much less five. He did not seem to be the homebody sort.

In that mood, you can lose the whole thing. Okay. So a happy singing drunk had been charmed by the happy face of a small boy and taken him for a ride, gotten timid—or sober—and dropped him in the park. Neighborhood teen-age clowns had wired the joke bomb on Glory's little car. Some twitch maniac, turned on with some kind of bug juice, had come looking for people to scrag and had settled for Ethel cat. One of Gadge Hairynose Trumbill's countryclub wives had boobytrapped the candy box as a sick little vengeance. Susan Kemmer had been bashed about by a hulk of a boyfriend.

Go home, McGee. It's too big and too scrambled and it happened too long ago. Smuggle Glory out of the polar regions. Take her home. Boat her, beach her, bake her, brown her, and bunk her. You too are a sucker for busted birds, starving kittens, broody broads. Healer McGee, the big medicine man. She's got that big fireplace out there, right? A stock of sauce, right? A fantastic grocery department, right? So go lay it all out and cry a little. She might even come up with an idea.

So in the endless twilight of noonday I went northward, locked into the traffic flow, listening to ghastly news from all over. Premier assassinated tax boost seen Wings lose again bombs deemed defective three coeds raped teen-age riot in Galveston cost of living index up again market sags Senator sues bowl game canceled wife trading ring broken mobster takes Fifth bad weather blankets nation . . .

The announcer was beginning to choke up. I turned him off. I couldn't stand it.

133

As I felt my way down through the Lake Pointe area, the wind was coming off the lake, bellowing and thrashing, and taking little plucks at the steering wheel. The driveway and the lighted house beyond was safe haven, and I slammed my car door, put my head down, and plunged through tempests. Anna Ottlo let me in.

"Ach! Thank Gott! Thank Gott!" she cried. She kept winding and unwinding her plump red hands in her napkin.

"What's the matter? Where's Mrs. Geis?"

It took me long minutes to piece it together. Anna had cleaned up after breakfast, and after she had finished the housecleaning, she had asked Gloria if it was all right if she went to her room and lay down for a little while. She had bad pains in one hip. She thought it was the dampness. The doctor was giving her cortisone. Her hip would stop hurting if she could get off her feet every now and then. She had dropped off to sleep. A little while ago, maybe fifteen minutes ago, she had awakened with a start and been shocked to find it was almost twelve-thirty. She had gone hunting for Gloria to ask her what she would like for lunch. Gloria was not anywhere in the house. Her car was in the garage. She thought perhaps she had gone walking on the beach. But she had never gone walking when the weather was this bad. She had been acting very strange. Anna Ottlo had been wondering if she should call the police when I had arrived.

"The wasser," she said, her eyes miserable, her mouth sick. "I keep tinking of the wasser."

So I took off into the whirling gloom. I would guess the temperature at thirty degrees, and the wind seemed to take the whole thirty points off it. The wind, hard and steady, but with sudden gusts of greater violence, picked sand off the lips of the dunes and dry-lashed my face with it.

I loped and bawled her name, shielded my eyes from the sting of sand, and stared up and down the shelving beach. Beyond the sand belt the spray whipped at me. There was no color in the world. Gray sand, gray water, gray beach, gray sky. I was trapped in one of those arty salon photographs of nature in the raw, the kind retired colonels enter in photography contests. Through watery eyes I saw somebody waving a flag at me, a hundred yards away. The somebody turned out to be a twisted and barren bush a hundred feet back from the smack of the lake waves. The flag, however, was a pair of pale green nylon briefs. Ladypants. Elasticized waist, some dainty bits of machine lace. Fresh clean new—sodden with spray.

Twenty feet beyond the bush was the touch of color in the gray world. Patch of dark red. Ran to it. Pulled it out of the sand. More than half of it was covered by the drift of sand. Dark red wool dress. Glory's size. Damned fool. Damned little fool with the broken heart. I wondered if the waves would shove her back onto the beach. As I started toward the beach I caught a movement out of the corner of my eye. I turned quickly and saw Gloria crouched on the crest of a small dune thirty feet away. Her posture was like that of a runner waiting for the gun. Her knuckles were in the sand. I could see a glint of her eyes through the sodden mat of hair. Her mouth hung open, the small row of bottom teeth visible. She was egg-naked.

I called her name and hurried toward her. She whirled and ran from me. It was the dreadful reckless run of absolute and total panic. She would stumble and fall and roll to her feet and as I closed on her, she would dart off in another direction. When I could get near her, I could hear the horrid sound she was making in competition to the sound of waves and wind. I was as desperate as she. That wind had to be sucking the heat and the life out of her. Finally I feinted one way and as she cut back I dived and got one hand on her slender ankle and brought her down. She kicked me in the face with her free foot.

She had fantastic strength. Her face was madness. As I struggled with her she suddenly snapped at my hand and got it between her teeth, right at the thumb web. With her eyes tight shut she ground with her jaws, making a whining and gobbling sound. I put my other hand on the nape of her neck and got my thumb on one side and my middle finger on the other in the proper places under the jaw corners and clamped, shutting off the blood supply to the brain. She slumped and rolled onto her back. I stripped my topcoat off, laid it down, put a foot on it so it wouldn't blow away, and lifted her onto it. As I did so I remembered long ago at Sanibel when I had first been surprised at how her small body which looked so trim and lean and tidy in clothes could have such a flavor of ripeness and abundance. I guess it was the ivory smoothness of her combined with a dusky, secretive, temple-magic look to the contours of breasts, belly, rounded thighs. Now perfection was abraded by sand, gouged and torn by the falling. I wrapped her up and ran for the distant house.

Once I got what I hoped was the right routine going—electric blanket turned high and heaped with other blankets, brandy forced past clenched teeth, I remembered who would have the biggest stake in giving her every attention she should have. I looked him up in the book and used the bedside phone. Her lips were blue. She made grunting sounds.

The office nurse said that Dr. Hayes Wyatt was with a patient and if I would leave my name and number. I have no idea what I said to her. I have absolutely no memory of it. I do know that the next voice I heard was that of Dr. Wyatt.

I got through it and he kept saying, "What? What? What?"

"Now goddam it, Doctor, pull yourself together. Gloria Geis had been freaking up and down this beach bareass naked God only knows how long, and I think it was the acid you let Fort Geis have, and she tried to chew my hand off and it scares me to look at her, so having you keep saying what what what isn't doing anybody any good at all."

Once he moved, he moved well. He got to the house ten minutes before the ambulance did. He took her to Methodist Hospital where the widow of Fortner Geis would get every attention in the book. I waited an hour before he came down and sat beside me in the lounge. He was a spare dusty tall remote man. He took off his glasses and pinched the bridge of his nose and sighed.

"We'll wait and see," he said. "She was all right last night and all right at breakfast. So as it wasn't repeated dosages we have to assume a massive dose. No matter how much or how little you take, it wears off in twelve hours at the outside. By ten o'clock tonight I should know a little more. She's in restraint now. She's being treated for shock and exposure. Did you notice her hands?"

"Yes."

"She chewed her arms and her knees badly, but the hands are the worst. I don't like that. It sounds as if the disassociation was total. Do you understand what I'm saying?"

"That she could stay out in left field from here on."

"Or come back in two days. Or two years. I should have gotten it back. I shouldn't have taken her word she'd gotten rid of it."

"She dumped it out. She must have found a new source."

He looked at me with surprise, started to protest, and then understood. "But I don't want to evade moral responsibility, Mr. McGee."

"Maybe Fort should have made sure it was dumped. Maybe he did. Maybe she found a wandering Mexican and bought mushrooms."

"Psychedelics have a legitimate scientific . . ."

"So does alcohol. And Demerol. And every day they pump out some little kid who eats all the aspirin in the house."

"You should be . . . an assurance salesman." He looked mildly pleased with himself. It was a joke. I do not think he had made many jokes in his lifetime.

"Doctor, with the best response you could hope for, how long would she be in?"

"At least ten days. At the very least. I'm going to stay right with her. I'll leave word at the switchboard that I will accept calls from you."

I phoned Anna Ottlo. I could hear her snuffling after I told her the score. I told her that as far as I could see, she could start closing the house, and packing up all Glory's personal gear. I said I would relay the news to John Andrus at the bank and to Roger Geis and Heidi Trumbill. She wanted to know how soon she could come and see Gloria at the hospital. I told her I'd let her know.

After I hung up I remembered I had forgotten lunch, and it was almost three-thirty.

ten

I had a sandwich and coffee at a twenty-four-hour place near enough to the hospital to get the random hours business of nurses and interns, clerks and dietitians, Gray Ladies and residents. There was a gabble of young nurses in a corner. The ceiling fluorescence was as bright as any operating room. My Formica tabletop was white as a surgical dressing. One young nurse had a lovely curve of temple brow, cheek, jaw.

I tried to contrast them with the spidery moon-painted fashion racks I had seen at the Ambassador, thinking that nursing seems to attract young women structured in a curious way—pretty and slender from throat to waist, and there swelling into sedate and massive hips, hefty peasant legs. Debutante riding along in an ox cart. Or, by analogue, some variant of the myth-man who, from the waist down, was horse.

Try as I might, I could not keep my mind twisted away from that great gray howl of beach where the pursuit still went on, the tall sun-bronzed man made clumsy by the scuttling and dartings of the little naked woman. That look of madness is ugly beyond belief when you see it on the face which once had shown you love. And, in my arms and hands, I had the tactile memory of how the total panic of the inner beast felt.

Once, long ago, I went drift fishing with friends for smallmouth black bass in the St. Lawrence River near Alexandria Bay, using live minnows and fly rods, pulling in the lines to run upriver, then drifting down again over the good places. At noon we beached the boat on a small island and cleaned and cooked some of the catch over a driftwood fire. One man cast a minnow from the shore and hooked and brought in a river eel perhaps two feet long, maybe a little more, and in thickest cross-section no greater than the average banana. My friend lived on the river, and he hauled the eel onto a bit of hard ground and told me to stand on it. I thought he was out of his mind. Two hundred and twenty pounds of man on two pounds of eel. I'd crush it flat. He insisted. I pinned it with one foot, then put the other and my full weight on it. As it writhed it kept lifting me an inch or so. I stepped off. It was undamaged.

In her induced terror, Glory had that same incredible muscular tension, so that if I held her too tightly, the muscles would break her bones, unhinge her joints, as sometimes happens under shock treatment. We use only the smallest part of the power of both brain and muscles. Even our senses are dulled in the state we call consciousness. Under hypnosis the good subject can read a newspaper across a room, hear sounds otherwise inaudible, detect differences in the weight of seemingly identical objects.

Perhaps it is merely sentimentality—that strangely unearned emotion—which makes us want to have the fates and fortunes of life favor the good guys. Glory was a good guy. She had had more than her share already. There is a grotesque and continuous tragedy about some lives which would be too extreme for even a soap-opera audience to stomach.

So I white-eyed a nurse into receptivity across forty feet of plastic restaurant, chomped down a plastic sandwich, gulped down acid coffee and plastic pie, and with accelerating stride got to the men's room just in time to whonk and brutch the belated lunch into a toilet. Homage to a one-time love. A sick heart makes a sick stomach. They had cleaned and dressed my hand. They do not give you a series of shots for girl-bite. Wasn't she the lucky one to think of asking you to fly up here and help her, T. McGee? You did great.

I shed coat and jacket and rolled up my shirt sleeves and drew a lavatory bowl of cold water. I wallowed and scrubbed and made seal sounds, and then found out that the management had thoughtfully provided one of those warm air tubes for the drying bit, the special kind that leave you feeling coated with grease rather than water.

Small children think they are fun. Every adult in the land hates them. They are part of the international communist conspiracy. A nation forced to dry itself in a machined huff of sickly warm air is going to be too irritable, listless, and disheartened to fight. Americans unite! Carry your own towels. Carry little sticks with which you can wedge those turn-off faucets open so you can get two hands under the water at the same time. Carry your own soap so you need not wash your paws in that sickly green punch-button goo that leaves you smelling like an East Indian bordello. Carry your own toilet paper, men. The psychic trauma created by a supply of the same paper stock used for four-color ads in *Life* magazine cannot be measured.

The cold-sweat sensation ended. I reassembled the hero, stared into his deadly mirrored eye, nodded reassuringly at the poor suggestible slob, and strode out into a blackening world where the wind had ended, where great slow flakes the size of quarters and half-dollars came falling down to melt into a black sticky slime on the sidewalks and on the fourteen million tons of scrap paper that littered the city.

At a drugstore full of games, toys, and sporting equipment, I downed a fizzing nostrum for ugly-gut, and from a booth got Heidi first. The fräulein was napping. I told her that Gloria Geis was hospitalized, that she had suffered a little bout of nervous exhaustion.

"Is my heart supposed to go out to her?" asked the ice maiden.

"I don't think that's what she had in mind. But tell your brother. Maybe you two can have a good chuckle over it. Mrs. Ottlo will be leaving for Florida when she gets the house closed. I imagine John Andrus will be in touch with you about odds and ends."

"I hope you and John Andrus understand that the little bitch is probably faking."

I quoted her word for word to John Andrus when I phoned him at the bank. He was shocked and concerned about Gloria, and I didn't tell him any more than I had told Heidi. I said Hayes Wyatt was on the case and any reports on her condition would have to come from him. John Andrus said he would swing into action about the house, the furnishings, storing Gloria's possessions, and finding her a place to live. Then he said, "Are you making any headway?"

"I wish to God I knew, John. I'll be in touch."

I got more change and went back to the booth and phoned the bus driver, Daniel D. DuShane in Galesburg. A woman answered and told me to hold on while she went to get him.

When he came on I gave Sergeant Ellis a new job. I put him in Missing Persons investigating a female juvenile runaway.

"Five two, about seventeen, blonde, about a hundred and twenty pounds, blue coat, blue scarf. She could have come into the city on number 83 last night. She might have had facial contusions and abrasions."

"Sure thing. She was on my load, Sergeant. You know, I been thinking ever since maybe I should have reported her as soon as I got in. No luggage, no purse even."

"Where did you board you?"

"It's a crossroads. From Peoria I'm routed up 29 on the west side of the river to Peru and LaSalle. There's a kind of village name of Bureau, where 26 comes in from the left. There's a crossroads gas station and lunchroom there name of Sheen's. It's like a hundred miles from Chicago, so I must get there usually about I'd say six o'clock, give or take some, depending. Once in maybe ten times I get a pickup there, and what Sheen does, he's got an amber blinker he can turn on and I can see it way down the road, so when it's on I hit the air horns and swing in and the fare comes running out, so it isn't too much time out of my schedule. I had the inside lights out, and she boarded and I turned on the front lights to take the money. She said Chicago and gave me a dollar and the rest of it all in change, and I gave her the ticket and looked up and the first thing I thought was she'd busted up a car and had to take the bus home. The light kind of shone up onto her face and it gave me a real jolt. She went back and took an empty, and later when I had the inside lights on at Ottawa, I saw her back there with her head kind of wrapped up in the scarf so it hid most of the damage. Runaway, huh?"

"Looks like her old man beat her up."

"Sergeant, I hope you locate her. It's no town for a kid like that to be wandering around in. And I hope you bend her old man a little. A guy who hits his kid like that is some kind of animal."

"Thanks for your help, Mr. DuShane."

"I guess I should have turned her over to the cops at the depot."

Back in my rental when I got the engine going and the heater on high and the wipers knocking the snow off, I dug an Illinois map out of the glove compartment and finally located Bureau. It was halfway between Joliet and Rock Island, and lay about eight miles south of Interstate 80. The legend said that from the size of the circle marking it the population was between zero and two hundred and fifty. The idea of a town of zero population bemused me. Should it not have been from one to two hundred and fifty? My eye, sliding, picked up the name of a town of the same size on the other side of the river. Florid. It looked like a typo. Florid, Illinois. The Florid Hotel. The Florid Bank. A community of fat happy little people suffering from high blood pressure.

So I had enough leverage now, properly used, to unlock Miss Susan Kemmer. And I knew I was sitting in a snowy automobile playing map games because I was reluctant to go use the leverage. Respect for the sanctity of the individual is a terrible burden in my line of work. I have seen cops whose greatest jolly is in taking your head apart and spreading all the pieces out on the table, under the interrogation lights. The totally dismembered personality can be put back together again, but the pieces never fit quite the way they did. And they come apart easier the next time. The old field strip.

Five o'clock and blundering old mother night had come in ahead of time to squat upon the city, upon two hundred thousand hair-trigger tempers clashing their way back toward good old home-heated television dinners, steam heat, the headachy little woman, the house-bound kids, and the dreadful feeling that Christmas was going to tear the guts out of the checking account.

I found a parking slot around the corner from Heidi's place, and as I was going to enter the downstairs foyer, I

142

turned on impulse and looked upward and picked out a big fat drifting flake, stuck my tongue out, and maneuvered under it. Consumer report: The snow is still pretty good. Cold as ever. Melts as fast. You can't hardly taste the additives.

She let me in through the red door, into lamplight glow. Her creative day had ended and she was austere and queenly in a white knit dress with long sleeves—an off-white, neckline prim, shift-like in the loose beltless fit of it, hemline just above the knees in that third-grade look which gives women with legs as good as hers an innocently erotic flavor, and gives women with bad legs the clown look of Baby Snooks.

"What a Christly ghastly depressing day," she said. She hiccuped. Astoundingly, she giggled. She looked appalled at herself, turned with careful stateliness, and said, walking away from me, "Don't think you've discovered some kind of secret vice, McGee. I felt chilly and I had some sherry. The work was going well and I kept drinking it and I didn't realize how many times I'd filled the glass and suddenly I was quite drunk. It isn't habitual."

"I'd never tab you as a wino, honey."

She revolved like a window display, hiccuped again, and said, "I shall be perfectly all right in a few minutes."

"How's your house guest?"

"Still sleeping. She must have been exhausted. Let's go see, shall we?"

I went down the short hallway with her. She turned on the hallway light. The room door was closed. She turned the knob carefully and swung the door open, hand still on the knob. I was right behind her. The wide vague band of light from the open doorway reached to the bed on the far side of the room. The young girl froze and gasped. She was standing beside the bed, and had obviously just taken off the borrowed nightgown and laid it on the bed and had been reaching toward the chair where her clothes were. The light was too shadowy to expose the facial damage. She had a ripeness, a pale heartiness in the light, and she quickly clapped one arm across her big young breasts and shielded her ginger-tan pubic tuft with her other hand.

A sound came from Heidi which turned every hair on the nape of my neck into a fine wiry bristle, crawled the flesh on the backs of my hands, and turned the small of my back to ice.

It was a tiny little-girl voice, thin and small, with none of the resonances of her maturity. It was a forlorn and sleepy little question. "Daddy? Daddy? Daddy, I'm scared. I had a bad dream. Daddy?"

Then she backed into me, banged the door shut. She stepped on my foot, turned into my arms, shuddered, and said, in that same infinitely pathetic little voice, "I'm going to tell on her. I'm going to tell on Gretchen! She was all bare!"

I held her. She was breathing rapidly, breathing a warm sherry-scented breath into my throat. Suddenly she slid her arms around my neck and held me with all her strength, crushing her soft and open mouth into mine, rocking and grinding her hips into me. There was so much frantic hunger from such a delicious direction, I was at least two-tenths of a second catching up to her. Suddenly she sagged, fainting limp, and groaned, and would have fallen.

I helped her into the living room. She coughed and gagged. She stretched out full-length on the couch and rolled her head from side to side. I turned out the lamp shining down into her eyes and sat on the floor beside her and held her hand.

"What happened to me?" she asked. The little-girl voice was gone.

"Listen to me, Heidi. I want to tell you a sad story about a sensitive and complicated little girl in a silent house. She must have been about seven years old, and there were nurses and the smells of medicine and the adored mother was dying, and she felt frightened and alone, and had nightmares."

She did not move as I reconstructed it for her. Her hand lay cool and boneless in mine. I finished it. There was no response.

"How vile!" she said in an almost inaudible tone. "How ugly and terrible."

"Sure. A lonely man, wretchedly depressed. A young

144

girl with a terrible crush on him. A slow-witted, amiable, romantic girl with all the ideas of soft surrender out of the love pulps and confessions. So she crept into his dark room and into his bed after God only knows how many nights of thinking about it. Soft, loving, willing young flesh and he took her. You came in on one of those nights to be comforted. She was just climbing out of his bed. There is a sexual undertone to every little girl's love for her daddy."

"No!"

"It must have terrified them to think that you might tell. But you went back to your own bed in another part of the house. And the doors slammed shut. It was too terrible a betrayal for you to endure. So it got pushed into a back closet of your mind, and the door was locked. But Heidi, you had to push other things in there too, and lock them away. The love for the father. And your own sexual responses. Slam the doors. Forget. The way you've forgotten how Gretchen looked, forgotten her voice. It turned you off, Heidi. Sex is vile. The world is vile. Love is ugliness."

"Amateur diagnostics. Christ! It's the parlor game I'm most sick of."

"Look at me! Come on. One more little minute before you run and hide. You reverted all the way back. You regressed to seven years old. Then you slammed the door. Then you came at me like a she-tiger. Like rape. You couldn't have made it plainer."

"No. No."

"Don't lie, damn you! Don't hide! Who *was* I?"

She closed her eyes. Her lips moved. "Daddy."

"Who were you?"

"I was . . . me. And I was Gretchen too. All in one."

"How did you feel?"

". . . Aching. Empty. Wanting. As if something secret and delicious was starting to grow, something that could grow and burst, over and over. Then everything went dark and dead."

"Poor chick," I said. "It's all bottled up. It's all twisted and strange. So that everything he did was a denial of you the way you denied him. Janice Stanyard. Gloria.

145

For about twelve fantastic seconds you started to break through. And you lost it. But it proves you could."

"No!"

"You want to enjoy your hang-up? You want to live a half-life in a half-world?"

She rolled her head from side to side and her hand tightened on mine. "No, but . . ."

"But . . ."

"It's no use. Gadge tried everything. Drinks, pills, different ways. It was just nightmare. Just all that terrible poking and jostling. So ugly." Her voice trailed off. "So stupid and degrading and . . .vile."

"Heidi, in that hallway shock turned your mind off, and your body came alive, and your body knew what it wanted."

"I don't want to be turned into an animal."

"Like Gretchen? You damn fool, do you know why that girl in there triggered it? Because she looks like her mother did eighteen years ago. She's your half-sister."

She stiffened, yanked her hand away, sat up and stared down into my face. "Oh . . . my . . . God! . . . Oh . . . my . . . *GOD*!"

"You sensed it, didn't you?"

"I could feel . . . something strange. Like an echo, like a memory I never had."

I moved up onto the couch beside her and took hold of both her hands. She looked at me, solemn and troubled, and extraordinarily lovely and alive. "And that girl in there is an animal?" I asked.

"No. No, of course not. She's a good person."

"So is Gloria. So is Janice Stanyard. So was your father. All this priss-prim condemnation act of yours is a by-product of what happened to you when you walked into that room at the wrong time, at the wrong time in your life and in your father's eighteen years ago."

She frowned. "It could be. Maybe. I don't know."

"Want to find out?"

"What do you mean?"

"After this is all over. After I'm through here, I'm going to find a place where the sun is hot and lasts all day. Come along with me. I'm the world's worst setup

146

for screwed-up broads. I hate waste. You're worth special effort."

She bit her lip. "All that again? No."

"You responded to me once."

"That doesn't mean anything."

"You must have some strong motivation to break out in some kind of direction or you wouldn't have let your pretty partner, Mark Avanyan, buddy you up with his musician friend—VanSomething."

She gave a delicate little shudder. "Anna VanMaller. She finally started to arouse me. It was creepy and terrible. I kicked her and I ran and threw up. She was furious. I'd rather be . . . the way I am, even."

"Even?"

She tilted her head, then blushed deeply and looked down and away, but she didn't pull her hands away. "I guess that was a little too significant, Travis. Okay, I'm aware of the deficit. It's probably lousy, but I don't know how lousy because I don't know what it could be like."

"Just one rule. If you say yes, you can't call it off. You endure it, until I give up."

"Gadge gave up."

"I'm not Gadge. You're twenty-five. You are a beautiful woman, Heidi. What if this is the last chance?"

She pulled her hands away, shook herself as if returning to reality, and stared at me with a little curl of contempt on her lips.

"So you'll make this terrible sacrifice, huh? Wow! I'm impressed. If you're the great lover who finds out how to turn me on, it gives you an ego as big as the *Tribune* Tower. And I can learn a wet smile, pose for a centerfold, and become a happy bunny. And if you try and try and I never make it, then you've had the loan of what I'm told is very superior equipment for God knows how long, and you can trudge away shaking your head and feeling sorry for the poor frigid woman. Tails you win, tails I lose, buddy. If foul-ups are your hobby, go find a different kind. I'm too bright to buy that line of crap, my friend. I'm not a volunteer playmate."

I got up and ambled around the semi-darkened room, scrubbing at my jaw with a thoughtful knuckle. She took very dead aim. She got inside. She made it sting. I will not fault my talent to kid myself.

I wandered, making bleak appraisals, and ended up standing behind the couch talking down at the top of her bowed blonde head.

"The first step has to be absolute honesty, Heidi. Okay. You are flat right, and you are flat wrong. Here's how you are right. I've got a plain simple old elemental urge to tumble you into the sack, on any terms. You have that cool remote princessly look in total contrast with a very exciting body and exciting way of moving and handling yourself. It intrigues. Man wants to possess. He wants to storm the castle, bust down the gates, and take over. But I think—I'm not really sure—but I think that if that was my total motive, I'm enough of a grown-up not to try to get to you by sneaking up on your blind side. Grabbing something because it looks great is kind of irresponsible. Life is not a candy store.

"Likewise, dear girl, life is not a playground full of playmates where all good men are supposed to come to the aid of old Hooo the Hef and dedicate themselves sincerely and with a sense of responsibility and mission to liberating the maximum number of receptive lassies from the chains and burdens of our Puritan heritage.

"I think my shtick, Heidi, is that I enjoy all the aspects of a woman. I like the way their minds work. I like the sometimes wonderful and sometimes nutty ways they figure things out and relate themselves to reality. I like the arguments, the laughs, the quarrels, the competitions, the making up. A nearby girl makes the sky bluer, the drinks better, the food tastier. She gives the days more texture, and you know it is happening to her in the same way.

"How this relates to Heidi Geis Trumbill is that I have the feeling it is a damned shame you stand outside the gates with a kind of wistful curiosity about what it's like inside. I want to be sort of a guide, showing off new and pretty country to the tourist. Life is so damned valuable and so totally miraculous, and they give you such a stingy little hunk of it from womb to tomb, you ought to use all the parts of it there are. I guess I would say that I want to be friends. A friend wants to help a friend. I want to peel away that suspicion and contention because I don't think it's really what you're like. If we can get friendship going, then maybe we can get a good physical intimacy going, and from that we can fall into a kind of love or fall into an affection close to love. If it happens, it adds up to more than the sum of the two people, and it is that extra part out of nowhere that has made all the songs and the poetry and the art.

"So it wouldn't be a performance. No great-lover syndrome. No erotic tricks, no Mother McGee's home-cooked aphrodisiacs. The only trick would be, I guess, to get you to like yourself a little. Then the rest would come.

"So you know what's wrong with the whole statement, just as I do. Why doesn't he get his own true permanent forever girl? Maybe it is some kind of emotional immaturity. Somehow I don't think so. I have a theory I can't prove. I know this. If I became one woman's permanent emotional stability and security, there would be a moral obligation on my part to change the way I live, because I'd have no right to ask her to buy a piece of my risk-taking. Yet risk is so essential to me—for reasons I can only guess at—giving it up would make me a different kind of man. I don't think I'd like him. I don't think she would. I don't know if all this is excuse, explanation, sales talk or what. I really don't know. It's what I *think* I think."

I stood there. She did not move or speak. I heard a deep sigh. Then in a lithe movement she turned, rolling up onto her knees, and stood on her knees looking up at me across the back of the couch. Her eyes were evasive. She put her hands out and I took them.

"So I'll try friendship," she said. "I've tried everything else. I don't even know very much about being a friend, Travis. I should make some gesture to seal the bargain, I suppose."

She uptilted her face, eyes closed, mouth offered. But I could tell that she was steeling herself. Her hands had a clammy feel of nervous tension. So, briefly and lightly, I kissed one closed eye and then the other. I released her hands and said, "Contract confirmed."

She looked startled, stepped backward off the couch, and said, "You kind of lost me a little with that risk-taking part."

"I conned John Andrus into giving me that card. I knew Gloria before your father did. They met down in Lauderdale. I stood up with them when they got married. She phoned me in Florida and asked me to come up and help. You could say I'm in the salvage business. Suppose some very sly, slick, sleek operator worked on you and suckered you out of the settlement Gadge made on you. The statutes are full of gimmicks. Semi-legal theft. I might be induced to give it a try. Whatever I could recover, I'd keep half. Half is better than nothing. No recovery, and I've gambled my expenses and lost. Make a recovery, and expenses come off the top before I split. Somehow people on a dead run with a jaw full of stolen meat react badly to having it taken away from them."

She sat and stared at me. "Half? Half of six hundred thousand?"

"Half of her end of it, and that would be subject to adjustment. The circumstances are always different. You can see how far I would have gotten with you if I told you who I was trying to help."

"She sent for you!"

"Surprise?"

"I want to be able to keep hating her, Travis."

"Then don't get to know her, if there's ever any chance left for you to get to know her."

"Do you know where the money went?"

"I might. I don't know. Susan Kemmer could be the key." She looked toward the bedroom. "She *knows*?"

"I don't think so. But she knows things I have to know."

"Poor little doll. I must have frightened her." She got up and went to the bedroom. There was a line of light under the door. I hung back. Heidi knocked and the girl said to come in.

In a little while Heidi came back out and left the door open and beckoned me back into the living room. "She was just sitting in there in the chair all dressed. Quiet as a mouse. I apologized for walking in on her before. I said I thought she was sleeping. She just shrugged and said it didn't matter. I told her you want to talk to her. Do you want me to be there?"

"It might help. But it might get ugly. Don't try to step in unless I cue you. The cue word is hell, said loudly. Then you hustle to her and hug her and comfort her and chew me out. You're the guy in the white hat."

I went in with her. Heidi sat on the bed. The girl had made the bed. I leaned against a chest of drawers. "Well, Susan, I guess we'd better start leveling with each other."

"There's nothing I want to talk about, Mr. McGee."

"I know that. But you have to."

"I don't have to."

"It won't keep me from finding out. It will just save me a lot of time and effort. I know you caught that North Central bus at Bureau, at the crossroads, at a place called Sheen's, a hundred miles from here. I know that Saul and Gretchen and you five kids left Chicago on Sunday the 22nd of August in the car Saul bought at the place he worked and fixed up. You were towing a U-Haul trailer. So the little family holed up a hundred miles west of here almost four months ago. Saul's parole period was over. That's just a sample, honey. I'm not going to tell you all I know. I'm going to hold back so that I can tell if you're lying to me."

She stared at me, startled, wary, worried. "*You* don't want to help me. You fooled Mrs. Stanyard too. You're after *him*!"

"The easiest way to attract attention would be to keep you kids out of school. And he apparently wanted to lay low. So all I have to do is drive over there with you in the morning and hit the high schools in the area and find out which one you've been going to. Then get the home address from the school."

"No. Please. *Please* don't."

"Why the *hell* are you being so stubborn, girl?"

Heidi hurried to her on cue, sat on the arm of the chair, and put an arm around Susan and glowered at me and said, "Stop bullying her!" Susan had begun to cry.

"Stubborn is bad enough without being stupid too."

"She's *not* stupid!"

"Sure she is. She takes after her mother. She takes after Gretchen."

"She's not my real mother!" Susan declared.

I shook my head sadly. "Honey, Gretchen is your real mother and Dr. Geis was your father. And your friend and protector there is your big half-sister. Say hello to Sister Heidi."

And Heidi stopped faking it. "Damn you!" she yelled

at me, her face pink. "What are you trying to *do* to her!"

"Shake her up. She needs it."

"Leave her *alone*!"

I smiled. "Okay, sis. You tell her the tender love story." I closed the bedroom door on my way out. I sat in the living room and picked up an art magazine and began leafing through it. I was a great guy. I did things to people for their own good. It gave me that nice warm righteous glow.

The art magazine told me that when abstract expressionism reflected utter disenchantment with the dream it still reverted to rhetorical simplifications even in its impiety, and that it is not a unified stylistic entity because of its advocacy of alien ideas on the basis of a homiletic approach to experience.

Funny I'd never realized it.

After I spent twenty minutes admiring my sterling character, Heidi came out red-eyed and wan and said, "It's tearing her to ribbons. She's had all she can take."

"Loan me your white hat and stay here," I said, and went in. The girl looked at me. It's the look the caged things have in small roadside stands.

I sat on the bed and said, "Growing up hurts, kid."

"You made everything awful."

"Your father was a fine man. Possibly a great man. Your mother was a sweet dumb sexy kid and she caught him at the wrong time or the right time, and there you sprouted. Miracle of life. Ah, sweet mystery. Et cetera."

"But why didn't he ever want to see me?"

"Let me see now. Could it be because he thought you might not be old enough to take that kind of a jar? And maybe you aren't old enough yet. He made the deal he thought best for you long ago. It didn't turn out so great. But he knew you did. He paid to have you checked out. He liked the report. I think it would be safe to say he was proud of you. But I have the feeling that his little affair with the housekeeper's daughter cost him a lot more than the annuity and paying to have reports made on you, and the ten thousand he left with Mrs. Stanyard. I have the feeling his little bout with statutory rape eventually and indirectly cost him just about everything he ever saved. Six hundred thousand dollars. And I think Saul Gorba got it."

"No! Oh, no, it wasn't anything like that. Honest. They explained it all to us kids. Saul tried to go straight, really. But there was a man at the body shop. He knew Saul had a prison record. So he started stealing. It was some way of putting the wrong amount on the bills and receipts. Saul explained it. Then the man put some forms in the back of Saul's locker and he found them and he knew what was happening, and he was going to be framed. Momma was so upset. Saul said that with his record he didn't have a prayer. He said he'd be sent back to prison and he said that he was pretty sure the welfare would take over and split us up and call Momma an unfit mother on account of they'd picked her up twice in Chicago on D and D and let her off with a fine, but it was on the record. He said our only chance was to just leave. He said he'd found us a nice place in the country, and we weren't to tell anybody we were leaving."

"It sounded logical to you?"

"It was the only way we could stay together as a family." She frowned. "I would be all right, but it would be terrible for Julian and Freda. I don't think Freddy cares one way or another. And Tommy is only six. He needs the rest of us."

"Where did you go?"

"Saul rented a farmhouse. It's RFD 3 Box 80, Princeton. It's off the Depue Road, all by itself at the end of a little dirt road. It's about two and a half miles from Bureau crossroads."

"Nice place?"

"Kind of shacky, but there's lots of room. Forty acres. Everything had grown up weeds and bushes. It had been empty a long time. They said we couldn't attract any attention. Our name was going to be Farley. And we had moved there from Chicago for Saul's health. We were going to farm it. We all had to practice the name. He put the Cadillac in one of the sheds and nailed up the door. He walked out and hitchhiked and came back the next day with an old pickup truck. He made a kind of workshop in another shed. When it was time to go back to school, he had our school records. He came back to the city and got them and he changed the names so you couldn't tell. They had driver's licenses and he fixed up birth certificates for us and everything. He said we were going to be the

Farley family for the rest of our lives, and we shouldn't ever tell."

"Did you mind that?"

"Nobody minded much. Anything is okay with Momma, the way she is. It made me feel bad that I couldn't write to my friends. They'd never know what happened to me. It was hard to get used to it being so quiet all the time. But after a while it didn't seem so quiet. You just heard other things. Wind and birds and bugs."

"Did your mother or Saul try to find work?"

"No. Saul would go away once in a while and be gone overnight. He'd go in the old truck. We all worked fixing the old place up for winter. Then one day when we came home on the school bus there wasn't anybody there. That was . . . just three weeks ago today. We thought they'd gone off in the truck. Saul came back alone in the truck and he wanted to know where Momma was. We told him she was gone when we came home. I looked and found that a suitcase and a lot of her clothes were gone. Saul cursed and stormed around. He said we'd just have to all sit tight and wait for her to come back. It bothered him a lot. I'd wake up in the night and hear him walking around downstairs."

"He did beat you up?"

"He was upset and he'd been drinking. All night maybe. He came into my room before daylight and he woke me up and handed me my coat and told me to come along and not wake the other kids. He said he had something to tell me about my mother. We went out to his workshop place. He had wired it for lights and he had a space heater going. He acted strange and he kept looking at me in a funny way. He had me sit down on the cot and he sat and put his arm around me and he was kind of half-crying. He said he was pretty sure that she had been gone so long now, she was never coming back.

"I told him I thought she'd be back and he told me she had threatened to go away for good because they hadn't been getting along. He kept rubbing his hand up and down my arm. He said there was just the two of us now to take care of everything. He said I was just like a regular mother to the other kids. He said I was a better mother in every way than she was. He said we had to stick together. I said I'd better go back to bed and I started to

154

stand up, but he got my wrists and pushed me down flat on the cot. He lay down beside me and put my wrists around behind me and held them there in one hand, hurting me.

"In a funny whispery little voice he said everything was going to be wonderful. He said he loved me, and we were going to be a little family, just him and me and little Tommy, and we were going to leave soon and drive to Mexico in the Cadillac, just the three of us, and he was going to divorce Momma and marry me and we'd live in a big house with a swimming pool and have servants. He said that on the way out of town when we were fifty miles away he'd call the welfare to take care of the other three and they'd be in good hands. He kept stroking me with his free hand and I was starting to cry and begging him to stop. He kissed my neck and told me I was his little darling and he had been watching me ever since we'd left Chicago, and he had just one more little thing to take care of and then we would go on a wonderful trip. Then he opened my coat and pushed his hand up under my pajama top and started squeezing and rubbing me. It scared me so I yanked my wrists loose and I hit at him and kicked him and he fell backward off the cot. I tried to get by him and get out but he grabbed me and pulled me down and then he got up and picked me up and threw me back onto the cot. He said I was old enough and big enough for it, so I better relax and enjoy it, because I was going to have a lot of chances to get used to it. I remember scratching and biting and kicking at him and all of a sudden he was on the floor again, kneeling, all hunched over, looking up at me and holding onto himself.

"His eyes are funny. They're sort of pale brown but when he gets mad they look yellow. Golden almost. He stood up slowly and when I tried to dodge around him he hit me in the mouth with his fist and knocked me down. He picked me up and hit me a lot more times, holding me with one hand and hitting me with the other. It all got blurred. He let go of me and I fell down and he kicked me a couple of times and went away and left me there. It was getting light. Pretty soon I could get up and I went back to my room. I didn't see him. I locked the door. Mr. McGee, I knew that if I went down to the road and hitched a ride into Princeton and told the police, he'd go to jail and the welfare would get us. And I knew if I stayed there, he'd keep at me until he got what he wanted. When the kids knocked on the door to find out about breakfast I said I was sick and I told Freda and Julian to help Freddy get breakfast for everybody. I stayed in there all day. After everybody was asleep, I sneaked down and got something to eat. I knew I was safe because I could hear Saul snoring. You can always hear him all over the upstairs part after he's had a lot of beer. I took food up to my room. Monday morning when Freddy knocked at my door I said I was better but I wasn't well enough to go to school. I'd remembered about Mrs. Stanyard. He reminded me, saying I better not go to her. I had the money I'd been putting away to buy baby chicks in the spring. I heard the truck go rattling out about two o'clock, so I got dressed and left and cut across lots and came out on the Depue Road and followed it to Route 26 and walked to the crossroads where I'd heard you could get the bus to Chicago.

"The waitress at Sheen's was nice. She let me lie down in back on a couch in a room off the kitchen, and she brought me things to eat even though I couldn't pay for them. I told her I fell downstairs. She said her boyfriend had a bad temper too. I think that when ... Momma comes back everything will be all right again. But he couldn't have stolen all that money you said."

"He had to steal something."

"What do you mean?"

"What did seven of you live on for four months?"

"Oh, it was hardly any rent way out away from anything in that shacky place, and we've always had that four hundred and thirty-three dollars every month."

"Not since August first, Susan. The company is holding four checks right now. The January one will be the last one made out to your mother. In February it starts to come directly to you, if they can manage to find out where you are."

She stared at me and even with the puffed lids she opened her eyes as wide as I had seen them. "But ... I thought that was where she got the money to ... to go on a vacation!"

"Did Saul quarrel much with her?"

"Oh yes. But it ..." She stopped and put her hand

to her throat. "No! He *wouldn't*!"

"Let's hope it's a lousy guess."

She said, "I have to get back there! I left Freddy a note. I said I was going to go off to get Momma and bring her home and not to worry, and be good, and help each other and not fight. If he ... if he ..." She could not continue.

"Sit tight, honey. Draw me a map so I can find the place. I am a registered licensed sneak. I'll go check on your clan, gather them up, and haul them back here. You've got more friends on your side than you know what to do with. Me, Heidi, Mrs. Stanyard. And there's always your grandmammy, Mrs. Ottlo."

"She doesn't like children very much," Susan explained. "I think they make her nervous."

Heidi spoke from the doorway, startling me. "She's right, you know. When we were little if we got in her way in the kitchen when she was busy, she'd do things that would hurt like fury, like snapping your ear with a fingernail, and giving a little pinch and twisting at the same time. She'd laugh but it was ... kind of a mean laugh." She tilted her head and frowned. "I remember once Gretchen showing us her back. She took her blouse off. She must have been about thirteen, and that would make me about four and Roger was probably eight. Anna had thrashed her with a belt. I can remember the marks still, the dark places and the little streaks where it had broken the skin."

"Please hurry," Susan said to me.

eleven

I took Heidi into the outside corridor beyond her red door and said, "Settle her down. Get a sleeping pill into her. I'm not going to go fumbling around in the boonies in the black black night. And I don't think he's going to

157

do any harm to those kids. I've got a hunch they might be there alone, and Saul Gorba may be rocketing south with the loot. The boy is fifteen. He should be able to cope."

"When are you going out?"

"In time to pick a nice observation post and see who gets on the school bus. I'll report by phone. Like having a sister?"

"I don't know how I feel yet. I like her."

"A staunch one. The kind that knows how to cope. Go in and be family. She needs it."

"Okay." She gave me a nervous smile. I guess it is the smile dentists see when the patient walks in and looks at the chair and the drills and then at the dentist. "I could need it too."

"So cozy each other, Heidi. Everybody has days like this."

The smile turned wry. "That's a little hard to believe."

I had noticed a change in her. The little provocative animal grace of her moments was gone. She had taken to walking like a stick doll. But at the same time she had stopped saying no. I knew she kept remembering the bargain she had made. But there was a certain little awareness mixed with trepidation. I had the feeling that if I made a sudden movement she would make exactly the same protective gestures Susan had made when we had looked into the room and seen her in the light from the hallway.

I rested my hand on the warm shoulder under the off-white knit and felt her tense up, and saw her throat work in a convulsive swallow.

I leaned and kissed her just to the starboard of the right eye and gave her shoulder a little pat and said, "Walk out there on that stage and give it all you've got, Gwendolyn, and I'll make you a star."

"Oh God, McGee, am I that obvious?"

"It's only terror, honey. No worse than a bad cold."

I drove famished to my hotel, ate hugely and well, and found no messages waiting. It was nine forty-five when I got to the house that Fort built, out at Lake Pointe. Bits of light shone through cracks in the drawn draperies and closed blinds.

Anna called through the door. "Ya? Ya?"

"McGee again, Anna."

I heard the rattle of chain and the chunking of the bolt, and she opened the door part way and said, "Comen in, please sir."

I slid through and she rebolted and rechained the door. She was concealing something in the folds of her dress and when she saw that I was aware of it, she held it out, a big ugly Army issue Colt .45 automatic pistol. She held it clumsily.

"Are you frightened of something?"

"Hear noises, maybe. Herr Doktor's gun."

I took it from her. Full clip, a round in the chamber and the safety on. I put it on the table beside the door.

"How is she? How is the dear little missus?"

"I'll phone from here in a little while and find out. Anna, we have to have a heart-to-heart talk. And it might make you very unhappy."

She accepted the formality of the situation. She invited me into the kitchen into the booth. She served us coffee and little cakes and eased herself shyly into the booth across from me.

I had to start by saying that I knew Susan had been fathered by Fortner Geis. It distressed her that I should know. She acted as if it was her own guilt, her own shame. She kept telling me how "goot" the Doktor had been, and what a "bat" girl Gretchen was. Very stupid girl. You have to do your best. Some people are "veak." Gretchen had a veakness for men. Five children, four fathers.

Yes, she said, she had made it a habit to go visit Saul and Gretchen every Sunday. If a daughter tries, it is a duty, *nein*? They had married officially at her urging. True, Saul Gorba was a criminal, a veak man, but brilliant. A pleasure to talk to. In prison he had studied many things. Languages. German. He had learned German so quickly. She helped him with his accent, with the idioms. She had the Germanic reverence for the erudite mind. She said she would take along small gifts for the *kinder*, help Gretchen cook the dinner, mend the clothes of the *kinder*, of them all a family to make.

Then poof. Shrug. Cast eyes heavenward. What goot is it? They are gone. No message, no word, no letter. Like animals of the forest. No consideration. It is never to try again with such a daughter, you can believe.

Key question. Anna, did you talk about Doctor Geis? Did you talk about Gloria and Heidi and Roger to Saul and Gretchen?

Deep blush, bowed head, contrite little nod. What is harm to talk? It is her life more with this family than that one, *nein*? A good man dying slowly, the dear wife trying to hold death back from him by love, his own children hating the wife, it is a sadness, and who else to talk to?

Did Saul encourage such talk? Did he ask questions?

Oh yes. Why asking?

And you know of the missing money?

She said with firmness that whatever the Doktor did, it was right. One should trust.

So it was time to pull the pin. "Anna, I am convinced that Saul Gorba used the information he got from you to extort all that money from Dr. Geis."

Much the same effect could have been achieved by cleaving her open from the crown of her head to the brow line.

"*Lieber Gott!*" she whispered. "Can not be. Can not *be!* The Doktor would not give to him!"

"I don't think the Doctor knew who he was giving the money to. Someone gave him some little demonstrations. Someone said, in effect, you are dying and you know it. Dying is at best a lonely thing. If you want to hang onto all the money that won't do you any good anyway, you can really die alone. I have shown you how easily it can be done. Your grandson, your second wife, Nurse Stanyard, your daughter Heidi, and the daughter you had by Gretchen will all predecease you. I think he made a logical decision. I think he sensed he was dealing with somebody merciless and perhaps a little mad. And I think he was strong enough to make his decision and then not let it bother him. He made sure Heidi got a good settlement from Trumbill. He saved out a single insurance policy for Gloria. Susan was already taken care of."

She mumbled and groaned about the cruelty of it, about how she could not believe it. Then her eyes widened and she said, "Ah! With the money he left. They ran far."

"Not very far. Now I have to ask you if you will take the responsibility for your five grandchildren."

"How do you mean, sir?"

"Gloria told me you plan to go to Florida and stay with your old friend Mrs. Kemmer. Let me see. Her son Karl fathered one of the tribe before he died, didn't he?"

"Freddy. Strong boy."

"Suppose I bring all five of them to you tomorrow and drop them in your lap. Susan's checks haven't been cashed for four months. There's a sizable emergency fund too. They are going to need stability and order. Susan is responsible and mature and devoted to the younger ones. There'd be money to set up a place here or in Florida. I couldn't promise anything, but I think there might be some financial help from Heidi to make college possible for Susan. How about it?"

"But there is Gretchen!"

"I don't think so. It's only a hunch, but I better tell you. I don't want to, believe me. I think she's dead. I think Saul killed her. She disappeared three weeks ago. And Saul has the hots for Susan. He gave her a very bad time. Gretchen drank. She wasn't smart. She was too friendly. She talked too much."

Anna Ottlo got up with astonishing agility and pulled her apron up over her head. It was a gesture I had heard of but never seen. She trotted into a sort of pantry arrangement off the kitchen and I could hear her in there whuffling and snorting and moaning. I ate a little cake. It didn't swallow readily. I washed it down with cooling coffee. She came trudging back, knuckling her eyes like a fat child. She plumped herself down and sighed and shook her head.

"I'm going to go jounce Gorba around some. He's going to get a real good chance to work on his languages if they don't electrocute him. He can pick up Croatian, Tasmanian, and Urdu. He can have a ball. But even with what all those kids have been through, this will shake them badly."

She sighed again. She looked down at her hands, at the palms and then the backs. "All the life," she said. "Verk, verk, verk. I have the arthritis. I have the high blood. Cook, clean, sew, scrub for children? Six years is the little one. How much more years of that? Nerves make the heart flutter like a bird and the eyes go black. No. I am sorry. After the long verk there is rest. I must have.

Susan is eighteen years soon, ya? With those checks I think the judge says she can have the brothers and sister, take care. Maybe the welfare comes and looks sometimes to make sure. She is young. She can do it. I know that one. She would want it. A good lawyer could fix, *nein*? Maybe I am selfish old woman. Too bad. Did I ask Gretchen to have five *kinder*? Life is too hard. Time to sit on the porch now. Rock the chair. Warm in the sunshine. Don't blame, please sir."

"Okay. I don't blame. W. C. Fields had a thing about children too."

"Who? Who?"

"Skip it." I looked at my watch. "Want to get on an extension while I find out about Gloria?"

"Oh yes!"

The operator at the hospital had me hold. I had a two-minute wait before Hayes Wyatt in his dusty, reedy voice said, "Mr. McGee?"

"Yes, Doctor."

"Bad news, I'm afraid. Pneumonia. Pulmonary edema, and we can't seem to hit it with antibiotics. Did a thoracotomy. Got her in a tent and a good team doing everything indicated, but we can't seem to make a dent in the fever. Almost a hundred and five, and if we get another three-tenths we're going to pack her in ice. So I haven't the faintest idea how much residual disturbance we've got from the dose she took, and the question may be academic. The first thing is to try to get her through the night. I better get back there, but here's someone who wants to talk to you."

"Travis? Janice Stanyard. I'm on the case with Dr. Wyatt."

"Is she going to make it?"

"If she's tough enough. I wondered how . . ."

"Everything is just fine. How would you respond to my dumping five kids on you tomorrow for an indefinite stay? Buy you some rollaways. Bedding, chests of drawers, cardboard closets."

"I would love it!"

"Go back to work, woman."

"Yes sir!"

"I'm just checking possibilities. Don't count on the kids for sure."

"All right, but really I would . . ."

"I believe you. When should I phone back to check?"

"It will go one way or another by dawn, I would guess."

Anna let me out. She was snuffling. She said Mrs. Stanyard was nice lady.

I placed my dawn phone call long-distance, from a red brick Georgian motel just off the Interstate west of Peru, Illinois. My heart sank when I was told that Dr. Wyatt had left the hospital. I asked for Janice Stanyard. She came on, her voice blurred and dragging with exhaustion. "She was tough enough, Travis."

"Thank God!"

"She's sleeping now. I'm about to go home and do some of the same. She's going to be very weak. And we don't know about the other yet."

I went out into a bright gray Wednesday world to find that a warm wind was blowing in from somewhere. Maybe all the way up from McGee country. I had driven through inches of sticky snow, but it had all been transformed into busy water, hustling down every slope it could find. I had no idea how early the school bus picked up the kids. I had forgotten to ask Susan. I did know that the coming Friday was the last day before Christmas holidays. And I knew the kids walked out to Depue Road and caught the bus there. The place was marked on the map Susan had drawn for me.

I knew that getting into position was more important than my morning stomach. It was flat lands, with a few gentle rolls and dips and hollows. It all looked bleak in the overcast morning light. There were some substantial farms, all trimmed and tended, and there were deserted places with tumbled buildings, fencing rusting away, leafless scrub tall in the silent fields, and it made you wonder how this one had made it and that one hadn't.

I parked by a produce stand on Route 26, shuttered and vacant. I was there a little while, and I had a forty-minute wait before I saw the yellow bus in my side mirror, coming around the bend. I let it get out of sight before I started up. I hung well back and then picked up speed after it made the turn onto Depue Road. Susan had said their dirt road was a mile from the corner and came in on the right, and I could tell it by the bright red paint on the post that held up the mailbox. There was no name on the mailbox.

I saw the red post all right. The bus didn't even hesitate. It rolled on by. I looked up the muddy rutted road and, half-obscured by a knoll, I saw what had to be the house, set way back, two stories, steep, swaybacked roof, stingy little windows and not many of them, clapboards painted a dirty gray white. Two shutters crooked, one missing. A cheerless and isolated place.

Once well past it I dropped back and kept the bus just barely in sight. I tried to figure it out. Okay, the procedure would be to slow down, maybe look up the road to see if the kids were coming on the run. Stop and blow the horn maybe. So the driver knew they weren't going to be there. So I'd better know what he'd been told.

Seven miles further, at the big central school complex, I found out the driver was a she, a brawny, likely, and clear-eyed lass in ski pants, mackinaw, and stocking cap, with shoulders like Arnold Palmer.

"Excuse me," I said, with my best civil-service smile and patronizing manner. "District survey. A little spot check on percentage of equipment utilization. Hope you didn't get nervous to have me following you."

"Nervous? What about?"

I glanced at Susan's map and put it away. "My route sheet shows that your first stop on Depue Road is a mile from the corner. Five children. Farley."

"Got on at Schottlehauster's. Four. One's sick. Oldest. High school senior."

"Got on where?"

She raised her voice as though addressing the deaf, and enunciated more clearly. "Shottlehauster's. Shottlehauster's. The big place on 26 three mile afore Farley's. They're staying there a time."

"Oh. I see. Thank you."

"Don't mention it."

So I went back a lot faster than I had come. I guessed that when she said three mile she meant three mile. But she had been wrong. It was three miles and one half of a tenth of a mile to the giant wine-red mailbox, "Shottlehauster" lettered in white in elegant script to a broad gravel drive, a long low white ranch-style house, and, beyond, the quonset equipment shed, white barns, triple silo standing against the wide march of rich and pampered farmland. I turned in, parked and got out, hesitating over whether to go to the front of the house or the back. I could hear a loud twanging and thumping of folk-rock. A bakery truck was parked at an angle near the back entrance. Darling Bakery. "Fresh as a Stolen Kiss." "Darling Bread is Triple Enriched." Bright blue and lemon-yellow decor.

At this time of day the back door would be more customary, I decided, for a hardworking credit-bureau fellow. To get to the back door I had to pass the kitchen windows. In the dingy morning the fluorescents were all on, bright enough so that it was like glancing through the tied-back café curtains into a stage set, the floor level in there maybe three feet higher than the level of the gravel driveway. I would say I was opposite that first window frozen in midstride for a second and a half. It took half a second to figure out what I was looking at, and half a second of confirming it, and half a second to get my direction reversed and get out of the way.

The Darling Bread Boy was bellied up to a long efficient counter top. Blue work shirt to match his truck. "Darling" embroidered in an arc across chunk shoulders. But the "a" and the "n" in "Darling" were covered by two gigantic vertical fuzzy pink caterpillars. Then beyond the edge of the center island in the kitchen I saw the lady feet in fuzzy white socks, clamped and locked together, pressing quite neatly the tail of the blue shirt against his butt. Saw one hairy straining leg with his trousers puddled around the ankle. Caterpillars became her sweatered forearms, her hands hooked back over the hanging-on place of the trapezius muscles, as though trying to chin herself. And over the Bread Boy shoulder was her effortful jouncing bouncing face, eyes squinched tight shut, mouth raw, like indeed with the struggle to chin herself on that horizontal bar of muscle. The twangity-thump of country git-ar with electronic assist came from the truck radio (paternalistic bakery management) and from the kitchen radio in unison, and for a couple of micro-seconds before I sorted the scene out I had thought he was attempting a crude, vulgar, unskilled version of some contemporary dance. But it was busy old rub-a-dub-dub, humpety-rump, dumpety-bump, with the counter-topped farm wife all wedged and braced.

I fled bemused to my rental. The idling truck made little pops and puffs of exhaust smoke. Where the hell did they think they were? Westport? Bucks County? Didn't they know this was the heartland of America? Didn't she know Jack LaLanne was the only acceptable morning exercise for the busy housewife?

I started the car engine and put the automatic shift into drive and kept my foot on the brake pedal. I wondered if maybe it was the architecture which had debauched her. I could not conceive of it happening in the traditional old farm kitchens. But she could see slightly glossier versions of her own fluorescence, stainless steel, ceramic island, rubber tile, pastel enamels, warm wood paneling in the Hollywood product on both Big Screen and home tube, so there she was on the set, and she had to say the lines, but after you said the lines enough times all of a sudden you'd get interrupted by something a little more direct than a commercial message from your sponsor. But it didn't count too much because it was as unreal sort of as a giant hand coming up out of the suds, or a washer going up like an elevator, or a nut riding a horse through the back yard and turning everything radiant white.

The instant Darling Boy came trotting into view I started ahead so that he could be certain he had glimpsed my arrival. Chunky redhead with a freckly, good-natured, clenched-fist face, carrying cheerfully wrapped bakery items in his big blue aluminum home-delivery basket. He gave me a glance, a happy morning nod and grin, and swung aboard his service van and rolled on out, a thousand loud guitars fading down the road, but still playing faintly inside the house.

The incident had decided me in favor of the front door. Storm door, then a big white front door with a narrow insert of vertical glass. Brass knocker shaped like the American eagle. Brass and pearl bell button which, when pushed, set off the biggest and most complicated chime set in the Sears catalogue. When it had played through to its finish, faintly heard through the doors, I felt like applauding. I waited and then thumbed them into encore, and when the presentation number was half over I saw her coming toward the door, patting her hair, hitching at her clothes, giving that sucked-in bite that goes with fresh lipstick.

She opened the door inward, pushed the storm door open six inches and with a cheery smile, said, "You want Harry, he had to go up to Moline again early, but he ought to be home by supper."

She was weathering the downslope of the thirties very nicely, a small sturdy woman with a wide face, pretty eyes, network of grin wrinkles, mop of curly dark hair with a first touch of white ones over her ears. Fuzzy pink sweater, denim ranch pants in stretch fabric. White moccasins, white sox. A shapely and durable figure, breasts rather small and abrupt under the pink fuzz.

"You're Mrs. Shottlehauster?"

"Yes, but honest to Betsy, if you're selling something I just haven't got the time, and you can believe it."

"I'm not selling anything, and you can believe it. I'm trying to get a credit report on some people named Farley on Depue Road, and I'm not having much luck. I found out their kids know your kids. I don't want to bother you, but if you could spare just a minute or two to answer some questions . . ."

"Heck, I can spare time for that. You come right on in, Mr . . ."

"McGee. Travis McGee, mà'am."

"Well, I'm Mildred Shottlehauster," she said, leading me through the entrance hallway into a two-level living room decorated in too many colors and patterns, and too densely populated with furniture, some of it good, and most of it borax.

"You sit right there and be comfortable," she said. "We've got those four Farley kids staying with us, and I certainly would like to know how long, not that they're any special problem or anything. I've got my six, and once you get up to six I guess it doesn't make too much difference if you have six or ten. And they're really good kids. They're almost *too* meek and quiet and polite. They make mine seem like wild Indians or something. Mine are sixteen, fourteen, twelve, eleven, eight and seven so . . ."

"I'd never believe it, Mrs. S."

"Well *thank* you, kind sir, she said. Anyhoo, the Farley children seem to fit right in and actually there's less fighting and squabbling when they're here. Harry and I are just doing the neighborly thing. Monday night it was, just on toward dark, you remember how raw and nasty it was, Mr. Farley came to the door and wouldn't come in. He hemmed and hawed and said that his wife had to go to Chicago, and Susan, the oldest—a perfectly darling girl she'd gone off to join her mother and he suddenly found out he had to go on a business trip for a few days and he didn't want to leave the other four alone and could we give them bed and board for a few days. He said he could pay for it. Well, we forgave him for offering money for a neighborly deed because . . . well, that family is right off the city streets and they can't be expected to know how we do things here in the country. When we said he certainly could bring them over, he said they were out in the truck, and so they were, chilled to the very bone. They came shivering in with their little bags and bundles of clothes and toothbrushes. I must confess I had qualms about my pack getting too friendly with those kids when they first came here. I mean they are sort of underprivileged, and you don't know what nasty tricks and habits children can pick up in the slums, and pass along, do you? It was last August my Bruce came racing home to tell me some family named Farley had moved into the old Duggins place. It's been empty three years since old Sam died, and he must have been older than God, and his only kin a sister in Seattle who couldn't care less, and nobody knew she'd even put it up for rent with that Country Estate Agency over in Princeton, but it's plain to see it's the kind of run-down place you could get for practically nothing, not like when you're nearer the city and they get picked up for vacation houses and so on. But you can believe it, those Farley kids, Freda and Julian and Freddy and Tommy, they're dandy kids. What did you want to ask me? Oops, I've got to go check the pies. I got stuck again. Four cherry pies for the Mission Aid supper and my dang oven thermostat is screwjee. Would you like some coffee, Mr. McGee? It's on the stove. Come on along."

I followed her out toward the whomping of the music, and she twisted the dial down to background size with a single expert tweak as she went by the radio. "I caught the coffee thing from Harry," she said. "He was in the Navy, so it's always on the fire, grind our own beans, never let it begin to bubble, like some people are about wine, I guess." And as she spoke she deftly assembled tall white cup and saucer, poured it steaming rich, slid it into position at the end of the center island which was a breakfast bar, put sugar and cream within reach. She went over and stood at her eye-level wall oven, all copper and chrome, and peered in through the glass front at her pies.

"The only way I'm going to be able to tell is from the color of the crust. Lousy thermostat. Hey, want a cinnamon pecan roll? The bakery just delivered fresh, and they're the special this week."

She poured coffee for herself, got out the butter and the rolls, and sat around the corner of the bar end of the island at my left.

"Marvelous coffee, Mrs. Shottlehauster."

"Specialty of the house, thank you kind sir she said. What is it the Farleys want to buy?"

"I don't know. We're a service organization and we work for a lot of different client companies. The point is are they a good credit risk up to such and such an amount."

She munched slowly, frowning. The pad of muscle at the corner of her jaw bulged with each bite. There was a flake of cooked sugar on her narrow underlip and her tongue slipped cleverly out and hooked it in. "I like to try to be fair to everybody. So I just couldn't say. It just depends on how much they can put into the spring planting, if they know what to plant, if they know how to go about getting help from the county agent and the state, if they're all willing to work like Arabian slaves. . . . I just don't know, honestly. Mr. Farley is well-spoken. You can tell he's had some advantages. I tried to be neighborly, and so did a couple of other women, but we spread the word that nobody else need waste their time. I stopped there last September and didn't even get invited in. They just stared at me, and I had the idea they were laughing at me somehow. You know? She's a big heavy woman, coarse-looking, and I don't want to hurt their chances, but she smelled like a brewery, and it was a hot day and she wasn't ... properly covered up. I guess that kind of thing doesn't mean much on a credit report."

"It's very helpful, really."

"I've been noticing what a wonderful tan you've got, Mr. McGee."

"I just got transferred up here from the Southwest. We get moved around a lot."

"I guess you must think I'm some kind of a nut, inviting you in and all, and being absolutely all alone here until the bus brings the kids back, but I've got a sixth sense about people, and there's a 16-gauge automatic shotgun standing in the corner there by the front door and you wouldn't have gotten a foot over the doorstep if I hadn't known right off you were perfectly all right, if I hadn't known I could trust you."

"I do appreciate that."

She smiled at me, and her pretty eyes had a slightly glazed look and they seemed to go in and out of focus. Her hand shook as she lifted the coffee cup. As she put it down she took a high quick shallow breath, shuddered, and her tongue hooked at crumbs that weren't there. Under the brightness of the artificial daylight I saw a little sheen of perspiration on her forehead and upper lip. A gentle sweet steam seemed to be rising from her. She hitched her hips on the stool and said in a huskier tone, "Since my littlest one started school and Harry took to being away politicking here and there, these winter days do seem to get awful long for an outgoing-type person like me."

No trouble diagnosing the problem. She was a little bit scared, and a little bit excited, and she wasn't accustomed to making a pass at a total stranger and she didn't know exactly how to go about it, but Bread Boy had not taken the edge off her and the only thing she could think of was how, without a total loss of all pride and dignity, she could hop back onto that counter top, sans moccasins, stretch jeans, and plain, practical briefs, and get rid of that aching weight, that burden teetering on the brink. She shivered again and gave a high tense artificial laugh and said, "Somebody keeps walking across my grave, I guess."

I looked at my watch and said, getting up quickly, "Holy Maloney, Mrs. Shottlehauster, this has been so pleasant I lost track of the time. I certainly do appreciate your kindness."

"Don't you have time for just one more cup of coffee?"

"I wish I did."

As I drove away from the impressive farm, I tried to tell myself I was a very decent and restrained chap, quite above the shoddy device of rationalizing it as an act of mercy. But I knew I was lying to myself. I knew from a little sense of heaviness in my loins that had I not had that startled moment of peeping tomism, I might possibly have succumbed to the environment, realizing for the first time the grotesque eroticism of a kitchen deed, amid rich good smells of coffee and pies baking and country woman, as if desire had a curious link with the homely processes of hearty food. A brisk and staunch and amiable little woman, fruitful as the land, her needs earnest and simplified and swiftly and with abundant energy gratified, without residual obligation or accusation. Trot off and set herself to rights and come back with the grace to blush a little, then pay off with a pat, a sisterly kiss, more good coffee and another thickly buttered cinnamon pecan roll.

So it had not been restraint after all, not a moral hesitation. It had been just my supercilious sense of my own dignity. McGee could not take over the morning chore where Darling Bread Boy had left off. Fastidiousness. A stuffy sense of social stratum, and of course no chance to exercise that jackassy masculine conviction that the lady would not have yielded to anyone less charming and persuasive.

Every day, no matter how you fight it, you learn a little more about yourself, and all most of it does is teach humility.

I knew something about her too. In any other part of the house it would be a horrified No. What do you think I am? The rest of the house gave her the sense of her value, wife of Harry, mother of six, doer of good deeds. The kitchen was her domain. There any little clinging web of guilt could be swiftly scrubbed away, like a thousand other things spilled and broken. Kitchens took care of simple hungers. Stir, mix, bake, and serve, then clean up the litter, polish, and scrub, and it is bright and new again—as if you hadn't cooked a thing.

I turned the nose of the car into the third of a mile of muddy ruts that led to the Farley farm. I stopped and stared at the road. I patted the slash pocket of the topcoat, feeling the little lump of the Airweight Bodyguard. Six rounds of 158 grain .38 Special. I traveled with it wrapped in a washcloth and tucked into a slightly oversized soap dish. This will not delude professionals. It escapes casual snoopers.

I fed the gas evenly and fought the eagerness of the back end to swing itself into the ditch on either side. Mud slapped up into the fender wells, but I kept the momentum all the way up the gradual slope, speedometer saying thirty and thirty-five, car going about eight or ten. Once over the slight rise the speed began to catch up with the reading, and I eased off and ran on into the dooryard and found a slightly less soggy place to swing around and aim it back out before stopping. I got out and with the motor dead the wet landscape had a silence like being inside a huge gray drum. The air tasted thick. I could hear the hum of my blood in my ears. There was no smoke at the chimney, no face at the window. An old pickup truck stood beside the house. Road salts had rusted fist-sized holes in it.

I squelched my way to the front stoop, stepped up, knocked on the door and said, loudly, "Mr. Faaaaarley! Oh Mr. Faaaaaaaarley!"

Cheery and jolly. Mr. Faaaarley, your kindly insurance agent has come to call, heigh ho.

Nothing.

And so I went around the side of the house prepared to see the empty shed where the salvaged Cadillac had been hidden. I got into mud that grabbed and held. Ruined the shoes. Added ten pounds to each foot and made me walk like a cautious comedy drunk doing the chalk-line bit, and made me sound like a hippo in a swamp. A shed was open. Boards had been ripped away, the door pulled back, hanging at an odd angle from one hinge. It revealed the pale luxury sedan, a front view, the hood up and the doors open.

"Oh, Mr. Faaaaarley! Yooo hoooo!"

My voice seemed to wedge itself into the heavy air, then fall into the mud. I got to the shed and stepped inside, stamped my feet, and had considerable cause for thought. Tools lay about. Somebody had undone, with very little finesse, most of Saul Gorba's work. Interior door panels levered off with pry bars. All the seats ripped loose, dumped out, slashed open. Overhead fabric slashed open and pulled down. The trunk was open. The front end of the car rested on the hubs and the back end was jacked up. All the wheels and the spare lay around, tires deflated, pulled halfway off the rims. The big air filter lay in parts nearby. There was a ripe stink of gasoline. The gas tank had been hacksawed open.

The car was a dead animal. Somebody had opened it up to see what it had been feeding on. There was a sadness about the scene. I could see that Gorba had been working on the car prior to its demolition. He had a set of body and fender tools. He had quart cans of enamel (Desert Dawn Beige), and baking lamps. He had two cans of that plastic guck they use these days to fill the dents. It is cheaper and quicker than beating them out with a rubber mallet and leading the rips and grinding the job to smoothness with a power wheel before sanding and painting. He had packs of sandpaper to smooth the goop down after it hardened.

He had been making it very pretty. There was some masking tape on the back window yet. Everything in the shed had been given the same complete attention as the car. I squelched my way to the house and peered through the windows. Everything I could see had been pried open, broken open, ripped open, and spilled widely. The kitchen was left the way the Three Stooges leave kitchens.

Total silence.

I tried the only other outbuilding with an entire roof on it. The door was open an inch. I pulled it open the rest of the way, using my fingertips on the wooden edge of it, avoiding the metal handle. That kind of silence and that kind of total and ruthless search can teach you a spot of caution.

The door squeaked as it opened. There was a gray and dusty daylight in his little work chamber. And an elusive stink.

He sat on a chair placed against the wall, erect as an obedient child. Hands high, the backs of the hands against the wall. Head up. Can that be you, Mr. Faaarley? How straight you sit! But of course, sir! That leather belt around your chest has been nailed to the studding on either side. And your ankles are wired to the chair legs. And that other band of leather around your forehead has been nailed to the old wood too, with the same kind of galvanized roofing nails, one over each ear, the same ones they drove through your wrists and palms before all the unpleasantness. My goodness, they dropped the cold chisel among your poor teeth, sir. And ripped away your pants for further intimate attentions which have left that faint stink of burning on the silent air. And there is just an ugly crusted paste in one eye socket, poor Mr. Faaaarley, but the other one is whole, a-bulge, and I saw an eye like that when I was very small, and crept on my belly to the edge of the lily pond intending to entice the granddaddy bullfrog to bite on the scrap of red flannel concealing the trout hook.

From the nightly ga-runk, I thought he would be gigantic, and he was, but I was not prepared to part the last curtain of the pond-side grass and find him not eight inches from my face.

And, Mr. Farley, then as now, I stared with awe into one froggy yellow eye. It was not the yellow-predator eye of the great blue heron or the osprey, or the intractable black panther. Its fierceness was not as aimed, not as immediate. Like yours it was a golden eye, and like yours it was a bland and diffuse venom, a final saurian indifference from across the fifty thousand centuries of the days of the great lizards.

One fearful yellow eye. A terrible hatred, so remote and so knowing and so all encompassing that it translates to mildness, to indifference.

Oh, they used you badly, Farley Saul Gorba.

I found myself leaning against the outside of the shed, breathing deeply, my face sweaty in the fifty-degree day, and with an acid taste of coffee in the back of my throat.

I made myself go back in. I made myself touch him. Death had stiffened his body. I could find no wound that could have caused death. But enough pain can burst the heart or blow the wall out of a blood vessel in the brain. And he had been in the hands of someone who enjoyed that line of work.

"Did you tell?" I asked him.

What do you think? said the stare of the froggy eye.

It was a good thing he was stiff, perhaps twelve or more hours dead. But I still had the problem of foot tracks, tire tracks, the motel registration, plenty of soil on shoes and car for analysis, testimony by the brawny bus-girl and the itchy farm wife.

I plodded to my car, only then noticing that the farm truck had been given its share of the attention too.

I put my hand on the door handle and wondered what it was in the back of my mind that was trying to claw its way out. Something did not make any sense. I had seen some contradiction and I did not know what it was.

I moved along the car and, in irritation, thumped a body panel with my fist and felt the metal skin give and spring back.

The thought got through and it brought me up onto my muddy toes like a bird dog. The body and fender tools and the loving care expended on that Cadillac did not jibe with the use of that plastic goop. And somebody must have had some feeling the money was in the car somewhere. I went back to the car in a muddy noisy lope. I saw canvas work gloves on a nail and put them on. I picked a big screwdriver off the floor and with the metal end played a tune along the curve of a front fender. Pang pang pang pank pock tunk. Grab a rubber mallet. Dig the screwdriver end in. Whack. The hardened goop chipped away. It flew out in large chunks. It exposed, barely visible through heavy pliofilm, an oval etching of General Grant. The packet was almost an inch thick.

Pang pang pang pank pock tunk. I got better at it. I

175

put the packets aside. I whistled between my teeth. Lordy me o my, I said. Treasure hunt. Here's another. And another.

Admirable idea. Take the rubber mallet, put a careful ding in the tailored metal wide, long, and deep enough to fit the pliofilmed money-package into it. Pack in the plastic glop and let it harden to hold the money in place. Then sand off the roughness of that first shaping of it to the curve of the metal, paint, and bake.

Gorba had the brains and I had the luck. I worked as hard and fast as I could, dug out eleven packets, couldn't find another place on the body that went tunk instead of pang. I'd had the luck to watch the process one day while roaming around a repair garage, and then to tell the manager what a cheap-ass system it was. He had the kindliness and patience to tell me some of the facts of life. Costs were going up so fast anything more than a gentle nudge would total a car. So be glad there was a new system that would keep the insurance cost from going out of sight a little while longer. If I wanted to complain about something, he said, I should complain about the shyster operators who'd buy one for dimes that had been in a head-on, then scour around for the same year and model that had been crunched hard enough in the rear end to be a total, saw both in half, weld the two good halves together, repaint and sell it a long way from home plate. The plastic just didn't fit the personality of a painstaking man very good with his hands.

I whacked the crumbs of hardened goo off the packets, stowed them in my pockets, ran to the car, carved the mud off my shoes with a sodden piece of wood, and made as good time as I dared driving over to Peru, a small city of about 9000. I put the car in a big gas station in town, told the man to fill it and see if he could hose the worst of the mud off. I bought myself a pair of shoes and, in the dime store, some wrapping paper, twine, tape, and mailing labels. I parked on a quiet street, put on the new shoes, dropped the muddy ones onto the floor in back, packed the money and the gun into the shoe box, wrapped it neatly and solidly, filled out the label, drove to the post office, and mailed it to myself at the Drake. Parcel post. Fifty dollars' insurance. Special handling.

I was hurrying through the things I knew I ought to do because I couldn't find any good handle on the main problem.

The main problem was all too vivid. Country areas have their own kind of radar, and it is as old as man, old as the first villages after he got tired of being a roaming hunter and sleeping in a different tree every night. Once Gorba's mistreated corpse was found, Mildred Shottlehauster would leap into the act, grabbing her little moment of importance, and she would call the sheriff, maybe calling him Ted or Al or Freddy or Hank darling, and tell him about this great tall suntanned pale-eyed fellow driving a such and such, calling himself McGee and talking about a credit investigation and finding out there was nobody at the farm, but maybe he went up there and somebody was there, huh? And when this got around, Brawn-Baby, the gauntleted girl bus driver with the shoulders, would connect and come up with something else, and the ripples in that little pond would finally lap at the doorstep of my Georgian motel where Hank darling would get the license number off the registration.

There was some merit in stopping it dead right at the source, right in Milly's kitchen before she started to make waves. I could hustle back there and make it before lunch, and play it cool, and tell her she'd been so helpful I thought I'd tell her I'd had to turn down the Farley family, and even though she had very probably been slowly turned off by the passage of time, with just a little firmness and insistence she would come back with a rush, and I could finish what Bread Boy had left undone, and later save her face with some sincere and solemn hoke about a sudden attraction so strong we really couldn't help ourselves. And then when she all of a sudden had an overwhelming urge to call Sheriff Darling Dear, doubtless a political buddy of her husband, she would yank her little competent hands back from that phone as if verily it were a snake. They could bring McGee back and he could answer the right question in the wrong way, and the earth would open and the Shottlehausters' farm and hopes would slide slowly in.

Could do. Even had she known Bread Boy for years,

the very basic rationalization was the same, the first hurdle overcome.

Listen, guys, let me tell you about the time I was up in Illinois and there was this little farm wife, six kids, and I'm telling you, I set her onto a counter top and she was as hot as a . . .

Not today, fellows. Not to save the McGee skin. Had I taken the opening being so tentatively and warily offered when I had been with her before, it would have left a tired taste in the mouth and bad air in the lungs and a sorry little picture in the back of the mind. But this was too cold-blooded to be even thinkable.

So, okay, stop off and see Mildred and tell her that I'd gone to the farm and Farley was dead in a very ugly way, and I didn't want to be brought into it, and if I was I'd have to account for all my time in the area, and I'd spent some of that time looking in her kitchen window and reading the legends and persuasions on the Darling truck. Sure. Rub her nose in it. Grind her right into the dirt. She who play kitchen game pay big price sooner or later, hey?

Think a little, you big stupid beach bum!

I finally got the rusty gears working upstairs, popped thumb and finger, and hightailed it for the Shottlehauster farm, rehearsing my end of the dialogue en route.

She was surprised to see me. I exuded total confidence. Something had come up. I needed her help. I'd lied about the credit investigation. Sorry. Have to do that kind of thing sometimes. Line of duty. I sidestepped her questions, borrowed her phone, and made a collect call to Heidi and, with Mildred at my elbow, I asked Heidi to put Susan on.

"Susan? McGee here. The kids have been staying with the Shottlehauster family since Monday evening. They're okay, and they're in school right now. But I think I'd better bring them back to Chicago. I just stopped at the farm. He's there all right. And somebody has killed him. Very unpleasantly."

At my elbow I heard Mildred give a gassy squeak. "Susan?" I said. "Are you all right?"

"I . . . I'm trying to be sorry about him. But I can't."

178

"Now would you do me a favor? Please talk to Mrs. Shottlehauster and ask her to help me get the kids out of the school here. This can be a very ugly thing and they ought to be well out of range. Don't tell her anything about me except she can trust me. Okay?"

I handed Mildred the phone. She stammered and said, "It's a t-terrible thing, dear. I'm so sorry." She listened for a little while and then she said, "Of course, Susan dear. You can depend on me. I'll pack their things and Mr. McGee can bring them along."

After she hung up I ordered her to sit down in her own living room. She was big-eyed and solemn. She said she knew who to call in the school system. She said she was a past president of the PTA.

"Here is what I want you to do. I know you have no training in this sort of thing, but you seem very understanding and intelligent. Here is your story. Susan called you from Chicago. She said a friend would stop by about noon to pick up the things her brothers and sister brought over here, and then go to the school and get them, and would you please arrange it, tell the school it is an emergency. Then she began to cry. You thought Mrs. Farley might be very ill. Mr. Farley had told you both of them were in Chicago. So you asked about Mrs. Farley. Susan then told you that her mother has been missing for three weeks and she thinks something terrible happened to her. So you did as the girl asked. A man came by and picked up the children's things. Just a man. He didn't give a name. But you knew he was all right because of having talked to Susan. Now, do you have a car here that you can use to get up that muddy road at the farm?"

"Harry's old Land Rover will go through anything."

"Do you mind seeing something pretty horrible?"

"I'm not a sissy, Mr. McGee."

"Back to your story. You will go to the farm because you thought Farley acted peculiarly Monday night. You wonder if he is there or Mrs. Farley is there. And you are a little uneasy about having made the arrangements on the word of a seventeen-year-old girl without consulting the parents. You'll find him in the first shed beyond the foundations where the barn was. I think he's been dead

179

since sometime yesterday, but that's just a guess. You will notice that the whole place is ransacked. So you will go to a phone and report it."

She nodded. "To the sheriff. Jimmy Tait. He's an old friend."

"Good. Now then, by the time he gets around to questioning you, I'll be well on my way to Chicago with the kids. You don't know where Susan phoned you from. Suddenly you will remember running into Mrs. Farley a month ago. Think of a logical place. She was tight. She seemed very upset. She talked strangely. It didn't make any sense to you. Something about the Outfit, and something about her husband thinking she was going to fink out, and something about pushers."

Solemn as a library child she said, "Outfit. Fink out. Pushers."

"And then she said something about old farms having their own graveyards and laughed in a crazy way."

"But why do you want me to say all that?"

"Mrs. Shottlehauster. Mildred. If you were trained in this work you could go ahead without question. But I am going to take the chance of telling you what we think. Believe me, it will cause me serious trouble if you tell anyone this. Your husband, anyone at all. We believe Farley is a known criminal. We have no I.D. yet. Last Sunday Farley made advances to Susan."

"His own daughter!" Scandal made her eyes sparkle.

"Only the smallest one is his."

"Tommy."

"Yes. When she resisted him, he beat her badly. She didn't let the other kids see her condition. She took a bus to Chicago Monday evening. She came to us and told us she believed Farley had killed her stepmother three weeks ago and buried her somewhere on the farm. She said Farley was hiding out there, and she had no idea why. I was sent to look things over. You know the rest."

"It's so terrible. Those nice kids!"

I looked at her with a firm official frown. "When you know things other people don't, Mildred, it's a terrible temptation to tell so that you can feel important. I trust you to resist that impulse. Your only reward will be the knowledge you lived up to your obligation as a good citizen. That will be in our files, but we can't thank you in any public way."

"Pusher means about drugs, doesn't it?"

"Please don't ask me any more questions because I've already told you more than I'm authorized to tell."

She glowed with her new responsibility. Her little jaw firmed up with resolve. She would hug her secret closely, cherishing the knowledge she was in our files. In my flush of success with her, I had the eerie temptation to tell her I was the man from A.U.N.T. Association Uncovering the Narcotics Traffic. But there is a limit to what you can make them buy.

She jumped to her feet. "I'll phone the school and then I'll pack their things, sir."

"Forgive me for lying to you the last time I was here?"

"Oh yes! You've got a *job* to do."

twelve

Five days later, on Monday morning a little after ten, I sat in John Andrus' office at the bank. A quiet paneled room. We were alone. The door was closed. He had told his girl to hold his calls. He was troubled. He frowned, sighed, shook his head.

"It's a very awkward situation," he said for the third time.

"It doesn't have to be. Just keep it clear in your mind what we keep on the record and what we keep off the record."

"As a trust officer I have certain . . ."

"I know, John. Fiduciary responsibilities. I gave you every last dollar I chipped out of that damned car."

"One hundred and seventy-eight thousand, six hundred

and fifty dollars. How am I supposed to account for it? How did I get it? Where's the other four hundred and twenty thousand?"

"You worry too much. Let's take it one at a time. I told you Janice Stanyard will lie beautifully if she has to. Geis gave her a package to hold for him. She forgot about it. She found it the other day on her closet shelf, opened it, found all the money, contacted Heidi at once, and Heidi said to bring it to you."

"Fine," he said wearily. "Wonderful."

"And when the estate is appraised next October, if the tax boys get sticky about it, you call that number I gave you, and you will get three characters who'll swear that for over a year the Doctor was going over to Gary once or twice a month and playing high-stakes poker in a fast game and losing very very heavily. That is, if we don't turn up the rest of the money somehow in the meantime. Which doesn't look likely. Those three will give you an expert performance, and nobody will break them down."

Staring at me he shook his head in mild wonder. "Where did you develop contacts like that, damn it? How can you so blandly and so confidently come up with people perfectly willing to perjure themselves about something that doesn't concern them at all?"

"I did a favor for a local operator once. He's the type who stays grateful. Maybe local is the wrong word. This is home base. He operates in a lot of areas. John, if nobody comes up with any more of Fort's money, how does the estate thing stand?"

He hesitated and then said, "Rough estimate. Seventy-five for Gloria and half that for each kid, Heidi and Roger.

"Nice if I could have picked up the whole thing out there. Or if they had found anything when they took the place apart, inch by inch. Of course it would have been a rough go proving it was Fort's money if they'd found the rest of it, but you could have swung it."

"Vote of confidence. Hah!"

"John, there's just too many possibilities. He took a lot of little trips. So he was stashing it elsewhere. Or whoever came after him, maybe because he talked just a little bit too much about making a nice score, found everything except what I found. I think it's over. They identified him as Saul Gorba. They know he had an aneurysm that blew under the high blood pressure pain gives you. They assume that whoever worked on him left with what they'd come for. It is obvious Gorba was hiding out. And it is a safe assumption he strangled Gretchen and buried her five feet under, suitcase and all. And they know the kids don't know anything about anything. Murder first, felony murder, by person or persons unknown. We got a little back. We pick up the pieces, the world goes on."

"Wonder why he killed Gretchen?"

"Maybe because she kept wondering where the money was coming from, and even though she wasn't too bright, she had been given enough twos to add to twos over a long time, and when the answer began to show, she didn't like it. She was an amiable earthy slob, but she wasn't crooked. And putting leverage on a dying man is pretty ugly. Or maybe he just decided the daughter looked a lot better. We'll never know."

"One comment, Trav. It really surprised me to have Heidi pick up the tab for that double funeral."

And one of the eeriest ones I had attended. Saturday afternoon. Two boxes. One floral piece on each one. Select little group. The five towheads. Gretch must have had muscular genes. The kids all looked alike. Fair, blue-eyed, round-faced, sturdy. Seeing them together it was an astonishment that Susan had been able to sustain her personal myth of a different parentage. In dark glasses, dark hat and veil, Susan's damages were obscured. So it was the kids and Janice and Heidi and John Andrus and Anna Ottlo and me, and a sonorous voice reading a standard service, and a tired woman diddling with the keys on a small electric organ. Anna whuffawed and snuffled and grunted her anguish. Some tears were shed for Saul Gorba, the tears of Tommy, his natural child. Most of his were for Gretchen, but he had some for Saul. There had been a relationship between them not shared by the others.

"Maybe Heidi Trumbill is mellowing. John, thanks for getting the law boys onto it and getting that money turned loose for Susan."

"She should get it by tomorrow."

"And thanks for getting the court order set up to have the kids stay with Janice."

"On this money, Trav, I have to escrow it until the estate appraisal is firm next October, but Gloria can borrow against it right here if she needs to. She ought to know that."

"When I see her this afternoon I'll see if I can get it through to her."

In a lounge at the hospital, in a low voice Dr. Hayes Wyatt explained it in layman's terms. "Think of the senses of sight, touch, smell, hearing, taste as being receptors, Mr. McGee. They have no analytical function. Think of a bundle of wires running from each receptor to the part of the brain which acts as a computer. The psychedelics are disassociative in that they loosen these customary connections between receptors and the analysis function. Messages become false and the analysis unreal. Hallucination. As the period of disassociation ends the connections grow tight again and the subject comes back into his familiar reality. The massive overdose she took tore all the wiring loose. It has to be fitted back, slowly and carefully. To continue the analogy you can say the wiring is hanging free and it is in approximately the right areas, so it touches and brushes the proper connection quite often. But there is a continual hallucination which of course creates terror, so it is best to keep her mildly tranquilized. There are motor defects. She will say a nonsense word when she means to say something quite different. This alarms her too. I think there is a certain amount of progress. I don't know how long it will continue, or if she will ever get all of the way back."

"Why did she do it?"

"She remembers wanting to take some. She can't remember the actual act. Possibly she is a semi-addictive, and even though LSD-25 is not physiologically habit-forming, the addictive personality has a tendency to overdose himself with any escape drug when depressed. She would be dead, of course, if you hadn't found her when you did. Even then it was terribly terribly close. Try to be perfectly natural with her. Cheerful. Confident. Ignore anything she says or does which seems out of line."

So I saw her, and her smile came and went too quickly and her eyes were strange. She called me Trav and she called me Howie, and she got scared of something on the bed I couldn't see. She dug her nails into my wrist and told me in a weak voice, "The cliffs are crooked near the edge. They wouldn't be that way home. They don't stop them here. They don't care."

I smiled my cheery way out and stopped a little way down the corridor and leaned against the wall, feeling more years than I had, more sourness than I was due.

I hunted up Hayes Wyatt and said, "So wouldn't she be able to hook those wires up faster where she knew what the hell she was looking at, where she knew the smells and the way things feel, and the sounds?"

"Home? Yes, of course, that would be useful, I think. But I understand that as a practical matter she can't afford the care she'd need there, much less maintain the house, so I haven't . . ."

"But you'd approve it?"

"Certainly, but not right away. A week from now perhaps, with a guarantee she'd be taken . . ."

So I hauled Janice Stanyard and Susan down to John Andrus' office. I gave my pitch. "The house is up for sale. Glory's personal stuff is in storage. Anna Ottlo has gone to Florida. Okay. The court recommended to Mrs. Stanyard here that she find a bigger place. Susan here has the annuity income. Gloria has the insurance income, and she can borrow against the seventy-five she's got coming if she has to. And Mrs. Stanyard has certain . . . resources. Financial. Aside from being a trained nurse."

"Which I insist be used for Susan and the others," Janice said with great firmness and dignity.

"And," I continued, "Dr. Hayes Wyatt says that Gloria's chances are going to be a lot better in familiar surroundings. The house is big enough. It's a fine house, a fine location. So it makes a crazy menage any way you look at it, but what I say is that Janice and Susan and Glory dump everything into the pot and dig in there, and everything has a lot better chance of working out all the way around."

So Susan scowled and scowled and then slowly lit up. The last stains of brutality were almost faded away. "Hey!" she said softly. "Hey now!"

And Janice said, "It just might . . ."

And John said, "I could see my way clear . . ."

Hayes Wyatt fudged the estimate of time by one day so

we could bring her home in the early afternoon on Christmas Day. Heidi and Janice and I and the kids had trimmed the tree the night before. And on the previous day, on Friday the 23rd, I had lost my wits, my judgment, and my self-control in Carson, Pirie, Scott.

She sat in a big chair, blanketed and feet up, and smiled and smiled and smiled, and had some bad times but not as many as we had been told to expect. John Andrus and wife stopped by, gift-bearing. So did Hayes Wyatt and wife. So, to my surprise, did Roger and Jeanie Geis and their kids. But Heidi told me on the side that she had gone and roughed brother up pretty good. He didn't like it, but he was there. He endured it. He wore a little obligatory smile.

Janice and Susan and Freddy, the oldest boy, had done a great job of settling them all in.

And so, all turkeyed up and tuckered out, I took the thoughtful snow maiden back to her shelter at 180 East Burton Place, and when she tried to end the evening with a friendly social handshake, I dug her private and special gift out of the car trunk and said that he who bears gifts gets a nightcap. And then she looked even more thoughtful and said she had a gift for me, so I should come on up, but give her a minute or two to wrap it.

Drinks made, she went off and came back in no more than a minute with a plain white envelope. In red ink on the front of it she had written, "A Merry Christmas to Travis McGee." In green ink she had drawn a small Christmas tree the way children draw them, in jagged outline.

She sat with brandy snifter in hand, my gift to her on her lap, and said, "You first. It wasn't going to be a gift. Maybe it isn't a gift, really."

I thumbed my gift open. Pale blue bank check. Certified. Eighteen thousand seven hundred and fifty dollars.

"What the hell, Heidi!"

"Why don't you just say thanks?"

"But you're under no oblig . . ."

"Hush. You explained it all to me. Half is better than nothing at all. You made the deal with Gloria, but you didn't go through with it. And Roger certainly wouldn't let go of twenty cents of his when he finally gets it. And out of family pride I just couldn't have you going around thinking of this as the Geis disaster. Please don't get all stuffy and noble and turn it down."

"Okay. So I accept it. Thank you very much. But only on condition that I lay a very good morsel of it on our little venture, yours and mine."

She went pale and her mouth trembled and she said, "But we aren't really going to . . ."

"Open your present, girl."

Her hands shook as she loosened the ribbons and the metallic paper. She stared down into the box. After she had unwrapped, in turn, the sun lotion, the giant beach towel, the big black sunglasses, the little beach coat, she had begun a dangerously hysterical giggling. And when she undid the last item, a bright bawdy little bikini that could probably have been packed into a shot glass without too much of it protruding, she stared at me and said, "But I couldn't ever wear . . . ever wear . . . anything . . . anything like . . ."

So hysteria was suddenly tears. Hands to the face. Gifts spilling. The wrenching hopeless hoohaw of vocalized anguish. Went to the lady. Brushed gifts out of the way. Picked her up by the elbows, sat in her chair, lowered her back down onto the lap, hiked her long legs over the chair arm, wedged resistant head into side of my neck, held tight. Said, "There there. There there now."

No gossamer she. Respectable girl-weight, bearing down on cushiony-warm bottom, all misty, humid, solid, sweet that bundle of tears, sob-time, fright. All unresponsive flesh, like those store-window dummies now fashioned of some kind of yielding plastic which you can bend slowly into a new position which they will maintain. No answers in the flesh. No questions. Dull plastic acceptance.

So as she slowly quieted there on that Christmas night, I graded my own final examinations in my own version of a severe Calvinistic morality. Maybe we all mete out to ourselves our little rewards and punishments according to our very private and unique systems of guilt and self-esteem. I had the fatuous awareness of having earned this lovely and inhibited bundle thrice over, by not slipping up on Gloria's blind side in a parody of comforting the widow that evening after I had first arrived and when in the ember-light we were both aware of all the small ways of saying yes, and by not accepting the full measure of Maurie Ragna's total hospitality and by not counter-topping the intensity and diligence of little Mrs. Shottle-hauster as had been inadvertently observed, an act which came complete with rationalization.

So when you skip the cream pie and pass up the chocolate shake and deny yourself the home fried, you begin to think that, by God, you have a right to the Cherries Jubilee.

Tears ended, she rested apprehensive upon me with all the nervous tensions of a jump-club recruit as the airplane makes its circling climb, and I knew that this was the wrong time and the wrong place and a certain guarantee of failure. So I set her on her feet, kissed the salttasty cheek, looked into evasive eyes, and said, "Sleep well. Get up and pack."

"But . . ."

"Pack!"

The tenth day of February. Three o'clock in the afternoon. Beach cottage. St. Croix. Sun coming through yellow draperies into the bedroom. Rental Sunbeam outside the door. Little sailboat pulled up onto the private beach. Excellent hotel a ten-minute walk away.

I awoke from the nap which was getting to be an almost insidious habit with us. Eyes half shut, I did some sleepy arithmetic and discovered it was our forty-sixth day of residence.

In the subdued golden afternoon light, Heidi came into my range of vision, elegantly nude, smoothly beach-browned swim-browned, sailing browned, topdown browned except for the narrow bikini areas which, when she had decided they were a sickly white, she had toasted to gold on the little walled patio off the living room. She started to walk past the full-length mirror set into the closet door, caught sight of herself apparently, stopped, and inspected herself solemnly, carefully, from head to toe. She faced it head on, and then without moving her feet, turned to present left profile and then right profile to the mirror. The tension made long firm flowing lovely lines, a complexity of curves from earlobe to delicate ankle.

There is an elegance of total unity, and an elegance in the smallest physical details of a truly great pussycat, a truly fantastic bird. Fine-grained texture of the skin everywhere. Little fold of the upper lid, curves and pads of the fingers, jeweler's precision of eyelash and brow. It is an elegance that makes for mystery somehow, so that finally the most complete intimacy merely hints at intimacies beyond, at promises unreachable.

She faced herself squarely again, brushed pale hair back with both hands. Sun and salt and wind had bleached it and coarsened the texture of it. She frowned at herself, underlip protruding. She patted her tummy and sucked it in. She squared her shoulders and, still frowning, cupped a hand under each breast, lifting it slightly. She took a step back, dropped her hands, tilted her head slightly, and then nodded at herself and gave herself such a broad, delighted, fatuous grin I nearly laughed aloud.

"Great merchandise," I said.

She whirled and stared aghast at me, mouth open. "Peeping tom!" she said. "Lousy peeping thomas!" Then came at me in a swift hippy hoyden run and pounced. After taking a certain amount of cruel punishment I managed to pin her wrists. She lay panting and grinning at me. The grin faded. I knew it was safe to release her. She nestled close and said, "It's what you kept saying, you know. About liking myself inside and out. Because if you can't there's nothing you can be proud of to give anybody, or share. It always used to make me feel crawly in a funny way to look at myself like that. Now I say Hey look! He likes it. It gets him all worked up. So it must be pretty good. And I own it. But, my God, Trav darling, I gave you a wretched time. Bless you. You are an infinitely patient man."

I held her quietly and thought once more of that descriptive cliché of comparing women to sports cars and violins and such, responsive to the hands of the master. What she reminded me of was the old yellow Packard phaeton with the Canadà goose on the radiator and the wire wheels which I had bought for sixteen dollars, a single-shot .22, and a block of Lindbergh airmail stamps during the year before I was going to be old enough to get a permit to drive. My father raised such hell about having that piece of junk in the yard, I spent all my time at first giving it the coats of paint, rubbing them down, fixing the rotten canvas, mending the torn leather seats, haunting the graveyards to find replacement parts.

I had thought that with the service manual on that year and model, I could get it started without much trouble. I finally got it to the point where everything was in order. Valve springs, fuel pump, coil, distributor, spark plugs, carburetor, jets, clutch plate, air filter. I'd sit in tense anticipation behind the big wheel, turn the key, step on the starter, fiddle with the choke, and it would go wheery-yurry, wheery-yurry, wheery-yurry, wheery-yurry. Not a cylinder would fire. And finally it would go yurry, yurry, yurry . . . yug.

Then I would walk up the hill behind the house and sit alone and stare desolately out over the valley and suck my barked knuckles and quietly despise the whole concept of the internal combustion engine. Then I would take the battery out again, put it in the red tin wagon of my younger days, and wheel it three blocks to the gas station for a slow charge, and endure stoically the gibes and taunts of the cretins at the gas station.

Then one day when I least expected it, she fired and turned over. For maybe eleven magical seconds she popped, banged, shuddered, and gasped before she stalled out. The next day it was almost twenty seconds. I was able to stop hating her because it seemed to me that that yellow Packard had a personality and that it had astonished her as much as me, and she was saying, in effect, "So *that's* what you've been after." When I had begun to despair of ever keeping her running, or ever getting her out of the back yard on her own power, I found that the firing order was wired up wrong, and after fixing that, I found that a lubricant with graphite in it had hardened on the bakelite outside of the distributor cap and some of the impulses were shorting down the outside of the cap.

Then came the day when I tried and thought it had not caught and then became aware of the deep hum of vibration I could feel through my fingertips on the steering wheel. Foot on gas pedal, I ran her up through the rpm's to such a roar of even, full-throated power it awed me. From then on, perfectly tuned, she would start at the slightest touch on the starter. I drove her when I passed my test. She and I went humming through many nights on the small back roads, taking the curves and grades in a perfect harmony. . . .

But now in all that golden light the holding had become nothing that could be called quiet, and in the strong and languid grace of sensuality totally aroused she turned and arched in presentation of self, her eyes huge in that listening look that measures the great slow clock of the body, and in the first taking of the gift her eyes closed, her mouth opened askew with tongue curled back, and she made a long soft vocalized exhalation, the haaaaaaah of small triumph, of search and finding. Then with a growly little she-lion chuckle, she shifted and settled and braced herself for the journey.

That night we drank, we ate, we danced one dance at the hotel, and came walking back along the beach, hand-holding, shoes in the spare hand, walking in the wet where the tide had run out.

We sat on the fiberglass deck of the canted sailboat and looked at the stars. "What can scare you," she said, "when you squeak through, when you know how narrow the escape was, is all the crazy accidents and coincidences that got you to where you are. You let me out of a dark room. I'd have stayed in there thinking it was just as dark everywhere. Son of a gun! If you hadn't found Gloria long ago and put her back together, if she hadn't gotten a job at that place where Daddy was staying . . . It can drive you out of your mind. There were so many choices and you don't know why, really, they went one way instead of another way. Even take something like Daddy not marrying Gretchen. It could have gone either way. Oh, how all the tongues would have flapped! But that wouldn't have bothered him. He was too busy to care what people thought."

I got up restlessly and walked about ten feet, sat on my heels, scooped up sand, and drifted it through my fingers.

"Is something the matter?"

"I don't know."

"Travis, for a week at least you've been going off somewhere. I have to repeat things I say. May I say something?"

"Why not?"

"If you're getting broody about this girl, don't waste yourself. I love you and I always will, in a special and private and personal way that is sort of . . . off to one side of what the rest of my life is going to be. One day this ends and I go back and I tear my painting all the way down to bedrock, and then I put it together again with some life and juice and fire in it, and I am going to look up and there is going to be some great guy there who wants the kind of life I want, and we are going to breed up some fat babies, and laugh a lot, and get old and say it was all great right up to the end."

"I wasn't worried about you turning into an albatross, kid. I'm worried about all the little things that didn't fit right. That Gorba thing is over and it isn't over. I got some answers. I got some salvage. I missed part of it. When you said that your father might have married Gretchen, I got a little resonance off that. Maybe she would have made him a good little wife. She got along with you and your brother. And she had her mama there to keep things to rights. Anna Ottlo had her widower employer in a great bind. But she worked out an alternate choice, the Kemmer boy. Why?"

"Well, wouldn't you say it was just that sort of . . . humility of the Old-World German? Respect for the learned doctor?"

"But she was in the New World where things are not the same. And you always want a better deal for your kids than you got."

"She was very harsh with Gretchen."

"And damned indifferent to her own grandchildren. It doesn't fit that . . . kind of hearty, hausfrau cook-up-a-storm image. Flour on the elbows, goodies in the oven, house clean as a whistle."

"Maybe she knew Daddy would never stand still for it."

"That's not my image of him. I think he had quite a load of guilt out of pronging that girl-child while your mother was dying, and the pregnancy meant more guilt, and marriage would have cleared it all off the books."

"Does it really make any difference?"

"With no life of her own really, except through your father, who was a damned busy man, and probably used the house the way other men use a residential club, you'd think Anna would want to be closer to her own daughter and the grandbabies."

"Oh, I think she had *something* else going for her."

"What do you mean?"

"I hadn't thought of it in a long time. Roger was home from school on vacation. He went to some kind of a party and then he went to a place where people parked and smooched. When he left he turned his lights on too soon. That's bad form. Lo and behold, they shone into a car and right on Anna. He didn't see the man. The next day he tried to kid her about it. She took such a clout at him it scared him. He barely got his face out of the way. She had a grater in her hand and he told me it would have taken the hide and meat off right down to the bone. He said it scared her too. She cried and said it was because she was so insulted. She was a decent woman. She did not do things like that or go to such places. He told me he was positive it was Anna. But he didn't try to argue the point or kid her about it, not after that first time. She was very upset. We agreed that she'd probably been out there. It seemed pretty hilarious that she should have a boyfriend. I'm just telling this to show that . . . she could have had other emotional outlets. I know *we* weren't one. She kept us warm, clean, and fed, and that was it."

"She was apparently very fond of Gloria. But she didn't tell Gloria that Gretchen and Gorba had made it legal, and she didn't tell her that better relations had been established and that she was visiting the family almost every Sunday."

"She was never one for talking about herself. I remember when we were studying World War II and the rise of National Socialism I tried to get her to tell me about Germany when Hitler took over before the war started and she just wouldn't talk about it. She said it was too sad and terrible. She said that she and Gretchen had been in a camp for a while and it was better to forget such things. Her husband and all her other relatives were dead and she wanted to forget it, not talk about it."

So I dropped it, admired the stars. We stacked our clothes on the sailboat and went skinny-dipping, and then went into the dark cottage and rinsed off the salt in a shared shower, and scrambled into the hasty bed.

As I was bobbling along in that dark current toward sleep Heidi walked her fingers along my chest and said, "Mister? You awake?"

"Oh, come *on!*"

"Don't leap to conclusions, friend. You haven't got the strength. I just remembered something. When we were helping get the house shaped up for Gloria to come back from the hospital, I was talking to Susan about the young kids, about relatives and so on. I asked about Freddy's grandmother Kemmer in Florida and if she'd let her know that her ex daughter-in-law had died. And Susan said that Karl Kemmer's mother had died back in nineteen sixty or sixty-one. So I said I was positive that was who Anna had gone to visit in Florida, her old friend. Susan said it must have been some other Kemmer. I was going to ask Gloria about it if she seemed up to that kind of talk, and then I forgot it completely until now."

So I was awake. Awake a long time. She drifted off. She purred into my throat. Her arm twitched and she muttered something. When I made the decision, I fell asleep. I told her in the morning over second coffee. Her face fell, but she tried to whip up a gallant smile.

"No, dear girl. Just because we check out of here doesn't mean you're going to get away just yet. I've got a shamefully neglected houseboat sitting up there in Fort Lauderdale, neglected mostly on account of you. You're going to earn your keep. You're going to learn how to chip and scrape and sand and paint, and when *The Busted Flush* looks brand-new, you can go back to Illinois."

The smile became real. "I work cheap. Board and bed."

"So okay. Start packing."

"You know, you keep saying that."

thirteen

Communication was far simpler back on the mainland.

I phoned Glory from the lounge of the *Flush* on Sunday a little before noon. She sounded a little more like herself, but uncertain, subdued.

"But where are you, Trav?"

"Back aboard the *Flush*. Taking my ease. There's a tall exhausted blonde puttering around in the background scouring the copper pots and muttering about mildew on the cabin curtains."

"We've all enjoyed her crazy . . . postcards. Darn it, I have to keep reaching for words."

"Otherwise?"

"Not so bad. Some bad little spots. Like the other day I was looking in the bathroom mirror and my face just started to sort of melt and slide off. It's like . . . parts of nightmares happen in the daytime. Heidi sounds happy as a clam."

"I beat her when she gets out of line. I'll let you say hello in a minute. Look, what I called about, where did Anna go?"

"That's a strange thing, Travis. I just don't *know*. I had an address she left, care of Mrs. Hans Kemmer in Winter Haven, and I wrote there and it came back address unknown, and then Susan said that Mrs. Kemmer died years ago. It's weird, isn't it?" .

"Very."

"I have a nightmare about her, over and over. She keeps clapping her hands in front of my face and telling me I'm burning up, that my skin is getting so hot I'm going to set fire to anything I get near."

"Maybe it was the fever you ran. How's your group there?"

"Great. Really great!"

I summoned Heidi onto the line. She took the phone and, talking, slid onto the long yellow couch and ended up in a teen-age posture, on her stomach, propped up on her elbows, sheaf of pale hair obscuring the phone, upright calves slowly scissoring. She wore white work pants with old paint stains thereon. The soles of her bare feet were dusty. One of the two snaps was undone on the back of her bandana halter. She and Glory compared climates, and she told Glory that St. Croix was the absolute of all time. I sat and watched her and pondered the disappearance of Anna Ottlo. When I paid attention again, Heidi was talking to Susan. I looked at her slender brown back between halter and waistband, at the almost invisible sunwhitened fuzz along that graceful curve that deepened and then lifted to the bisected heartiness of the splendid bottom. I felt the inner wrench, the sideways slide, the feeling there was not quite enough air in the whole lounge to fill the lungs of McGee. I moved over and wedged beside her and she slid over to make room. I ran a slow thumb down the crease of the strong back across the little knots of the vertebrae. Her breath caught and broke in the middle of a word and picked up again and when I rested my hand quietly upon her I felt that inner humming that had begun, like the inaudible idling of the great engine of the yellow car of long long back.

Keep this one, I thought. It'll keep well. It has one hell of a shelf life.

At the final good-bye, I popped the single snap with my thumbnail and the two halves of the halter slid away. She faked collapse, face down. "Nothing but work, work, work," she grumbled. "Jeeez!" Then rolled around grinning to reach out with both arms, and the phone bumped onto the rug and was tugged toward the desk by the coiled accordion phone wire.

Monday morning I phoned Dr. Hayes Wyatt and he phoned back in a half-hour and I found out he had not heard Glory's dream about Anna Ottlo. He said she was coming along nicely and if she could keep on coming back at the present rate, she should be quite herself by June. The dream interested him. I asked some questions.

"Yes, Mr. McGee, under any of the psychedelics the subject is extraordinarily suggestible. If she could be made to believe that her body heat was such that her clothes and the things around her were beginning to smolder, she might very well run out onto that winter beach, shedding her clothes."

"What about the hand clapping?"

"Yes. Acceptable technique to capture and hold the attention long enough for the suggestion to be made and accepted."

I looked down at my brown hand at the two pale little puncture marks, still visible, the scars from the bite of the terrified thing in the howl of wind on that beach. I explained the curious thing we had learned about Anna. I asked him if he could find out if Gloria could remember anything that could have happened the morning of that day or the evening of the day before which might have given Anna some cause. He said he would try, but if Gloria began to get agitated he would have to wait for another time.

When the call came through at four o'clock, Heidi was over on the beach with a hairy friend of mine named Meyer. The wind had died and the Florida day had warmed up, but not enough for swimming. When Meyer had first seen her he had shaken his head slowly from side to side. He had clucked. He had sighed. He had said, "Now if *Vogue* only used a centerfold girl." He pointed a thumb at me, his eyes still on hers. "That one. He shouldn't have such luck. He shouldn't have such good taste. He brings you around and all of a sudden I am a bitter old man."

In resignation he had put his hand out, and she had laughed, moved in, kissed him a good hearty smack, and said, "I hate shaking hands with bitter old men, Meyer."

"I swoon," he had said. He offered his arm. "Come with me to a saloon. I need sustenance. Let this aging beach boy here stew in his own jealous venom." And off they had gone, laughing, the best of friends. Instant Meyer.

Dr. Hayes Wyatt called back and apologized about being tied up and not getting to me sooner. "But I don't have much. It's all pretty shadowy in her memory. Seems she got up very early that morning. Much earlier than usual. And she found Mrs. Ottlo in Fort's study, sitting at his desk, just putting a handwritten letter and some kind of legal document into an envelope. As she was holding it, running her tongue along the flap, the envelope was toward the doorway, a pre-printed business address, quite gaudy. All she can remember is something like Mark Bay or Macko Bay, and a palm tree, and a row of airmail stamps. When she saw Gloria, she started violently and slapped the envelope face down onto the desk. She seemed agitated. That's all. I'm sorry."

"Not much to go on."

In the middle of the night something came sliding into my mind and slid right out again before I could grab hold of it. At breakfast I caught a glimpse of an edge of it in the back of my mind and caught it before it could get away and pulled it into sight.

Your retirement paradise! A planned community for the senior citizen. Live the golden years in the golden way. And it wasn't Mark or Macko, but she had been close. Marco Bay and Marco Bay Isles, between the mysterious Everglades and the glorious Gulf. Marco Bay Development Corporation.

"What's with you?" Heidi demanded. "Something wrong with the eggs, dammit?"

"They are beautiful eggs and you are a beautiful girl and I think I can lay a hand on Anna Ottlo. We're going for a nice long ride."

"But we were going to go fishing with Meyer, honey."

So we stopped and told Meyer it was off. I said we were going over to Marco Bay, between the mysterious Everglades and the glorious Gulf, to see if, perchance, a good cook I had met in Chicago had settled herself there to live the golden years in the golden way.

We took a cab over to the garage. Heidi was enchanted with my old stately transportation, name of Miss Agnes, one of the really big old Rolls-Royces. She had suffered a curious trauma, perhaps during the Great Depression, when somebody had converted her into a pickup truck and painted her bright blue.

In the bright clear cool morning we struck west across the Tamiami Trail, sitting high above the squatty and more frangible products of later years, Miss Agnes going along with stately rumble and faint wind-hiss, floating up to her mild and amiable eighty miles an hour when I had clear pieces of road.

And so at eleven-thirty I parked in a broad lot next to the sales office of the Marco Bay Development Corporation. I left Heidi by the truck and went into the office. It looked like functional slices of three kinds of jet aircraft fastened together with aluminum windows. The salesmen weren't in. A Miss Edgerly was. She was all wrists, eyebrows, and big rabbity teeth, and determined to be helpful if it killed both of us.

"Gee now. From Chicago in late December." She went trotting from file to file. She was about eleven inches across the shoulders and forty inches across her secretarial butt, making the pink blouse and madras shorts less than totally attractive.

"With a thick German accent? Gee now. Well, heck, I can check it by date but that's about the last way left." She riffled through more files, pulled out a sheet. "Gee now, actually the only sale from the Chicago area was Mr. and Mrs. Hennigan, and that was just on account of our handling the resale of the Torbadill house at the end of Citrus Lane. Poor Mrs. Torbadill had . . . well, catering to an older group we often have to handle the resale of some very excellent properties."

I knew why she looked distressed. It's the old sun-city syndrome. Instead of fun in the sun in the golden years the oldsters find they've locked themselves into a closed society with a mortality rate any combat infantry battalion would find impressive. You have to make friends fast because they aren't going to be around long. Spooks in the sunshine. Change the club rosters once a week. For Sale signs sprout as fast as the pretty tropical flowers and trees.

"I guess that's it," she said. "I'm terribly sorry. Over here are some pictures at the Welcome Party. Everybody who moves into Marco Bay has a Welcome Party at the Golf and Tennis Club. I think this is . . . yes, this is Mrs. Hennigan." And with the eraser end of her yellow pencil she tapped the fleshy smiling face of Anna Ottlo. "But of course she just doesn't fit the sort of person you are describing." She leaned close, squinting to read the typed legend taped to the bottom edge of the glossy color print. "Perry and Wilma Hennigan are retireds from Chicago, all right."

"I suppose there's the off chance they might know where the other lady is, if they know her at all. Long as I'm here I might as well ask. How do I get to . . ."

"Well, hey, come look here at our wonderful map that's just been brought up to date!"

It was so big I hadn't seen it. Vivid green plaster for the grass. Blue mirror glass for water, in the bay, the canals, the community pools, the private pools. Some kind of gray flexible strip for the roads, complete to yellow center line.

I followed the pencil eraser. "Right down Mainway all the way to Grapetree Circle, and then three quarters of the way around it and down Osprey Lane to the end where it runs into Citrus Lane, and then take your right and go to the end." She bounced the eraser off the roof of an L-shaped house on a point of land that jutted into the bay. Most of the houses sat shoulder to shoulder. The one she indicated, and a very few others, had a lot of lateral privacy. "You can't miss it!" she cried, spinning toward me, beaming, and smelling of peppermint.

"Looks pretty elaborate."

"Oh, it *is*! It's one of our Adventure in Living series, the biggest one. Tropic Supreme. It's thirty-one thousand nine hundred and ninety-nine, plus the lot, but including closing costs and title insurance, and the poor Torbadills added the Kingway Pool, a second Florida room, and marvelous, absolutely marvelous plantings. They picked one of the choicest pieces of land, and they bought these three additional lots for privacy. They furnished it beautifully too. Why, I would say they had at least, at the very *least*, sixty thousand in it. It's really the nicest home in the entire development. And just when they had it exactly the way they wanted it, poor Mrs. Torbadill . . . well, that's another story, isn't it?"

"The Hennigans must be pretty well-heeled too."

"It was a fantastic bargain, actually. Forty-nine five for *everything,* even including the boat poor Mr. Torbadill bought and only used twice."

"It still adds up to big monthly bite though."

"I heard they paid a *considerable* part of it in cash."

"You've been very helpful, Miss Edgerly."

"That's what we're here for. To be of service."

When I went back out to the lot, Heidi was standing leaning against Miss Agnes, hands in her skirt pockets, ankles crossed. When someone has become very dear it is rare that you get a chance to see them anew, as though for the first time. I saw her before she saw me approaching. She stood there in her relaxed and slender elegance, chin up, expression cool, looking perfectly capable of buying the entire project and moving everybody out and building herself a castle.

I told her the whole bit. "Darling," she said, "are you quite certain it was Anna?"

"Positive."

"But how absolutely *weird*!"

"So we find out what goes on."

I drove the route pointed out to me. A pickup truck means a service call, even if the basic vehicle happened to cost three thousand pounds back in the days when a pound was worth five dollars. So the glances were casual. The separate generations belong together. No matter how lush the flowerbeds, how spirited the bridge games, the shuffleboard competitions, the golf rivalries—nor how diligently the Hobby Center turns out pottery waterbirds, bedspreads and shell ashtrays, this kind of isolation still makes a geriatric ghetto where, in the silence, too many people listen to their own heartbeats.

I had noticed a small community bayfront park at the intersection of Osprey Lane and Citrus Lane, so I pulled in there and turned Agnes off and reached across Heidi into the back of the shallow shelf under the glove compartment and took out the little canvas zipper case, extracted the Bodyguard, and worked it into my right-hand pants pocket.

"To see Anna Ottlo?" she said incredulously.

"Hear dem bells. In the back of my head. Better safe

than sorry. A stitch in time. A penny saved. Hell, dear, I'm cowardly."

"But clean."

"You wait here. Think pretty thoughts. Paint a painting in your head."

Circular drive. Double carport. Dark blue Buick station wagon in one stall. Power mower and golf cart in the other. Drops from the sprinkler pattering off elephant ear leaves. Birds yammering. Blue bay beyond. Sizable cinderblock house, awning windows, Bahama gray with white trim, glaring white roof.

When I pressed the button the chimes came loud and clear through the screening of the door. They were not as ornate as the Shottlehauster set. When I heard a female voice call, "Coming," I moved a little to one side, turned my back toward the door.

"Yes?" she said. "Yes? What is it?" I heard the spring creak on the screen door and I turned and caught it and faced her.

"Hello there, Anna!"

She had been somewhat thinner in the Welcome Party picture, and since then she had lost a great deal more weight. Her white hair had been dyed a peculiarly unpleasant shade of building-brick red, and cut into a style that would have looked cute on a young girl, the bangs curving down to eyebrow level. She wore dangling gilt earrings, a yellow blouse, purple pants, and zoris. It was a grotesque outfit for a woman in her middle fifties. The meaty face had lost no weight, and the pottery-blue eyes were the same.

"Anna, what happened to the vaudeville accent?"

She frowned and shook her head. "Young man, you apparently think I am someone else."

"I think you're trying to be someone else."

She turned and shouted into the sunny vistas of the house. "Perry! Sweetheart! Come here, dear. There's a man here saying the strangest things. Hurry, sweetheart!"

"Cleverness isn't enough," I said. "It takes luck too."

"You must be insane, young man." I realized how perfect a place she had picked. Guaranteed respectability. Immediate group identification. She was wearing the uniform of the day. Again she turned and shouted over her shoulder, "Will you please come out here at once, Perry, and help me with this. . . ."

It covered any small sound he might have made when he came up behind me. Something flickered in front of my eyes and then as I gasped with surprise, the standard reaction, something was yanked to a fatal tightness around my throat. I spun to grapple with whoever had sneaked up behind me, and I saw a plump bald man hop nimbly backward. But the pressure on my throat did not lessen. I could not take a breath. My ears began to roar. I tried to get my fingertips under whatever it was, but it was sunk too deeply into the flesh. I reached to the nape of my neck and felt some kind of a clip device and felt of the free end that dangled down my back. I fumbled with the metallic-feeling clip. The screen door had shut. She stood watching me through the screen. He stood with the same expression—interest and mild concern. Vision began to darken. I thought of the gun and I willed my hand to go down and take it out of the pocket and put one through the screening and one into the plump belly. But my hand was more interested in trying to dig enough meat out of my throat to get to the tightness and pull it free. Roaring had turned to a siren sound. I felt a jolt and a faraway pain in my knees. The world went from dark gray to black and I pitched from my kneeling position, face forward over the edge of the world, spinning down and down and down. . . .

Brightness shone through my eyelids. My chin was on my chest. I tried to swallow the gravel packed into my throat but I couldn't budge it. I opened my eyes and tried to sit higher in the chair and saw at once why I could not. It was a tubular aluminum lawn chair, the kind with a double bar for the armrests. My forearms were fastened with wide white surgical tape from wrist to elbow to the chair arms, wrapped around arm and armrest, tight and overlapping, so that my hands had darkened and puffed. My legs were straight out, heels resting on terrazzo, pants cuffs hiked up by the same kind of tape which had also been used to fasten my ankles together.

I lifted my head. I was on the sort of jalousied porch

locally called a Florida room. Anna sat ten feet away and a little off to my left. Behind her was a picture window from ceiling to floor and ten feet wide, framing the swimming pool beyond. There was a row of little white seahorses on the glass to keep the unwary from trying to walk through it. I could see a dense hedge of punk trees, tailored grass, concrete pool apron, redwood picnic furniture, a stone barbecue, a wall of pierced concrete block painted white. A blow-up duck, big enough to ride, floated high on the pool water, being drifted in random turning patterns by the light breeze.

On the table beside Anna was my undersized .38 special. She was using yellow needles and knitting something out of bright blue yarn.

She gave me a merry little glance and said, "You're very heavy, Mr. McGee. It took both of us to drag you."

I started to speak, but it was a rusty whisper. I cleared my throat and managed a guttural rasp. "Was the code word *sweetheart*?"

"Hoping we'd never have to use it. You certainly had good luck. But when you add stupidity, what good is the luck?"

"Where *is* sweetheart?"

"Taking a little stroll. He wants to know how you got here and if you brought anyone along."

"Nobody important. Some state cops."

"I hardly think so."

"Not a trace of accent. You're very good."

"Thousands and thousands of hours, Mr. McGee, in my room, listening to your damned dreary radio programs, practicing into a tape recorder, playing it over and over and over, correcting it each time. Discipline. Endless self-discipline. Endless patience. And now, you see, we are quite safe. You are an annoyance only."

"You dosed Gloria, didn't you?"

"I knew where it was and what it was, and knew it would not change the taste of her morning orange juice. It was interesting, but it was just a little bit careless. I indulged myself. When she asked me what I was mailing to Marco Bay, I should have made quite sure, don't you think? Perry is very annoyed. The silly sentimental little bitch was quite amusing, gasping and panting and slap-
204

ping at her clothes to put out imaginary fires."

"Anna, wouldn't it have been a lot easier to live the lush life by marrying your daughter off to the Doctor?"

The needles stopped clicking and she stared at me. "My *daughter*! If I'd ever had children, my dear man, I can assure you they would have had considerably more intelligence than Gretchen. But then again, had she been brighter, perhaps she couldn't have been persuaded to believe I was her mother. I had her on my hands only seven years, thank God. A tiresome child. Oh, you asked about the marriage. If the man in that untidy situation had been very rich and very obscure, it might have been an acceptable solution. But Fortner Geis was somewhat of a celebrity, and it would have been a treat for your dirty-minded newspapers, and I could not risk their prying into my personal history, of course."

"What are you wanted for?"

She saw me start and look beyond her. She turned and saw the bald man bringing Heidi around the house. He had her hand in his and she walked quite rigidly, with a twist of pain on her lips.

"Heavens!" said Anna Ottlo. "What a small world it is after all."

The man opened a jalousied door and pushed Heidi in and followed her. Heidi massaged the hand he had been holding and she stared at me and then at Anna and then back at me. "Trav, what are they . . . He walked me and said such terrible things to me. Anna, my God, what are you trying to . . ."

"I asked her name and she told me," Perry said. He stood beaming. His bald head was sunburned and peeling. He wore a sport shirt of pillow ticking, dark blue walking shorts, white canvas boat shoes. He wore his stomach high. It looked solid. He had meaty and muscular forearms, and spindly, hairy, pipestem legs. He had little brown eyes, a broad flattened nose, and a heavy sensuous mouth. "She made it too easy. I see you're breathing again, sonny," he said, turning toward me and giving me a quick little wink.

Anna shook her head. "How perfectly delicious, Perry. Dear Heidi. The arrogant bitch of all time. Why make her bed when old Anna could do it? Drop the clothes where you take them off. Never carry a plate to the kitchen. The cool, golden, superior princess."

"Anna! You don't have any accent at all."

"What a marvel! What a miracle! Stupid housekeeper. What a treat to have you here, Miss Heidi."

Heidi lifted her chin. "Stop this nonsense at once and take that tape off Mr. McGee."

Anna faked vast astonishment. "Is that an order?"

"I think I made it quite clear."

"Perry, if you could teach this child to sing us a little song, I think her manners would be better."

"My pleasure," Perry said, with a little bow. He moved over in front of Heidi, his pudgy back toward me. He hooked one arm around her and yanked her close and busied the other hand between them. I could see the elbow turning and working.

Heidi gave a harsh gasp of shock and outrage, then her eyes and mouth opened wide and she flapped her arms weakly at the plump shoulders of the man and gave a squalling sound of pain and fright.

He let her go. She staggered, going so pale her tan looked gray-green. Her face was shiny with sweat. She took two weak steps to an aluminum and plastic chaise and half fell onto it and bowed her head all the way to her knees, flax hair a-spill.

"A pretty little song, dear," Anna said. "Now mind your mouth." She spoke to Perry in a fast guttural rattle of German. He answered and seemed to ask her a question. She thought, shrugged, gave a longer speech and he nodded, gave a short answer, gestured toward Heidi. Anna responded and he went beaming to her and picked up one hand and hauled her to her feet.

He put an arm around her and led her into the house proper. She gave me a gray, lost, hopeless look as he led her by me. In a cooing little voice he said, "Tender little dearie. Dainty little dearie."

"Hardly little," Anna said. "She's a half-head taller than he is. You couldn't have made him happier."

"Look. She got a case of the hots and I made the mistake of letting her come back to Florida with me. She doesn't know anything about anything. She's a clumsy lay, and she's a bore."

"Perry won't be bored."

I heard a sharp thin high scream from somewhere inside the house. Anna looked irritated and yelled some kind of an order in German. He answered in a placating tone.

"Now he'll go get your truck and bring it around," she said. "All he was supposed to do was secure her in there. They have a charming little practice here in Marco Bay, Mr. McGee. We all have these little round signs on sharp sticks that we can stick in the ground out at the end of the driveway to show we are taking naps. They say *Hush, Friend* on them. Nobody ever violates the rule. Perry stuck ours in when he went to get Miss Heidi."

"Did both of you work on Saul Gorba?"

"Just Perry. Saul was a fool. Very smart and very sly, but careless and impulsive. Hard to control. He couldn't see why it was best he should marry Gretchen. We did not wish to alarm him by telling him that if the Doctor became stubborn it would be necessary to arrange certain accidents so that in the end Susan would be the only heir. Perry is very skilled at such things. But the Doctor decided not to be stubborn. I knew how much money there would be. I knew how long he thought he might live. I knew his warm feeling for Mrs. Stanyard, and knew when she visited her husband. I knew many useful things. Perry found that farm for them, a place good for our purposes. We needed Saul Gorba for certain risky things, like taking Branty for the ride, like breaking into Mrs. Stanyard's apartment to do the thing with the cat. And he was very good at documents. Perry and Wilma Hennigan are very well-documented people. Saul had a great greed for money. It was amusing to discuss it with him in German. Stupid Gretchen had lost almost all of her German. Saul taught me how to wire the noisemaker to Gloria's little automobile. And, of course, when the gift of candy was in the house, I opened it carefully and fixed a special treat for Miss Heidi."

"Why did Dr. Geis set up Mrs. Stanyard for Susan to go to if she needed help?"

"There was a certain threat made against the girl, a nastiness to be done to her. This was over the telephone, you understand. That is how negotiations were handled. A whisper over a pay telephone, by Saul, of course. We told him what to say. We frequently . . . encouraged the Doctor in that way." She bit her lip. "I could not say.

Perhaps Saul was a little too convincing when he spoke of the girl. At any rate, I saw the letter before it was mailed to Mrs. Stanyard. I told Saul about it, and the fool told Susan he knew where she'd go for help, after he had beaten . . ."

Perry came out onto the sun porch from the main part of the house. They carried on a lengthy conversation. I got the impression she made a suggestion he did not like, and he made a series of alternate suggestions. She turned every one down, firmly. He pouted like a fat child. She gave him a little lecture, a teasing tone in her voice. He shrugged, smiled, brightened up and went back into the house.

Anna said, "Poor disappointed man. He has all the rest of the day and into the night for both of you, and I have told him that under no circumstances must you be marked, either of you." She got up and came over and bent to peer at my throat. She rubbed it briskly with the flat of her hand and went back to her chair saying, "That will not be noticeable." She sat down and picked up her knitting. "We have decided to hold your faces down in a basin of salt water from the bay so that the lungs will be proof of death by drowning. And tonight late we shall undress you both on a quiet beach we found that is twenty miles from here, and put your clothing on the seat of that truck of yours and push you into the sea and drive back in our car together. A blanket on the beach and perhaps some beer, that will add conviction."

I heard Heidi's voice whimpering and pleading.

Anna smiled. "I told him it is a test of his ingenuity. Many things can be managed. At least he has time, not the way it was with Gretchen when Saul called up in panic to say she had guessed what he had been up to and was threatening to take the children and leave. He had only one hour with her."

A sudden harsh hoarse cry of anguish from Heidi sickened me. It sounded effortful enough to tear her throat.

"His little bird sings well for him. You understand, course, about people like Perry. I like a bit of it, amusement. But to him it is necessary. A sexual orien tion, I suppose. First there must be the gross humiliatio the unthinkable violations of the precious citadel of se with pain as the spice and fright as the sauce. But he will have to do with what variations he can invent on that theme, because he cannot have what he likes best, to create those moments of ultimate hopeless horror when his companion experiences damage she knows cannot be undone, cannot be mended, and then begins to wonder how long he or she will be forced to sustain the burden of consciousness and of life itself."

Out of the silence Heidi began to make an explosive sound, a kind of squealing grunting sound repeated over and over in abrupt jolting rhythm, then dying slowly away.

Anna listened with tilted head, half-smile. "Ah, he is a rascal, that one!"

My heart was breaking for Heidi. All the silky luxuries of her, and the sense of fun, and all her quick sure hungers . . .

"Listen, Anna. Make him stop. Please. I'll make a deal. I got to the farm before the police did. I found what Perry couldn't find. Maybe the figure is proof enough. A hundred and seventy-eight thousand, six hundred and fifty. I kept it. I'll make a deal. If she has to die, okay, but no more of him. Make it easy for her and I'll tell you where it is and how you can get it in absolute safety."

She put the knitting aside, next to the revolver on the table beside her chair. "Poor Saul thought he would keep that money. He could not know he was only holding it for us until it was time to leave. Then he lost his silly head over that juicy little wench and after beating her in a temper, let her sneak away. So when he found out she was gone, he went to a pay phone and called me late that Monday afternoon and I told him to get the children out of the house, to leave them with friends."

"God! God! God!" Heidi cried, her voice rusted almost shut.

"Stop him," I yelled.

"Where was the money, Mr. McGee?"

"Hidden in dings he put into the fenders and body and covered over with plastic and painted. Stop him. Please!"

With half-smile and half-frown she said, "But I'd have to give him a reason. Saul died after just a few hours. Perry was furious. He searched as long as he dared and then came back. It would be nice to have that money, but not really essential. I think you must have given it to Mr. Andrus anyway. If I called Perry and told him such nonsense he would just say that when he finishes with her and gets to you, you will tell him everything you know anyway, so what is the point? I wouldn't think of spoiling his pleasure."

Then came a cry from Heidi more horrid than anything which had gone before. It was a wild straining, climbing, gargling croak that stopped with a sickening abruptness.

Anna pushed herself to her feet, scowling. "Now I don't think he could get *that* much effect unless he has . . ."

The blackest anger and total despair can give you what you need for superhuman effort, if you can focus it and direct it. I yanked my feet back, lunged up, and stood in precarious balance, hunched in the aluminum embrace of the chair. And I went at her, hoppity-hop, grunting, fighting for balance. I had the vague idea of charging into her, knocking her down, and getting my teeth into her fat neck. With a look of alarm she turned to reach for the pistol. I had lost my balance on the last hop and as I started to fall forward, I gave a final thrust and felt my head ram the softness of her belly, heard the air grunt out of her. I fell onto my side, the aluminum clattering onto the terrazzo, and saw her stagger back, turn half around to catch her balance, trip as one foot came out of a zori, take two little running steps, head down, and then dive.

Her brick-red head hit the window wall section perhaps two feet from the bottom. It punched a huge shard of glass out onto the grass, and ran diagonal cracks all the way up to the top corners. Small pieces sprinkled down onto the terrazzo. She lay face down with her throat across the sill where the plate glass had been puttied in. The top section was suspended. It shimmied. It creaked. Pieces of dry putty fell, then suddenly the great plate of glass worked loose and fell like a great blade, straight down.

She humped her purple hips high and smacked them down. The final grind and bump. The falling glass had made an enormous sound. The brick-red hair did not go well with the spreading puddle of bright red blood.

I hitched myself with frantic effort toward the small

table by her chair. I hooked my feet around a table leg and yanked it over. I could hear him coming. The gun spun to a stop five feet away. More lumpy hitching spasmodic effort, like a legless bug.

"Fredrika! Fredrika!" he called in a voice of anguish and loss. He was behind me. I could not see him. I got my fingers on the gun. I could barely feel it. My hands were numb. I fumbled at it and my right hand would not pick it up.

Something yanked my chair back. He bent and picked up the gun. He was bare to the waist, oiled with sweat, his chest hairless, his breasts fatty as a woman's. His mouth worked and he sobbed and he aimed the snub barrel at the center of my face. He was bending over me. There was a strange sudden sound, a damp, smacky little chunking sound. He straightened up and stood very still as if listening to something a long way off. The Airweight slid out of his hand and clanked on the floor. Then he puddled down slowly, with a tired sigh, and stretched out on his back, his head lolling toward me, eyes half-open, only the whites showing, and with a small, very neat, very very round hole punched through the bone of brow an inch above the left eyebrow, and on the curve of forehead into temple. A single blood-drop ran an inch away from the hole and stopped at the end of its pink snail-trail. Belly gas rumbled and then made a little snore sound as it came out through the flaccid throat.

I had a view of the lawn beyond the broken glass from a vantage point about as high as a rabbit's eye, and I saw two men come across from the direction of the punk-tree hedge. It was an arty director's angle at combat technique. They came toward the house, running swiftly, widely separated, constantly varying both direction and speed, weapons held in a familiar readiness. The ultimate and grotesque contrast was in the way they were dressed—neat dark trousers, dress shoes, white shirts, neckties.

"It's okay!" I shouted. "It's safe."

They dived and disappeared. "What is your name?" one of them called. Veddy British.

"McGee. Travis McGee. They're both dead."

They appeared suddenly, much closer, standing upright, stepping through the great hole where the glass had been, avoiding the blood. Trim-bodied men in their early thirties. Tough and watchful faces, an air of special communication between them. As they quickly checked the bodies of the man and the woman, I said, "The girl needs help. She's somewhere in the house."

One gave the other an order in a language I did not understand and then went into the house. The order-taker set his weapon aside and righted the chair with me in it with an effortlessness that shocked me. He took out a pocket knife, inserted the blade near the aluminum arm, and with one keen stroke sliced the tape open from elbow to wrist. He put the knife down, paused, shrugged, gave me a gold-toothed grin, and said, "No Englitch," and ripped the tape loose in a single yank that took the hair and felt as if it had taken the skin too.

As he was slicing the other arm free, the other one came out of the house onto the porch and said, "D'you know the lassie quite well, McGee?"

"Yes. How is she?"

"Bit hard to tell. Better see if you can settle her down."

I winced as the other arm was ripped loose. I massaged my hands and a painful prickling began to penetrate through the numbness. The gold-toothed one squatted to slice my ankles free.

The one standing gave the dead man a casual kick and said, "I suspect the old sod merely scuffed her up a bit. The Captain here had to take the clean shot before he blew your face off with this silly little weapon. Too bad. We wanted a chat with Wilhelm."

"Captain?"

"On leave. From the Israeli Army. Spot of sightseeing here and there." He helped me to my feet. I wobbled and then steadied. "Tend the lady while we look about," he said. "She's in the bathroom."

Heidi lay naked on her side in the corner beyond the shower stall, on a floor of yellow and white octagonal tiles. Her knees were pulled up to her chin, fists hugged between her breasts, smudged eyes closed, hair matted with drying sweat. There were two doors into the bathroom. Her clothing was on a hanger on the hook on the closed door, arranged with a deadly Germanic neatness. Damp towels were strewn about. The man's pillow-ticking shirt was on another hanger.

I squatted beside her, touched her shoulder, and said, "Honey?"

She gave a convulsive start and scrabbled her way into the corner and kept scrabbling as though to push her way through the wall. With wide blue-gray eyes focused on me but not seeing me, she said, "Please not any more, please, oh God, please no." It was a sugary sweet little gamin croak, a humble little voice for begging, and it sounded like the husk of a long-ago movie star whose name I could not remember.

"You're all right now, honey. It's me. It's Trav."

She looked very dubious. Very skeptical. Her teeth chattered. Incongruously I remembered the fate of the Packard phaeton after my dear old buddy Buzzy borrowed it and didn't make a curve. He took me out the next morning and showed me. He had missed a tree and a telephone pole by narrow margins, had gone down a forty-degree slope and torn a swath through scrub alder and then hit the almost dry creek bed. It had gone a hundred feet along the creek bed. The water-smooth boulders were the size of peck baskets and bushel baskets. The sturdy old car had rearranged a few dozen of them. Everything that could possibly be shaken loose had flown off the car, including both sides of the foldback hood. Axles, drive shaft, frame, engine block, and all four wheels broken.

"It's like a miracle all I got was just this one little bump on the head," said Buzzy.

We salvaged the parts worth salvaging. It squatted there among the stones and during the spring torrents from the snow melting up in the hills, it disappeared completely.

She let me take her by the wrists, and she did not resist very much as I pulled her to her feet. She leaned against me and in her tiny croak said, "He kept . . . He made me . . . He put . . ."

"Easy, honey. It's all okay."

"It hurt so," she said. "It hurt so bad."

It was like dressing a child who is just learning about

213

buttons and sleeves. She would help a little and then forget. I took her into a bedroom. She walked like a convalescent taking the first trip down the hospital corridor without the wheelchair. I sat her on the edge of a neatly made bed, lifted her feet up onto the spread. She lay back and looked at me out of child-eyes and I said, "Rest a little while, honey. Then we'll go."

"All right."

I found them in the living room, the Captain watching while the Englishman went through each drawer, looking at each piece of paper.

He looked up and said, "How is she?"

"Shaky. I made her lie down and get a little rest. Suppose you start with the beach that night in December. Who hit me and what with?"

"My dear chap, we don't have to start with anything and go anywhere."

I stood over him and said, "I have been goddam near choked to death. I have been tricked by two old folks, and I have listened to that girl screaming when I could not do a damned thing about it. With pure courage and brute strength and great skill I managed to kill a fifty-six-year-old woman in purple pants. Now stop the secret-agent act, buddy, and give me the score."

He spoke to his friend, the friend shrugged and said something, and they both laughed.

The Englishman went back to his search. He began speaking, stopping for a few moments when he came to any piece of paper that interested him. "I was eight years old, thereabouts, when our dead friends out there made the list. The names won't mean anything to you. Fredrika Gronwald. Wilhelm Vogel. He was one of the Munich bully boys. When The Thousand Years began, they became an interrogation team. They sifted the camp lists, picked up people who looked useful, worked the last crumb of information out of them, and made confidential reports to Himmler. I can assume they were ambitious, but their methods turned too many stomachs, Gestapo stomachs even, a very considerable accomplishment. Both of them would have given a clinical psychiatrist weeks of good fun.

Aberrant types. Opportunity reinforces the aberrations.

"The list grows very short these days, McGee. Those two eased out so cleverly it took a long time to piece it all together. They fell out of favor in late 1942, and they were sly enough to sense how the war was going. While they still had interrogation privileges they searched the camps—not the death camps—for new identities. She found an Anna Ottlo, same age and build, some facial resemblance. She'd been in since thirty-seven. Her child, Gretchen, was in another area of the camp and hadn't seen her mother in the whole five years. From what we can gather, they took the Ottlo woman and extracted a complete personal history from her before finishing her off. Maybe she had remaining relatives who had to be done away with also in order to be safe. Perhaps the test was the reunion with the daughter, not a terribly bright child. When the daughter bought it, Fräulein Gronwald knew the child was her ticket through the interrogation by the other side. We suspect that Vogel did much the same sort of thing. They duplicated the camp identity tattoos, slipped into one of the underground escape routes, and made it all the way to the Land of Liberty.

"Four years ago we got a recognition report on her from Chicago, and it moved her name up to the active list. There was a certain clumsiness a year later which alerted her. We debated bagging her then before she made a run, but the powers that be are far more interested in Vogel. We can't move swiftly, unfortunately. Limited resources. No phone taps possible. One must have a taste for the hunt. Once they knew, or sensed, they had been spotted, I imagine they thought it essential to extort funds from her employer. Vogel's work on the Gorba chap was as unmistakable as a signature. Incidentally, you did a respectable job of work tracing them here, McGee. I imagine you have a good amateur instinct for it. We traced it through the shipping arrangements she made for her two crates of personal possessions. An intricate pattern, but not intricate enough. In earlier years she would have had the sense to abandon such things. Ah! This looks promising."

He showed it to me. It was a receipted statement for almost two hundred dollars for installation of a barrel safe in the utility room.

It had been installed in the floor. The circular cement lid with recessed lift-ring was hidden by a grass rug. The Englishman gave an order when the safe was exposed, and the Captain went out and came back quickly with a tool case. He opened it and took out a little aluminum chassis case with a speaker grill, toggle switch, and volume dial. The single lead was a suction-cup mike. He pressed it against the safe above the dial, turned the rig on, turned the volume high. It made a continuous hissing sound. He turned the safe dial slowly to the left. There was an amplified grating sound and then a sharp clack. He turned the dial to the right until it clacked again, then to the left until the third clack. He tried to open it but it was still sealed. He went the second time to the right. After the fourth clack he tried again and opened the safe. As he turned the amplifier off and pulled the suction mike loose, the Englishman knelt and began reaching down into the safe and taking the contents out, examining each item. He opened a thick manila envelope, thumbed a double sheaf of currency over three inches thick, slipped the red rubber band around the envelope, and flipped it to me, saying, "Your affair, I believe."

I caught it, hefted it. "But shouldn't you take some of it, at least?"

He smiled up at me. "My dear chap, there would be a positive wilderness of forms and reports to complete, absolutely weeks of desk work. If you do feel some intense obligation, suggest to your principals they send some over as a contribution to the Irrigation Plan, or some such.

I made protest but he didn't hear me. He had found a little tattered pocket notebook. Their heads were close together as they turned the pages slowly. They made excited comment to each other.

He stood up. "Bit of luck. Seems to be some five-number groupings that could be what we call the Argentina code. Still a few of them holed up down there. Getting quite

216

old. Sly as old foxes. Constant condition of fright, and bloody well justified. I think you'd best gather up your lady and be off. We have a spot of stage management to do here." His smile was the coldest I have ever seen. "Rearrange the meat, plausibly."

"But won't they . . ."

"Don't worry your downy head, dear fellow. After all, it's our game, isn't it?"

With Heidi in a huddled silence on the seat beside me, I passed their parked car after I turned out of the drive. It was a pale green sedan with New York plates. Gold lettering on the side door said, "Freddy's Exterminator Service" with an Albany phone number.

I drove eastward through the bright day, in tourist traffic. Herons and egrets fished the canals, as did people with cane poles. I had never thought that an ugliness of so long ago could ever reach into my life. I had thought it was all history-book stuff, and that all that Eichmann hooraw had been an anachronistic after-echo of it.

It gave the same feeling as if I looked over across the saw-grass flats dotted with cypress hammocks and saw one of the great carnivorous lizards rise up onto his steaming haunches, with scaly head big as a Volkswagen, scales gleaming like oiled metal in the sunshine, great tearing fangs of the flesh eater, and the cold yellow savagery of the ancient saurian eye.

I could not have guessed that any fragments of that old evil were still around, and still claiming victims. Gretchen, Gloria, Saul Gorba, Fortner Geis, Susan, and the silent, wretched, violated girl beside me. Know-it-all McGee. I'd been a damned fool prancing in total naïve confidence around the edges of disaster, like a blind man dancing on a roof.

"Hungry at all?" I asked her.

Out of the corner of my eye I saw her shake her head no. I drove on, contemptuous of myself and my comedy automobile and my sybaritic nest of a houseboat, and all my minor skills, and all the too-familiar furniture of my life and my brain.

fourteen

Three days later, after making the necessary phone calls to set it up, I got an early jet to Chicago from Miami International with a firm reservation for a flight back that would get me in at ten that night.

It was three below zero at O'Hare. Janice Stanyard met me and I drove her car out to Lake Pointe. All the kids were in school. Big logs were crackling in the fireplace. Jeanie, Roger Geis's wife, had come over to be with Glory while Janice went in to get me.

Gloria hugged herself to me, and laughed, and tears spilled at the same time. She looked better than I had been led to hope. John Andrus arrived ten minutes after I got there. I had given him the total of the second piece of salvage over the phone, and he brought along a work sheet of the probable estate-tax bite.

Gloria and John and I closeted ourselves in Fort's study. I took the money out of the briefcase Meyer had loaned me and put the banded stacks on the desk. Personally counted and banded by McGee.

Gloria sat in Fort's leather chair. She studied the work sheet. "So, in round numbers, John, it makes an additional hundred and twenty thousand for me and sixty each for Roger and Heidi."

"Approximately. We're still way short of what's missing."

"But there won't be any more," I told him.

"As I told you on the phone, John, Travis gets sixty thousand of my share. Half."

"Just a minute, Glory . . ."

"Minute nothing. You wouldn't take any of that first part. I know your rules, Trav. I knew them when I yelled

218

for help. And even if I didn't, it's worth more than sixty thousand to know that . . . that damned woman gave it to me, that I didn't take an overdose. I don't care how you arrange it, John. Just arrange it."

I said I would take absolutely nothing. She said she would force me to take it all if I made her any angrier. Impasse. So I reached over and took one slender packet with $10,000 printed on the band and tucked it into the inside pocket of my winter jacket and said, "I must have made a mistake counting it. Pretty stupid, I guess. What I actually recovered is ten thousand less than I told you, John. Count it and see."

He looked at me in horror. "But you can't just pick up ten thousand dollars and put it in your pocket, man!"

"I didn't see him do that. Are you out of your mind, John? Did you pick up any money, Travis?"

"Certainly not! Do you think I'm low enough to steal from a poor little woman who has five kids to ̄educate?"

"But," he said. "But . . . oh, the hell with it! I am going to take this to the bank. I am going to put it in the vault. Then I am going to the club and I am going to sit at the bar for a long long time."

After Andrus left I showed the women the clip from the Naples paper. Tragedy at Senior Center. Wife dies in freak accident during quarrel. Husband slays self, leaves note.

I didn't answer their questions very well. I didn't know too much about anything, just that it seemed she was some kind of a war criminal or something and she'd been in hiding for all those years, and Gretchen wasn't even her daughter. We'd been there when a couple of men appeared to settle old scores.

"But why wouldn't you let me talk to Heidi on the phone?" Gloria demanded.

"It was all pretty sudden and pretty violent and it shook her up badly. Sensitive, you know. Artistic temperament. She's started going to a good man. Talk it out. Get steadied down." I patted my pocket. "When she gets a clean bill, I think I'll tote her back down to St. Croix on this money."

"Have you ever considered making an honest woman

of my sister-in-law?" Jeanie Geis asked sweetly.

Gloria snorted and said, "If she was honest they wouldn't have anything in common, dear. And I believe she did try marriage once."

"Dear Gadge," Jeanie sighed. "Well, do have fun. I have to run. Give Heidi a hug for me. Keep well, Glory. Jan, dear, I'll try to remember to phone about Tuesday, but if I forget, you call me. Let's all see if we can't settle down into some kind of nice quiet predictable life, shall we? Ciao, everybody."

We flew over and settled into a two-bedroom cottage on a Thursday, the second day of March. We were a couple of miles closer to Christiansted, the cottage not as attractive or as well furnished, the beach narrower. But the sea was the same, and the flowers and the smell of the air. And I managed to rent the same kind of car and lease the same breed of small sailboat.

The doctor had recommended that I try to create the same scene as closely as possible. It is both unpleasant and difficult to sit across a desk from a grave and bespectacled man and tell him in clinical detail just how one had managed to introduce the repressed lady to enjoyment and untie the knots that had kept her so hung-up. There is a temptation to skip parts of it, and to go into an aw-shucks routine. He solemnly told me the obvious as though it were news, saying that her previous sexual repression with its neurotic basis was what was now preventing her from recovering from the emotional damage of being abused in crude fashion. He said that I should not, under any circumstances, make any direct or indirect sexual advance to her.

And no matter how deliciously lovely she looked on the St. Croix beach or on the sailboat, or how painfully and often I would be spitted by a shaft of pure aching old-timey lust, sharpened by the bursting health of beach and sea, sailing and swimming, and one of my periodic programs of physical conditioning—easy on the sauce and groceries, push-ups, sit-ups, duck walks, sprints on land and in the sea, I was not going to lay a hand on the damosel, not after two gestures of physical affection back aboard the *Flush* before I knew how deep the fright was. Each response was a convulsive leap. Once she spun into the wall, hands upraised, face sweaty and drained of blood, staring at me but without any knowledge of who I was or where she was. The second time she ran headlong over a chair and finished on her hands and knees, facing me, backing into a corner and trying to keep backing after she got there.

It is difficult to describe properly what our relationship was like during those weeks of March. We used separate bedrooms. Perhaps the best analogy is that we were like the only two passengers on a freighter. Because we were sharing meals and the long voyage, it would have been ridiculous not to go through the polite ceremonies of acquaintanceship. We could share the sea view, relish the weather, play deck games.

She was often listless, lost in her thoughts, looking up from a book to stare for a long time at the far edge of the sea, white teeth pinching into her underlip. At other times she had energy to spare. She was ripe with health, her hide taut and glossy, a blue tint to the whites of her eyes.

And then, one night, as the world was gathering itself to roll on into the fragrance of April, I was slowly awakened by her. I had been asleep on my back. She was beside me, braced to look down into my face, angled so that there was the warm silk of her against the side of my leg. Her face was in the steady silver of the moonlight, unreadable eyes pockets of shadow, the two sheafs of hair hanging to brush the sides of my cheek and neck. Moon made a single catch-light on the curve of underlip.

A scalding tear fell onto my upper lip near the corner of my mouth, and with tongue tip I hooked in the small taste of her salt. When she leaned slowly down and lay the soft acceptance of her mouth onto mine, I did not dare touch her. Each time she bent to kiss, I felt the weight and sweetness and warmth of her bare breasts upon my chest. Slow kisses and slow tears, and I dared hold her, but there was no start, no tension, just a slow and dreamy sensuousness, turning gently for me, with small urging pressures, to lay as I had been and lift in a waiting readiness, fingertips on my shoulders bearing no more weight than the moonlight, and in the slowness of joining her catch of breath was almost inaudible, and the following sigh as soft and fragrant as the night breeze.

In one lifetime how many times can it be like that, be a ceremony that becomes so unrelated to the flesh that I had the feeling I floated disembodied in the night sky, halfway between sea and stars, looking down upon a tiny cutaway cottage, at two figures there in the theater of moonlight caught in a slow unending dance to the doubled heartbeat, a counterpoint in offstage drums. But there is a time to fall out of the sky, and a fall from that height makes long moments of half-light, of knowing and not knowing, of being and dying.

When I felt her beginning to leave me, I caught at her to hold her, but she whispered, "No." I let my fingertips trail down her arm as she went out of moonlight into the darkness and back to her own bed. That single whispered monosyllable was the only word she had said. I could feel my mouth smiling as I slid toward sleep. Total and unflawed smugness. Patience, understanding, and self-control had done it, boy. She has turned the corner. And now day by day and night by night we would build it all back, into all our old moods and manners of making love, of hearing her little soft chuckling laugh of pleasure as she felt herself beginning to begin.

I slept later than usual and when I came yawning out in swim trunks, with a piece of tissue pasted onto a razor nick, she was just finishing her packing. I asked what the hell. She looked very groomed and brisk and competent. She said she had phoned and made flight reservations. If I'd put on a shirt and slacks we'd have time to drive to the hotel and have breakfast with a comfortable margin to get to the airport for her flight.

I kept saying Why often enough to sound like some kind of rotor that needed greasing. She looked pale. She snapped the catches on her second suitcase and looked around with that Got-Everything? look. Then she marched to me and stuck her hand out like a lady ambassador.

"We'd better say good-bye here, Travis."

I tried to pull her into my arms but she begged and demanded and I gave up. "Then answer the question," I said. "Why?"

"Because I have to have my own life."

"Oh, great!"

"I'll never never forget you. You'll always be . . . part of me, part of whatever happens to me."

"Thanks a lot."

"Don't scowl so, darling. Please. Remember when you told me in Chicago I was standing outside the gates looking in, wistfully? So you opened the gates. Huge heavy gates with rusty hinges, and you led me in to where all the gardens are. I thank you with all my heart. Darling, if it had stopped there, I could have survived beautifully, and kept my own identity. But don't you understand? I got thrown out into the darkness again. I nearly lost my mind. And you had it to do all over again, but differently, because I knew the second time what it could be. And, bless you, the gates are open again, just a little way. I squeezed through. I'm standing just inside the gates. But I can't go see all the gardens with you."

"Why not?"

"Because then you would own me, every atom of heart and soul and body forever, and life would have no meaning except as it related to you. It would be a total dependency as long as I might live. I do not want that kind of life or that kind of love. But if you want me on those terms, Travis, if you want that responsibility for another human being forever, say so, and I'll cancel the reservation and unpack. I am fighting like hell for emotional survival, and I'm right on the edge of surrender. I think if I am going to be a whole person, now that I am inside the gates again, I had best go the rest of the way with some man I have yet to meet, but know in my heart I will meet. Shall I phone?" Her stare was intent, direct, searching. Her mouth was trembling.

So I put on shirt and slacks and put her bags in the car.

Meyer keeps telling me that I did exactly the right thing. He keeps telling me that she knew how a dependence that total would have suffocated me. But when he looks at the painting she sent me, his voice loses conviction. A small painting. She sent it air express from Chicago. It is an enchanted picture. At close range it is an abstraction, an arrangement of masses and light and color. But when you get back from it you realize you are looking through the black bars of an ancient iron gate, into a place where there are black limbs of old and twisted trees. The sky is a heavy dreary gray, but there is a shaft of sunlight shining down on a vivid brightness of gardens, a small place you can see beyond the gate and the trees.

I think that when he looks at the painting Meyer has the same suspicion I have, that maybe all along this was the one, and that she got away. I am outside the gates and there is no one to open them.

So then he tries to lift our mood and he makes his jokes, and when I sense that he is trying too hard with the jokes I manage to laugh a little.

Otherwise he'd just stand around looking like Smokey the Bear watching all the forests burn down.